The

Wisdom

of

Winter

The
Wisdom
of
Winter

Annie Seyler

atmosphere press

A Note from the Author

I believe in the possibility of harmony.

I believe in the power of dreaming.

I believe the differences between us make the discovery of our similarities so very interesting.

I believe I am accountable for my actions and words.

I believe in our ability to change the world.

For the Seylers and the Peltons, here and "gone"

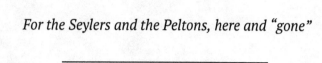

Part I

CHAPTER 1

She used to be still. For hours we'd lie outdoors in the tall grass beneath the sugar maple, her fingers drawing circles on her belly. Peaceful. Restful. At times she hummed or sang, and we vibrated.

We didn't speak, but we were familiar to each other in the way people sometimes are in the early days before falling in love. We both knew ours was a reunion, not a beginning.

I would have stayed there with her forever, but she grew restless . . . fidgeting and shifting often. At one point I had spun myself around, hoping to make more space for her. Deft hands, accustomed to obedience, poked and pressed to force me back. Finally, they let go.

Now her heart no longer answers mine; it gallops ahead. The still waters, once gentle and stirring, whip with warning. I have nowhere to go but forward.

I surrender to the pull, not by hands or forceps, but by the life ahead of me. The family I will thrill and disappoint; the rush of love and the crush of rejection; the ground I will skip over and the roots I will trip on; the words I will say and the ones I will withhold.

Double breached, upside down, and backward inside my mother's womb, I understand the perfection of the life to come.

Becoming. Forgetting. Remembering.

She calls me by name . . . *Beatrice* . . . and suddenly my knowing fades. I search but there's only blankness.

Something is about to happen.

Something wonderful.

Something terrible.

Still, I go.

CHAPTER 2

She's singing about a big yellow taxi again; it's taking away her old man.

I lie still as my mother's silky voice floats up through the floorboards and tempts me into the new day. Grit clings to my ankles. A twig tickles my neck. *No bath last night.* I smile and fling off my top sheet. It soars and swirls to the floor, blanketing the herd of stuffed horses I had cast away in the night. I rescue each one and rearrange them together on my bed, a lineup of manes and tails and glassy black eyes gazing out across a bedsheet sea.

"Chickens, Beatrice," my mother says from the kitchen below. She knows I'll hear her through the gaps and cracks. Our farmhouse doesn't like us to have secrets.

I pull on denim overalls and rummage for my swim goggles, then race to the bathroom and onto the wooden step stool. Mom sings again about the taxi and the screen door slamming, her voice sliding like cool water across the bathroom tile. I soak in every word while I brush my teeth, my eyes locked on my reflection in the mirror. Staring back are a mouth full of baby teeth, fiery blue eyes, and a head of dark curls that grow like bush beans toward the sun. *What if I never get older?* Stuck at six years old. My legs never reaching the gas pedal. Forever excluded from grownup mysteries like bras and black coffee and why so many songs are about people leaving.

The long staircase creaks and groans beneath my feet. The house squeaks just about everywhere I go. Dad says our farmhouse is more than a hundred years old. I guess that's why the floor in the corner of our living room bobs like a trampoline. I haven't told my parents that I bounce there. Maybe the house is trying to.

At the kitchen doorway, cinnamon and peaches mingled with heavy heat from the oven greet me. Mom wears a sleeveless dress with a tight bodice and a skirt that fans wide. She's like the marigolds in our garden, bright and bold in a color that can't be ignored. Barefoot, with ruby toenails, she glides from oven to counter, setting tins of morning-glory muffins and mini loaves of sweet bread to cool on a maze of wire racks. A band of Vermont summer sun inches across the black and white checkered linoleum. Stacks of mixing bowls teeter in the sink. Most of the cupboards are open. There's flour on the ceiling.

Mom is spotless. The eye of the storm. She bends over to brush something off her knee, then lifts the scalloped hem of her dress. Her upper thigh is pale underneath, almost fragile compared to her deeply tanned legs.

"I got so dark this summer," she says. I don't think she can see me standing there but she grins at me, then straightens, her raven hair tumbling past her shoulders. She is prettier than all the other women in town. When she's nearby, it's hard to see anything but her.

"You're wearing your swim goggles to collect the eggs?" she asks.

I nod.

"Are you a fish out of water?"

"I'm a mermaid wearing girl skin."

She raises a shapely eyebrow. I imagine my overalls are a sheath of watery, shimmery scales.

"Prettiest mermaid I've ever seen," she says and as her loving gaze travels over me, my forked tail flutters.

A wasp dive bombs over her head and lands on a cinnamon-raisin loaf. She points at the mound of magazines on the kitchen table that Dad built out of scrap wood.

"Grab me one of those, Beatrice," she says.

I choose *The New Yorker* because it has cartoons. The wasp wizzes to the countertop. Mom tears the cover off the magazine, knocks the flour off a measuring cup, and traps the wasp beneath the dome. She slips the magazine cover underneath and breezes to the screen door with the makeshift trap pressed between her palms. With a bump of her hip the screen door swings wide. She opens her hands toward the sky, waiting patiently, arms extended, until the wasp rises and zigzags away. I've never seen her kill anything.

"Where's Dad," I ask. Most mornings he's here, hovered over his students' homework, wearing a grownup shirt with sleeves and a collar, khaki pants, and a belt. Always buzz-cut, clean-shaven, and dressed in calm earth tones, he's like the evergreen trees that can hold on to their leaves year-round but only get to show off one color.

"He's at the university," Mom says and steals a raisin from the bread loaf, leaving a noticeable crater behind. She pops it in her mouth and motions me to approach her. She smells of fresh laundry. I smell like everything I did yesterday. She untangles the swim goggles that are coiled around my neck and she reaches for my hair, but instead of tamping down the tangle of willful curls, she slips her fingers in and tugs gently so the whole cloud gets bigger. At her touch, my scalp tingles and my eyelids snap shut. Her fingers rake through the chaos one more time and when the shivers pass, I open my eyes to find her face inches from mine. The summer sun has left freckles on her nose.

"Chicken coop. Eggs," she whispers and beams at me.

My chest hurts with all the love. *Can a person die of love?*

The old-fashioned rotary telephone clangs to life on the wall behind us. With each deafening ring, the phone knocks and vibrates as if it's struggling to break free. I scurry out of its reach and grab my father's fishing cap with ear flaps from the hook by the screen door. Mom rescues us mid-ring with a singsong "hello."

The yard shimmers in the morning light, the dewy grass sparkling like fairy dust. A layer of fog sits low and thick in the distant fields, giving the night creatures extra time to find hiding places. The only breaks on the horizon are our empty corral and stable, Dad's wood shop, and the art barn. Mom calls it the art barn because her painting studio takes up the second-floor loft, but since her Mercedes consumes the whole first floor, I think the art barn might be a garage. Mom's Mercedes is white. The last one was blue. Grandpa sends her one every two years. Dad won't touch them.

I flip up the bill of Dad's fishing cap so I can see better. Avoiding the stone path, I cut toward the chicken coop across the newly mowed grass, enjoying the tickle as the loose blades glue to my toes and ankles. I'm aware that I'm surrounded by movement but not sound. Cauliflower clouds tumble over the Green Mountains. A garter snake darts for cover in the buckthorn. Squirrels bound up the trunk of a maple. There's no wind, so the trees are strangely quiet. I can hear myself breathing.

Tires crunch on gravel and a silvery-gray Lexus SUV with

an out-of-state license plate crawls up our driveway to the art barn. I halt mid-stride. The driver's door opens and a skinny woman in tight jeans and a scoop neck shirt slips out. Her long blonde hair hangs smooth and flat. Big dark bug-eye sunglasses rest on a perky, narrow nose. Her lips gleam glossy pink. I've never seen sandals with heels that high.

I pretend that I'm invisible.

The woman scowls as she scans our farmhouse. I follow her gaze and realize that Dad spends more time building things for inside the house than fixing things outside the house. The paint is faded and chipped. A gutter sags. Deck railing is missing. Mom's lacey bras and Dad's undershirts are pegged to a clothesline. I wonder if that's bad, too.

The woman glances my way and flinches. "You startled me, little boy," she says as her hand flies to her heart. A diamond ring winks from its golden perch on her finger.

"I'm not a . . ." is all I get out before Mom pops through the screen door and onto the lower of the two rear steps.

"May I help you?" Mom asks the woman. The house appears drab and weary compared to her dazzling smile and marigold power. The woman appears to relax at the sight of her.

"I'm sorry to bother you. My family and I are vacationing in Stowe, and I thought I'd take our daughter out—you know, explore Vermont. We've been driving for a while. I hoped we might find a mall or something, but we haven't had any luck."

Mom nods encouragingly. She hates malls.

"I left my cell phone at the rental house so now we're lost in these . . ." she motions toward a stand of birch trees, ". . . back woods and my daughter needs a restroom. Can she use yours?"

Mom ignores the stone path and cuts across the yard through the wet, clingy grass. Her feet soon look like mine— covered in grass fur. I smile beneath the fishing cap.

"Yes, of course," Mom says. When she reaches the woman, she extends a slender arm. "I'm Lily."

"Julie," the woman says and shakes Mom's hand. Julie motions toward the hulking gold-trimmed Lexus behind her. "And this is my daughter, Mia."

The tinted windows don't lower. A door doesn't open.

"Mia, angel, get out of the car and come say hello to Lily."

Nothing.

Julie and my mother exchange tight smiles.

"Right now, Mia," Julie says.

A rear door unlatches and creeps open. All I can see are rail-thin legs and a pair of pink ballet flats gradually descending. The toes touch the gravel, then recoil, as if gravel is foreign. When the ballet flats finally land, a girl about my age with honey-colored hair comes forward wearing a black halter-top sundress and a tiara. The lifelike doll that's crushed beneath her crossed arms is dressed in the exact same outfit. The girl doesn't look at her mother or at my mother or at the art barn or the farmhouse; her eyes are fixed on me.

"What's your son's name?" the Julie woman says.

At that I pull my swim goggles on. The world turns blue.

"That's my daughter, Beatrice," Mom says, and winks at me.

The woman's eyes grow wide. "Your *daughter*? How nice," she says in a high, thin voice that suggests it's not nice at all. Like the way Dad says "Delicious!" whenever Mom bakes crustless tuna quiche for dinner.

I lower my cap so only the strangers' calves and feet are visible. A ladybug drops onto my arm. It stays put for only a few seconds then takes flight and lands in the grass. I drop onto all fours to search for it. My palms and knees sink into the earth.

"Hi Beatrice," the woman calls out.

"Hi," I say.

She rewards me with a little wave.

I spot the ladybug nestled in a patch of clover. I crawl over and gently offer her my finger. She crawls on.

"She doesn't look like a girl," Mia says.

At that I stand, my finger extended. The ladybug creeps over my knuckle. My damp overalls cling to my knees.

"Be polite," the Julie woman says.

Mia forges on. "She looks like a boy," she says and uncrosses her arms. By her side, the matching doll now dangles by its honey-colored tresses.

Heat floods my face. The ladybug weaves through the tiny blond hairs on my forearm. I step backward and my feet sink into warm mud. It feels like pudding.

My mother speaks. "She's six years old."

"She's not wearing a shirt," says the girl.

"Mia," the Julie woman says.

"Overalls are for boys," the girl says.

"Don't you ever play outside?" says my mother.

I want to run away, but I can't move. The pudding has me.

"Yes, but not dressed like *that*," says the girl.

Tears rise behind my eyeballs. I drop my gaze to the ladybug. It flies away.

Don't look at the girl. I tell myself. *Just don't look at her.*

I look.

She glares at me. The doll too.

My mother's gentle voice rings out and spellbinds me. True and smooth, it can lure me from my most faraway places.

"Mia," my mother says.

The girl ignores her.

"Mia, eyes on me please," my mother says.

The girl obeys.

"Think of what a sad, dull world this would be if all little girls were alike," Mom says.

A rush of energy travels through me. My feet lift from the pudding mud. I tug off my father's cap and as I spin away, sunlight kisses my face. I skip, then run to the laying hens who eagerly await me.

CHAPTER 3

Ginny and I sit alone on the rear steps, looking out across the darkened lawn and distant barn. A faint golden glow clings to the edges of the sky while the ground lies drenched in shadows. It's the in-between time when night is trying to settle in, but day doesn't want to let go.

I watch the smoke as it leaves Ginny's lips and tangles with the crisp September air. She lets me hold her lighter, a tiny gold box engraved with her initials. I know the lighter isn't for children, that it's somehow dangerous and forbidden, but rather than return it to her, I run my thumb over its sleek finish, trace its smooth edges, and fold it securely inside my palm.

Ginny visits Mom once a year and dresses a little differently each time. I fear I stay the same. She wears black linen slacks, a black blouse, a plush pink shawl, and black leather ankle boots. I'm wearing my tie-dyed pajamas with feet.

"Is that a bat?" Ginny says and freezes, the cigarette inches from her mouth.

I catch sight of the acrobatic flyer. "It's chasing insects."

"Look at you," she says. My chest puffs with pride.

She tugs on the sleeve of my pajamas. "Did your mother make those?"

I nod. "Do people make their own clothes in San Francisco?"

"People make clothes to sell. To make money."

"Do you have a yard in San Francisco?"

"No. I have an apartment with a view of the San Francisco Bay."

She draws on her cigarette and makes smoke rings as she exhales. I didn't know humans could do that.

A swarm of fireflies flash by.

"Are there animals?"

"Sure," she says. "Dogs. Cats. I saw a racoon behind a dumpster once."

"What can you do there?"

"So much. You can eat Italian cannoli for breakfast, a Salvadorean tamale for lunch, and sushi for dinner. Right outside your door are trains, trolleys, and taxis to take you anywhere you want to go—to the theater, a museum, shopping. The city is full of people from all over the world. It's exciting and invigorating and you can be anyone you want to be there. No questions asked."

She takes a long pull on the cigarette then crushes it beneath the heel of her boot.

"What's cannoli?" I ask.

She twists to face me, her eyes wide. "You've never had cannoli?"

I shake my head.

Her eyes linger on my face as if she sees something unexpected.

"It's sweet and delicious pastry," she says and pushes my hair off my forehead. Her brow scrunches in concentration. She lifts my chin with her index finger and fluffs my hair forward to make bangs. Unsatisfied, she tries to tuck my hair behind my ears, then makes a ponytail on top of my head. Finally, she whips off the clip that neatly binds her auburn curls and tugs, gathers, and twists my hair into a potato-sized lump at the base of my neck. After lots of wrangling and wrestling, the clip clicks shut. My scalp prickles in protest.

"Let me see," she says.

I move my head slowly fearing my hair will rip out.

"You should wear your hair like that," she says.

"I can't breathe."

"It makes you pretty."

"Dinner is ready!" My father calls from indoors.

Ginny rises and brushes off her slacks. My forehead throbs.

"Really pretty," she says before she disappears into the house.

Crickets chatter. Night has won. My belly grumbles in hunger. I run my fingertips over Ginny's clip while her gold lighter hums in my other hand. I don't know why but I feel I have to choose: not one or the other, but both or none. Laughter erupts in the kitchen. I don't hesitate. By the time I'm seated before a steamy bowl of rice, chicken curry, peanuts, and coconut, I've forgotten about the lighter, the hair clip and the "pretty" I left behind, set neatly aside on the rear steps.

Dinner is eaten amidst a flurry of Mom and Ginny's laughter. I watch speechlessly, riveted, hoping to catch a glimpse of the girls they were when they were my age. My father, still wearing his college professor outfit—khaki pants, brown shirt, and knit tie—is also a spectator, sitting relaxed in his chair and smiling at my mother often. At times, he rises to silently serve food or clear dishes or pour wine, but he never interrupts their rhythm. I can't read him and I've nearly given up trying. I know he's the one who folds the clean laundry that Mom has left on the guestroom bed for six days. I know he's the reason there's always milk for my cereal. And I know that when he emerges from his shop after hours of carving and sanding a side table or a rocking chair, he appears taller, brighter, and the sawdust speckles in his hair give him a king's crown.

He carries the last of our dishes to the sink and returns with a fresh bottle of wine. He refills Ginny's glass, but Mom covers hers with her palm.

"I'm done," she says and smiles up at him.

He kisses the top of her head. She wraps an arm around his waist and snuggles against him. He rubs her shoulder in slow, looping circles.

"You know I'm the reason your parents met," Ginny says to me. I perk up. "We were all at Cornell together and one night during our senior year I dragged your mother away from her easel and made her go to a party with me."

"It was barely a party. There were nine people. Eight if you don't count the DJ." Mom's face remains bright, but her voice has grown tighter.

"There were enough people there for you to make a love connection," Ginny says then purrs like a feisty kitten.

Normally Mom would rise to the bait, but she falls strangely quiet.

"Love at first sight," Dad says. He tucks his tie into his shirt, rolls up his sleeves and fills the sink with hot soapy water. His eyes find mine. "Your mother asked me to dance," he says.

"Brazen hussy," Ginny says.

"I was shy," Dad says.

"Wanton minx," Ginny says.

"I'd seen your mother's art show in Sibley Hall, so I knew who she was. Everyone on campus knew who she was."

"We all thought Lily was headed to the Sorbonne after graduation," Ginny says to me.

Mom pulls me into her lap.

"You had that string of incredible shows junior year and

then senior year that one stupid critic . . . what was his name?" Ginny says.

"Mitch Markwell," Mom says. Her nose sinks into my hair. She breathes me in.

"Mitch Markwell! He was the only fool who couldn't see what you were doing with your portraits. My god, you were a magician with color, Lily."

Ginny takes a sip of wine. Her voice softens. "I didn't see you for days after Markwell's review came out."

Mom locks me in a tight embrace.

"What's a Sorbonne?" I whisper.

"A famous art gallery in Paris," she mumbles against my head.

"Then suddenly you're pregnant," Ginny says, eyes wide.

Mom reaches around me and refills her wine glass.

"Beatrice was the surprise of our lives," my father says as he scrubs a dinner plate.

Mom stiffens.

"I had to decline the forestry program at Berkeley and accept the teaching position at The University of Vermont," Dad says.

Mom's chest rises and falls against me. Her heartbeat drums.

"I wouldn't change a thing," Dad says.

"You could have painted while you were pregnant," Ginny says. "You could have painted and been a mother."

"I paint," Mom says and sips her wine.

"I built her a studio," Dad says.

"She paints trees," I say.

"Time for bed," my mother says and sets me on my feet.

A short while later, I lie under the covers and whisper goodnight to the horse posters on my wall. Morgan. Belgian. Arabian. My eyes linger on the midnight mustang racing across a tumbleweed prairie, and as the fog of sleep rolls in, my mother's voice, unusually strained, floats from my parents' bedroom next door.

"I can't keep lying to him," she says.

My eyelids fly open.

"I know it's been six years."

I'm six.

"It's eating me alive."

Hers is the only voice in the room. *She's on the phone.*

"I don't know what he'd do."

Fear creeps across my skin.

"That's so 1950s."

I hold my breath.

"Having another child is not the solution," she says.

CHAPTER 4

The sky hangs low and gray. A biting wind whistles through the empty chicken coop and barrels across the crisp, glossy snowpack. The weathervane points north.

I zip my parka and bury my boots in the deep powder. Snowstorms in April don't have the teeth they had in January. Mornings after those squalls were muffled and still, but today the cardinals are already chattering and tulips peek through the snowdrifts.

My boots cut a wide trail. I stomp extra to the left and the right to make it easier for the foxes and rabbits to find their way through the snow. In the distant field, beyond the weathered stable and corral, a herd of deer emerge from the forest and plod along the tree line. I pause to survey our white-capped farmhouse and scan the windows for my father. In his teaching tie and collared shirt, coffee mug in hand, he has watched me cross the yard to Mom's painting studio every morning during my April school break. This morning the curtains are drawn.

The wind picks up and forms a tornado-like funnel that climbs the hill behind our house, whips around the story bench, and disappears. Last September, after Ginny left, Dad made the bench from a maple that lightning had struck. Mom told me stories up there, like when she was my age buying clothes with her mother at Bergdorf's in New York City. Or riding alone in the back seat of a long, black car singing *Frère Jacques* on her way to school.

I tug off my wool hat, stuff it in my pocket, and trudge to the art barn, a dark red stain against the milky countryside. The heavy rolling door squeals as I drag it along the track and with each step, the headlamps and grille of Mom's Mercedes come into view. I don't think it likes being shut in.

I tiptoe alongside the monstrous car, a restless, sleeping dragon. Tall, satiny shopping bags with rope handles crowd the rear seat. When Grandma visited last week, she and Mom redecorated the guest room and spent hours shopping together. Sometimes Mom buys extra. I press my nose against the car window. Seven bags. These must be the ones she doesn't want Dad to see. *Her secrets are my secrets.* Even when I don't understand them.

Light spills from the loft, smothering the stairwell in a golden glaze. I shrug off my parka as I clamber up, wooed by the purr of a space heater. Floor lamps blaze in the airy, open loft, warming the pale walls and paint-speckled floor. A ceiling fan whirs, giving flight to a mobile of glass swans. Flickering purple candles pump the air with lavender.

I climb onto the chair at the center of the room, drop my parka on the floor, and twist around to say hello to Mom's trees. Her paintings fill an entire wall: forests after logging— cemeteries of stumps; branches stretching to reach the sunlight; felled trees with a creature's face etched in their bark. There are no bold yellows or popping reds or creamy oranges; all the paintings are black and white and touches of gray. Mom wears colors but she won't paint with them.

I watch her slender arm reach from behind the easel and select a thin wand from a jar of brushes. Her trees remind me that there are parts of her I'm not allowed to see. Parts that are just for her. Knowing this doesn't push me away; it draws me closer. No activities at school, no playmates my age are nearly as interesting as the mysteries of my mother.

"Is this the fifth time?" I ask. From where I sit, bellbottoms and wool socks are all that's visible of her.

"The sixth," she says. Her hand re-appears, rifles through a pile of gnarled acrylic paint tubes and rags, and retrieves a black-handled palette knife.

"You're painting me," I say.

"Yes, a portrait."

"Like what you painted in college."

"Good memory. Yes."

"Will I be sad like the trees?"

At that she leans out and scans my face. I think she can peer inside my mind. I hold still so she can see better.

She disappears behind the easel.

"What are those paintings?" I ask. A tower of canvases fills the corner of the studio.

"Mom found them when she and Dad had their guest cottage renovated. She brought them when she drove up last week. They're my paintings from college."

"Will you show me?"

"Someday."

"Why don't you hang them with the trees?"

"I don't want to look at them."

I don't ask why. By her tone, I know the reason is off-limits.

She sets her brush aside, comes out from behind the canvas, and gives me a smile. It lands. Hits its target. I tingle all over.

"Hi," she says.

I forget what we had been talking about before. "Hi," I say.

She walks over, rests one hand on her enormous belly, and gently lifts my chin with her fingertips. The sight of her bulging tummy renews my dread. I don't want a sibling.

"Mom," I say.

"Hold there," she says.

"Can I tell you something?"

"Of course."

"I don't want . . ."

She inhales sharply and doubles over. I pop up off the chair. She reaches out and rubs my arm to soothe me. The space heater ticks off. Her skin reddens.

My mother is dying.

"Honey," she says.

Who will raise me?

"Beatrice," she says.

Dad won't know how.

"Listen," she says.

Please don't leave me.

She squeezes my hand.

Our eyes lock.

"Go get your father," she says.

Hours later, my father and I sit in a windowless waiting area with glossy floors and blinding overhead lights that turn Dad's gentle eyes into ghostly shadows. We sit side by side in hard plastic chairs and hold hands. Our palms have grown sweaty, but neither of us lets go. His right knee won't stop bouncing.

Across from us, nature photos hang from the dull, puddy-colored wall. "What's that black and white bird with checkerboard wings?" I say.

"A loon," he says.

"Do we have them at the house?"

"No, they live on lakes and ponds."

"What do they sound like?"

Dad glances in both directions of the empty hospital hallway, then releases a loud, trilling call. I'm about to ask him to do it again, but the door to Mom's room flies open and a slim nurse appears in the doorway.

"You can come in now," she says and steps aside to make way. My father leaps to his feet, thanks her and disappears into the room.

My body moves slowly, each footstep in quicksand. I make it as far as the doorway then stop. The nurse's blue scrubs are close enough for me to touch. I sense her eyes on me and I expect her to hurry me along with a hand on my shoulders, but she doesn't touch me. My gaze falls to the seam in the linoleum floor that marks the end of the hallway and the beginning of Mom's room. The tips of my boots touch the line and I realize that the hallway is the past when it was just me, and the room is the future where I have to share them. Share my parents.

I float up out of my body. Alone. Rising. I can see my parents on the bed below me, but I can't reach them or call to them. I simply drift, weightless, a forgotten balloon, until a hand settles on top of my head. The touch is gentle. Solid. I peer up and find the nurse watching me. I search her face. Kindness.

"You're okay," she whispers. I can't reply. I can't even nod. Her hand on my head is my only tether to Earth, to "okay" land.

"Beatrice."

My father's voice breaks through. He sits on the bed at my mother's feet. I won't look at her, only at my father.

"Come meet your brother," he says.

The nurse's hand stays put. It's as if she wants me to be the one to break away first. Dad pats the space beside him. His loon call rings in my head. I take a step and the nurse's hand falls away. I cross to the bed and Dad lifts me up, draws me close, and wraps an arm around me. Head lowered, I stare at the small tear in the knee of his blue jeans.

A wriggling, blanketed creature is laid in my lap. My father's long fingers part the fabric and I see him. The baby. The boy. My brother. Instantly I land. I return to my body, sitting cross-legged on a hospital bed with my family the morning after an April snowstorm.

A white-coated, gray-haired man appears at the bedside and asks my mother questions about how she's feeling. I hold perfectly still so my brother doesn't slide off my lap.

"But Dr. Morris, she didn't need painkillers after Beatrice," my father says.

The sound of my name draws my attention.

"I'd like to send your wife home with enough tablets for a week, and if she needs more she can refill the prescription," Dr. Morris says.

"Painkillers seem excessive," my father says.

"Every delivery is different."

"Still . . ."

"Your wife is older."

"She's not even 30."

"I'll take them," my mother says and the window rattles.

CHAPTER 5

Birdsong lulls me out of my dream. As the story fades, I cling to the edges.

My face pressed against glass. My new classroom is on the other side. Miniature desks and chairs in a circle. My teacher writes on the blackboard. It's Ginny . . . but not Ginny. My classmates file in. They're not young like me; they're grown-ups. Class begins. I tug on the door. I can't get in.

Anxiety follows me into wakefulness, but instead of the lemony walls of my bedroom, I awaken to dapples of sunlight and the thick bough of an oak. A Monarch butterfly flits past. The story bench is just long enough for my body to fit, head to toe. I wonder if Dad knew that when he built it. I roll onto my side. The September breeze carries the smell of McIntosh apples and cider donuts from the picking orchard up the road. A squirrel scurries into the brush. It's the weekend. No school.

My mind retraces the morning: waking to the crunch of gravel under my father's pickup truck tires as he left for the grocery store. Oliver asleep in his crib. Mom's bedroom door closed. The mess in the kitchen: baby bottles and nipples, the stench of dirty diapers, half-drunk mugs of coffee, a magazine open on the floor. Life interrupted. Everything unfinished.

In the coop, the hens had left me seven eggs. I took them

with me to the story bench, hoping I'd catch sight of the fox again. I lay on the bench so he wouldn't be frightened by me. I must have fallen asleep.

My gaze drifts to the fresh eggs in the grass below. The light brown Rhode Island Reds and the slightly darker Plymouth Rocks are smooth and clean, as if the hens got up early to wash them for me. Feathery fuzz sticks to pebbles of poop on the pale, blue-green Araucana eggs. Dad once said Araucanas have digestion problems like Grandpa. Even Mom laughed at that.

I leave the smallest egg for the fox and start toward the house, my mind whirring. The outdoors still makes sense. The drum of overnight rain. Fingers of sun in the garden. A cloudless sky. But in the months since Oliver was born, my parents have stopped hugging. We hardly ever eat meals together. Nights are broken up with their soothing and feeding Oliver. By day, Mom is slow to smile. I pour my own cereal now and wash my hands without being asked. I have conversations in my head more than out loud. I fade into the walls and pass through rooms without them noticing me.

I watch. And listen.

With the egg bundle against my belly, I tramp down the hill to the farmhouse. The screen door creaks and the door sticks and when I step into the kitchen, my mother is on the floor. Legs out straight, her rust and gold floral dress fanned out like a puddle, she sits propped against the wall staring blankly at the still unvarnished cabinetry. Wispy tendrils of hair escape her French twist and spiral past her ears. A tear spills from her long lashes and drips dark with mascara. Her eyes fix ahead, her face slack.

At first I'm frozen, but then my body moves without me asking. I set the eggs on the floor, pull a kitchen towel from the drawer by the stove and blot her damp cheek like I've seen her do. Her misty eyes find mine. I smooth her head the way I pet Lemon Drop, the pudgy Beagle at the country store. Long, slow strokes. A faint smile tugs at the corners of her mouth. She pulls my hand to her lips and kisses my palm then presses my hand against her check and holds it there.

A picture flashes in my mind: Mom loading up the Mercedes and driving away with a mound of glamorous dresses in the rear seat. Fear coils inside my chest. She rubs my forearm. Her eyes appear distant and haunted. I wish I knew what I'm supposed to do.

"I messed up," she says, still pressing my hand against her cheek. "I messed it all up."

My throat goes dry. Words crackle from my lips. "Messed what up?"

"My life. My whole life," she whispers.

Sickness slinks into my belly. She pulls my hand from her face and gently kneads my palm and fingers with her thumbs. I see the Mercedes again. A streak of white as it drives away.

"It doesn't change how much I love you," she says. "Or your Dad. Or Oli."

Her words feel true but not true, like my teacher in the dream . . . Ginny . . . but not Ginny. I flash to the story bench with the dappled sunlight and the oak's bough and the cider donut air. Only my body stands here in the kitchen. My stuck child body.

"Beatrice," she says.

I snap to the present. I wish I was older. I wish Dad was home. She's so different now. *What's wrong with her?*

"Will you sit with me?" she says and pats her lap.

I move toward her. Her face brightens but as I'm about to climb in, Oliver cries out from upstairs. She covers her face with her hands and brings her knees up to her chest until she's small and tucked. She leans forward and drops her forehead to her knees. Her French twist is inches from me. Stray hairs hang loose and call for me to tuck them back in. As I reach out, Oliver howls. I withdraw my hand. Mom covers her ears.

You have to choose.

The thought startles me. Impossible. How could I choose? It's always been Mom. It will always be Mom.

As if she's reading my mind, her head pops up. The world seems to pause. She opens her hand to me. Her fingers are inches from mine. Oliver cries out. Our eyes lock and I step backwards. I've never felt so sad. She slides onto her side and curls up on the floor.

The stairs squeal under my pounding feet. Oliver's howls soften to hiccups as I approach his crib. He flails like a beetle on its back. His cheeks blaze with red splotches. The front of his sleeper is wet with tears.

I had watched Dad build Oliver's crib out of maple, driving long bolts into the sturdy wood and reinforcing the frame with metal rods. I choose the end without the mobile of ducklings and find an easy foothold in the "V" of two struts. The crib creaks as I climb over the frame and lower myself onto the mattress. Oliver wiggles and clucks. I inch over, curl on my side, and draw my knees to my chest just like my mother downstairs.

With my nose against his cheek, he smells like baby chicks and spring grass and rainbows—pure and raw and fragile. I rest my hand lightly on his chest, feel the rise of his lungs and look out at the world as he does, through bars.

CHAPTER 6

Cowboy is all that stands between the five of us and the five of them. His suede chaps hug his narrow hips and flair wide at the base so only the triangular tips of his dusty boots are visible. He tightens the straps at his waist with two quick tugs. His silver belt buckle catches the sunlight and sends off laser sparkles.

He rolls up the cuffs of his long-sleeved shirt, revealing dark brown skin and muscular forearms. Silver snaps line the front of his shirt instead of buttons. I check out his hands and his thick fingers. *Can fingers be too big for buttons?*

He sets his hands on his hips, taking the same stance as my brother's action figures. He isn't tall. Dad is taller. Neither man is overweight. But Cowboy takes up more room than my father.

He stands motionless, but there is power in it. Suction. Our eyes are on him. Next to me, the woman in denim, another visitor to the ranch, has finally stopped talking. Cowboy crosses his arms. Oliver slips his hand into mine and slouches against me.

"Hi, Oli," I say.

"Hi," he squeaks.

Cowboy lifts his hat and runs his fingers through tight black curls. He surveys us. I straighten, hoping to appear older. I inch away from the denim woman and her husband and son. I don't want Cowboy to think we are part of their family.

"Now I'm going to match each of you with your horse," Cowboy says, motioning over his shoulder. His voice is low, like a singer.

I've been studying the five horses at the far side of the corral since they were led out . . . fixated as the handlers saddled them, picked their hooves, and slipped bridles over their heads. A gray Mustang. A brown Mustang. Two chestnut Quarter Horses. And the tallest horse I've ever seen. Completely white. White mane. White tail. If it had a horn, it would be a unicorn.

"My handlers will help you saddle up, check the tack, and give you basics about riding so nobody gets hurt. Not you, not the horses."

Injury had never occurred to me. It is a foreign object in the fog of my excitement.

"Rest easy," he continues. "You don't have to be experienced to ride my team. My horses have walked this trail a thousand times. They know where we're going. They know each other. The only thing they don't know is you," Cowboy says.

Beside me, Oliver kicks the sand with his hiking boot as if willing it to fly off his foot. I admire him in his Superman T-shirt and blue jeans, a mop of midnight curls hanging over his left eye. He cried when Mom made him put on the square-toed, heavy-soled boots this morning amidst the searing Arizona heat. We've been camping for nearly two weeks, working our way from Vermont to California to see Ginny. This morning was the first time he'd cried since we left home.

"Wendy," Cowboy calls out. The denim woman giggles, then fans her face as if to cool a sudden blast of heat. Cowboy smiles but not wide enough to show teeth. In riding boots as red as garden tomatoes, the denim woman trudges across the deep sand to Cowboy. I strain to hear what he says to her, but it's just a low rumble of manly voice. She hurries over to the line of horses.

The handler by the brown Mustang extends his hand to shake. She ignores it and throws her arms around him. He stiffens inside the hug.

Cowboy calls on the denim woman's husband next and sends him to the Quarter Horse with the dark mane. Then their teenage son, gangly and quiet, eyes hidden behind his bangs, is sent to the gray Mustang.

Only the blonde Quarter Horse and the giant unicorn remain. The unicorn has got to be mine.

Cowboy strides toward us. He closes the space in three steps and stands near enough for me to see that his eyes are golden brown, he has a pencil-thin scar on his chin, and he is much, much taller than my dad.

"Beatrice and Oliver, right?" he asks, his eyes squinty.

I nod. My voice is suddenly not working.

"Like I said, my name is Cowboy," he says, touching his chest and then squatting so he is closer to my brother's height.

"My name is Oliver," my brother says, touching his own chest. Cowboy smiles. Still no teeth.

"How old are you?" he asks.

"I'm five and Beatrice is eleven," Oliver says.

"You ever been on a horse before?" he asks us.

I shake my head.

Oliver speaks up. "No, but Beatrice has posters of horses all over her room."

Cowboy raises an eyebrow. Our eyes lock. A million questions flood my mind but get stuck, clogged in the neck of the funnel.

"Today you get to ride two of my favorite horses: Winter, the white one, and Topaz, the speckled one. You'll be right behind me at the front of the line," he says, then straightens and extends his hand to Oliver, who drops mine instantly for Cowboy's.

Together they trudge through the corral's deep sand— Cowboy in slow motion, as if he's waist deep in water, and Oliver speed walking in rapid-fire bursts. Oliver's head bobs and bounces as he talks. Every few paces, Cowboy nods.

They reach the horses. Cowboy lifts Oliver onto Winter. My horse. The unicorn. My disappointment fades quickly.

Oliver grabs the saddle horn with both hands and sits ramrod straight while Cowboy adjusts the stirrups. Winter is a mountain of muscle; Oliver is a dollop of whipped cream on top. My brother's shoulders are up around his ears. His eyes are as big as donuts. *Should I tell Cowboy that my brother is terrified?*

Just then, Cowboy stops and lays a hand on Oliver's calf, pushes his hat off his hairline, and says something. Oliver nods. Cowboy talks. Oliver nods. Cowboy runs his hand along Winter's shoulder. Oliver lets go of the saddle horn, leans forward and presses both hands on Winter's coat, like he's hand painting.

I wonder what Cowboy said to him. I wonder if my parents saw what just happened. I spot them easily in the visitors' lean-to. Mom, in blue jean cutoffs and one of Dad's T-shirts, a bright-red L.L. Bean windbreaker tied around her waist, and a camera over her shoulder, leans against the frame, eyes closed, shoulders sagging, her hair bound in a messy ponytail. Dad stands several feet away, trim and tidy, studying a road map. I give them a quick wave. Neither of them notices.

Topaz seems to get larger as I get closer. Tiny, Topaz's handler, cups his hands for me to step into, but I don't want to put my dirty boots on his clean skin.

"It's okay," he says and lifts me easily. He rapidly adjusts my legs and the stirrups, tightens the girth, and trudges beside me along the perimeter of the corral calling out instructions. I hang on his every word.

"Those reins connect to the tender part of Topaz's mouth, so don't yank. Think of *asking* Topaz to slow instead of telling him. Soft hands," he says, holding imaginary reins and easing them toward his body as if his forearms were shock absorbers.

"Soft hands," I say.

"And use your voice. '*Whoa.*' Clear like that."

"Whoa," I say, like I do when Oliver and I play horse.

"No, say it like you mean it, but you're not angry."

I clear my throat and speak from my gut. "Whoa," I say and Tiny gives me a thumbs up.

Minutes later, Cowboy leads us away from the corral and from everything familiar: my parents, our dusty Saab with the French fry grease-stained state park maps, Oliver's treasured blue blanket, and the diary I write in when I have thoughts that I don't know what to do with.

Parent-less.

On my own.

Entering unfamiliar territory.

Something tells me I ought to get used to it.

CHAPTER 7

As we leave the corral, Topaz's ears flicker as they track sounds. I watch Winter's rippling hind quarters beneath my little brother, and Cowboy's relaxed posture atop his Buckskin, who is the color of deer but with a black mane, tail, and "socks."

There's more sky here than in Vermont, more sky than I ever imagined. And around me, instead of grass, there's sand for miles, a dry lake with lily pads of brambles and rock. Absent are the maple trees and oaks that grow around our house. Here, the trees are cacti that look like distant relatives who don't eat enough vegetables.

The horses' scent—sweet and musky—fills my nostrils. I draw the raw, animal smell into my lungs. Beneath me, Topaz troops sure-footed and steady. It's already easier . . . moving with him, letting him lead me. His sweat dampens my jeans where my calves and his belly touch. Near the saddle horn, a light patch of mane grows short and wiry instead of long and flowing like the rest. I lean forward and stroke the short hairs as if there was a wound there.

We are six in a row: Cowboy, Oliver, me, the teenage son, the husband, and the denim woman. The horses snort and nicker, saddles squeak, tails swoosh, and hooves clack. Strangely, it's not noise to me, it's closer to silence, like when

I'm underwater in the pool at the YMCA. Although the world is loud and echoing outside the water, all I hear is my own heartbeat.

I close my eyes and imagine I'm Topaz. *Hooves driving into the sand. Legs strong and swift. Fearless. Free.* My body softens. I seep into everything around me. The horses. The air. The sand. I forget that sixth grade starts soon in a different building with a new teacher. I forget that the older I get, the more rules there about how to look and how to act and the harder it's becoming to not follow them. I forget that Mom sleeps all the time.

Around us, the flat desert has morphed into swells and jagged rocks dotted with shrubs and cacti. We see prairie dogs, lizards, and snakes. Cowboy twists in his saddle to tell us about the animals, how they survive here, why the plants enjoy it here, and what the weather does. The way he explains it sounds like a puzzle. Everything fits together.

In front of me, Oliver's hands rest on the saddle horn while he admires the scenery. Cowboy must have tied off the reins somehow so that Oliver wouldn't have to hold them.

Cowboy slows his horse so he's riding alongside Oliver. "How ya doin'?" he asks.

Oliver says something I can't hear.

"Winter is six years old," Cowboy answers. "She was born right here on my ranch. Her mom, Lightning," stroking the mane of the Buckskin he's riding, "showed up in the middle of the night during the worst lightning storm I ever saw. She was pregnant, her belly out to here," he holds his hands about two feet from his flat stomach, "but she was skin and bones. Took me a while, but I got her into my barn and gave her hay and grain and stayed up with her all night." He pauses. "I named her Lightning after the storm. A few days later she had her filly," he says.

"Did you name the filly 'Winter' because she's all white?" I call out.

"Nope. I named her Winter because around here, snow would be a miracle. And Lightning surviving on her own and giving birth to Winter . . . in my book, that's a miracle."

A miracle. I get choked up, so I lower my head and scratch at nothing on my jeans in hopes that nobody will notice the sudden flush on my skin.

Soon the ground levels out and the shrubs thin and then disappear. We are on the flat sand again, winding through harsh patches of brambles and thorny brush. In the distance, I see the corral and the lean-to. The horses lengthen their strides.

The denim woman shouts from the end of the line. "Almost home!" I flinch but she bothers me less now.

As we approach, Tiny holds the gate open and we enter the corral single file. Cowboy, Oliver, me, and then the three others. Nearly all six horses are inside when it happens.

Mom, in her fire-engine red windbreaker, jumps out from the lean-to and snaps a picture of Oliver with the old-fashioned camera her father sent her. Sunlight bounces off its shiny metal. The flash attachment hurls a pulse of silver light and releases a crackling electrical "pop."

Lightning, closest to the flash, hauls up on her hind legs like a tidal wave, but instead of toppling over, Cowboy sinks low and forward, glued to the saddle. Winter bursts right. Topaz explodes left.

Somehow, words erupt from my mouth. "Whoa!" Topaz ignores me and trots. "Whoa!" I holler and pull on the reins. Topaz trots on. *Soft hands. Ask don't tell. Like you mean it.* "Whoa," I command, and Topaz comes to a halt.

In front of me, the denim woman flails her arms, signaling toward the open desert. Cowboy and Lightning race off and Tiny runs the gate closed behind them.

I whirl around.

Denim woman. Husband. Son.

Me.

Winter is gone.

CHAPTER 8

There's movement on the horizon. Everyone in the corral—riders and handlers—freezes and gawks.

It takes me a moment to understand what I'm seeing. An empty saddle. Winter running awkwardly, as if she's injured her hind leg and can't bring it forward.

I search for my brother but he's nowhere. I scan the horizon, then cut to Winter, who's still cantering. At last, my brain lets me see. Oliver has left the saddle but hangs upside down, arms above his head, trapped in a fall that won't end. His belly is bare and his Superman shirt coils around his neck.

Winter canters while Oliver dangles from one stirrup . . . dangles from one hiking boot. But Winter's gait is not normal. It's as if her hind leg—the one Oliver hangs from in front of—isn't coming all the way forward. Then I understand. *Winter is trying not to kick him.*

"That child is dead," the denim woman mutters.

Cowboy and Lightning lope across the desert, setting off mini explosions of sand. Winter trots awkwardly, cutting at an angle away from them. Cowboy and Lightning ease to a walk then halt. Winter loops out wide but continues to glance over her shoulder at them. Trotting. Watching. Trotting. She throws her head, tosses her mane, whips her tail, and slows to a rapid walk. Oliver's arms fall open. His body is an inverted "T."

Cowboy slips off the saddle as smoothly as water streaming from a glass and stands beside Lightning. Winter walks, her head high, her ears cocked.

Lightning is still. Cowboy is still. Winter circles around to face them.

Lightning is still. Cowboy is still. Winter lowers her head.

Lightning is still. Cowboy is still. Winter limps to Cowboy and halts.

Cowboy calmly reaches out and places his hand on Winter's neck. She drops her head until her nose is nearly touching the sand. She shifts her weight, lifts the hind leg by Oliver off the ground, then gingerly lowers it.

Tears rush over my face. I wipe them but my hands shake so badly, I have to use my forearms.

Cowboy rubs Winter's neck and leans into her, as if he's whispering something, and then he steps slowly around her side, bends, and slips an arm beneath my brother's rag-doll body. Cowboy only takes his hand off Winter long enough to lift Oliver up, free his boot from the stirrup, and lay him gently across his chest and shoulder. Oliver slumps against him and goes still.

Tiny and another handler appear by their side. Tiny takes Lightning's reins and starts toward the corral. Cowboy hands over Winter's reins and walks alongside them with my brother in his arms.

Mom and Dad cluster by the corral gate. I can hear Mom crying and mumbling something. The camera and the windbreaker are nowhere in sight. Dad's arm circles her waist. I haven't seen him hold her like that for a long time. His other hand meets his forehead, pressing, like something is about to fall out. Something he won't ever get back.

I'm suddenly cold, as if an air conditioner flipped on inside me.

Winter hobbles, her coat gray with sweat, a tangle of rivers crisscrossing her belly and hindquarters. Cowboy, holding Oliver, steps through the gate. Mom and Dad rush to him and they all huddle. There's no movement. Their heads are nearly touching. I hold my breath.

Then I see it.

Oliver hauls his upper body off Cowboy's chest and swivels his shoulders toward my father. His arms seem to be glued to his body. Cowboy lowers slightly and Dad scoops Oliver up as if he is weightless, no longer a five-year-old boy, but an infant, a bundle.

Mom wraps her arms around them both and I shake. Tears drip from nose, slip over my lips and chin and drop to my chest, my lap, everywhere. I tremble and shudder. I want to be over there with my family, but my limbs won't listen.

"Beatrice." I hear a voice from somewhere far away. I'm underwater again at the YMCA and a voice is calling from up there, out there, where the air is.

"Beatrice." Again, it calls. Something grips my leg. "He's okay," Cowboy says.

"What?" I ask.

"Oliver. He's okay," Cowboy says again and strokes Topaz's neck.

I forgot I was on Topaz. I forgot he was even there.

"Oliver is scratched up and he's going to be sore, but that's it."

I wipe my cheeks with the heel of my hand. "How can that be?"

"Winter was tall enough and Oliver was small enough that his head never touched the ground. And somehow Winter didn't kick him."

Cowboy's eyes rest on Winter. He lifts the front brim of his hat, rubs his forehead, and says in a low voice so only I can hear, "I don't know. Maybe it's another miracle."

We remain in silence together—me, Cowboy, Topaz, and the miracle—until the denim woman approaches. Cowboy shakes his head at her and she spins away.

"Why?" I ask, watching one of the handlers put ointment on Winter's legs. My mouth is dry. I taste sand.

"Why did Winter run?" Cowboy asks, as if reading my mind.

"Yes."

"She ran because she was scared. Your mom's red jacket. That camera flash. The pop. She didn't know what was happening. She did what she thought she had to do to survive."

"Run."

"Yup."

"Why didn't you gallop the whole way? Why did you and Lightning go out there and then stop?"

"If Lightning and I had run after Winter, she'd have just run faster. She'd think she had a good reason to run, if we were running too. The only way to tell Winter that she didn't need to be afraid was for Lightning and me to show her that *we* weren't afraid."

I lift my hand and wipe my cheeks, my gaze settling on my family, then over on Winter. "All my life I've loved horses, even though I didn't know them," I say. "But now . . ."

Cowboy squeezes my foot. "Beatrice, horses need you to love them more than ever now."

"How come?" I ask, tears flowing again.

His face softens and he smiles so wide that his perfect snow-white teeth show. "Because now you see them for who they really are. Powerful and brave and full of fear. It's one thing to love something because of how it appears on the outside. All pretty. But it's another thing when you get in real close and you see the cracks and flaws. And instead of walking away, you love them more."

His words don't enter through my ears. They enter through my heart.

Love them more because of their flaws. My eyes cut to Winter, then to my mother.

CHAPTER 9

Along the dusty road leading away from the ranch, Oliver naps in his car seat beside me. The ointment Cowboy smoothed on his belly and face smells like an old boot. I stick my head out the window like dogs do and let the wind flood my skin and take my hair. In my mind, I say goodbye to the horses. I wasn't allowed to say it in person.

We pass a shabby farm stand with a handwritten sandwich board advertising corn, tomatoes, and melons. A woman with sunken cheeks sits out front in a folding chair, smoking a cigarette under the shade of a makeshift umbrella. She seems almost part of the landscape—as if she's been sitting there her whole life. Resigned to her post. Resigned to her life. I spread my fingers in a wave so subtle I don't expect her to catch it, but she lifts her arm high and straight in return and we hold ourselves that way until she's just a bump on the parched terrain and I'm two red dots of taillight.

"You couldn't have known Oliver's horse would spook," my father says to my mother as I pull my head inside the car. The atmosphere feels heavy and strained. *Maybe the farm stand woman is happier than we are.*

"It was an accident," Dad says. Mom studies his face as if to gauge if he's telling the truth. She tilts away from him and rests her head against the window.

"I could have killed him," she says.

The undeveloped land gives way to a smattering of short strip malls, fast food drive-throughs, and a church, then a half dozen towering signs advertising "Howdy Corral" trail rides for the whole family. On the signs the horses are cartoon characters—mother, father, son, and daughter—standing upright in matching human outfits. One of them drinks a soda. Another licks an ice cream cone. They all wear ten-gallon hats and have goofy wide-eyed expressions and oversized teeth. Nothing about the cartoon horses matches the animals I just experienced, but when we pass, the Howdy Corral parking lot is packed. I continue to feel like an outsider in the world. More and more I just want to retreat.

"Remember the horse farm near campus?" Mom says. "We used to pass it when we drove to Cayuga Lake."

"I was more interested in you than the scenery," Dad says.

Mom sits up and gives him a sly smile. "Me and your truck."

Their flirtation sparks hope in me. I watch transfixed.

"160,000 miles on that truck," he says. "I said a prayer every time you rode with me."

"You loved that thing."

"I was proud. A farm boy like me at an Ivy League university with a beautiful girlfriend and my own pickup truck?"

Dad beams in the rearview mirror.

"I'd never been in a pickup before," Mom said.

"The only time it conked out was the morning of graduation. We were parked at the Falls."

"You ran up that steep path in the sweltering heat to flag for help."

"Rural New York. A sweaty guy in a suit by the side of the road. Nobody stopped. They probably thought I was a Bible salesman," he says.

She smiles at him and my breath catches in my throat. He rests his free hand on her shoulder. She drops her cheek to meet it. I go still.

"You were a vision in yellow," he says and tucks her loose hair behind her ear. "A human daffodil." Her smile widens. "And four months pregnant."

She lifts her cheek from his hand. The connection breaks.

"The most beautiful woman I'd ever seen," he says. She gazes out the side window.

"I miss who I was in college," she says.

"You're still her."

"No," she says. "I'm not."

Dad's hand drops from her shoulder and moments later, we turn onto the rutted road into the campground. We drive past the RV sites with onboard kitchens and toilets, TV antennas, and his and hers folding chairs with beverage holders until we reach the tent sites, neat and silent, with coolers, battery-powered lamps, and clothes drying from tree limbs.

We pull into our site and the Saab sputters and pops as the engine shuts down. Dad scoops Oliver from his car seat and hugs him tightly against his chest. Mom comes round and reaches out to take him, but Oliver resists and drops his head to Dad's shoulder. I'm struck by Mom's bony shoulders, elbows, and knees—her shorts and T-shirt billow on her frame. *When did she get so thin?*

"He needs to sleep," Mom says.

Dad whispers something to Oliver. My brother nods, and Dad lowers him to the ground. Mom laces her fingers into his and they head for the tent.

"Wait!" I call and they both turn. Mom's face is puffy and blotchy. So is Oliver's, but his is also a bit like Frankenstein with a patchwork of spindly red scratches across his forehead, cheeks, and chin.

"We have to rest, Beatrice," Mom says. She must see the hurt in my face because she adds, "We won't be long." She lets go of Oliver, unzips the rain flap and inner screen, and crawls into the tent.

Oliver stands there, facing me. I walk over, drop onto my knees, and trace his Superman emblem with my index finger while I hunt for words. Heat flushes my cheeks. My eyes mist over. Oliver reaches out and lays his hand on my shoulder, as if he's a grand king knighting me with his sword.

The action takes me by surprise. I burst into laughter. Oliver grins. Mom's arm coils around his waist. Oliver gives me a little wave as Mom's hook draws him backward into the green dome.

At the picnic table, I drop onto the bench across from Dad. He passes me the water jug and I take a long drink, not stopping even when a trickle erupts at the edges of my mouth and soaks the front of my T-shirt.

"How long are they going to nap?" I ask, nodding toward the tent.

"I don't know," he says.

"Mom naps for hours these days. Is it going to be that long?"

"I don't know," he says. He's not much help. Maybe he should nap.

"Oliver is okay now, right?"

"He will be."

I wonder if I'm okay.

Dad stacks the plastic cups and bowls that have been drying in the sun and slides them to the corner of the table. "We're turning around tomorrow instead of continuing on to California," he says.

"What about San Francisco? Ginny?"

"We'll see Ginny next time she comes east. We're going to spend a few days with your grandparents at their summer place in Martha's Vineyard. They haven't seen you kids in a while."

I squeeze my eyes shut and drop my forehead to the picnic table. Ginny's words have never left me: "You can be anyone you want to be in San Francisco. No questions asked." The farm stand woman materializes in my mind. Sunken. Sad. Stuck. *Will that be me?*

A light breeze blows my hair off my neck. I wish it would take me away. Suddenly sparked into movement, I lift my head and untangle myself from the picnic table. My thighs throb. My shoulders ache.

"Where are you going?" Dad asks.

"To hear about the animals," I say as I limp away. We found the outdoor theater the night before. It isn't fancy, just a circle of boulders with log benches in the center, a dirt floor, and a slide projector.

"Don't go, Beatrice. This isn't the end of the world," he says, but I've already spotted the trailhead.

The worn path winds behind the tent sites to a flat area at the base of a hill. A park ranger whom I haven't seen before is speaking, but he's wearing the same thing the woman ranger wore the night before—green shirt, khaki shorts, and hiking boots, a sort of outdoor version of Dad's teaching outfit.

Clusters of grown-ups and children take up the first several rows of benches. Something passes over their faces when they see me. *Shock? Concern?* I'm not sure. Even the ranger pauses mid-sentence.

It's not until I'm sitting alone in the last row that I realize what they were reacting to—my knotted hair from sticking my head out the window like a dog, my sweat-soaked jeans and T-shirt covered in hair from riding a horse, and tear-streaked cheeks and neck from when I thought my brother was dead.

The ranger clicks a button and the image on the projection screen changes. It's a gray lizard on a rock. "This lizard has a special ability," he says.

The ranger seems much happier than the teachers at my school. Maybe because he doesn't have to wear a tie.

The ranger clicks a button, and a split image comes up. On the left is a lizard on a light rock. On the right is a lizard on a dark rock. Both lizards match their rocks.

"These lizards are different shades, but they are all the same lizard," the ranger says. "This lizard can change color depending on the color of its environment. Can anyone tell me why?"

A boy about my age sitting beside an older man in the front row shoots his hand into the air. It sure seems like school now.

"Go ahead." The ranger urges the boy.

"So predators don't see it?" the boy asks.

"Yes! This lizard can blend into its environment by changing color. It adapts so it isn't eaten."

Adapt so you aren't eaten.

Dad appears and sits on my bench just a few feet away. I pretend not to notice. He slides over until our thighs touch. I stare straight ahead. He curls his arm around me and kisses the top of my head. I want to resist. I try to resist. But in the end I break and relax against him.

Adapt so you aren't eaten.

CHAPTER 10

Outside, the Atlantic Ocean tumbles and crashes. It's as if the water, wild and free, refuses to surrender quietly to the island's rigid shoreline.

My grandfather's office smells of Lemon Pledge and dirty spices. If I sit perfectly still in his stiff leather chair, close my eyes, and tell myself that I am outside playing on the beach, I'm hoping that when I open my eyes I will be outside playing on the beach.

"Hello, Beatrice," my grandfather says. My eyelids fly open.

"Hello, Grandpa," I say, disappointed that I still haven't figured out magic.

Grandpa's camel-colored shirt sports epaulets that make his shoulders appear broader than they are and hides a belly that rarely misses a hot meal. Despite his formidable girth, Grandpa crosses the silk Persian rug without emitting a sound. I know the rugs in the house are silk and Persian, but I don't remember when I was told.

It might have been the talk about not wandering through their home eating a very berry popsicle or the one about not running or skipping—with or without food—or not yelling through walls or floors to ask someone a question, or not playing chopsticks on the grand piano, or not leaving the toilet unflushed even if all I did was pee.

My grandfather settles across from me in a chair that matches mine, but he doesn't appear lost in it; he's a king on a throne. If he's surprised to see me waiting, he doesn't show it. He must know Mom requires me to join him here in his office once every time we visit.

"How are your studies?" Grandpa asks, as he holds a match to his pipe and puffs until the embers glow. His fingernails are short and clean. His lips glisten with wetness where they meet the pipe stem.

Along one wall of the study, beneath windows that open onto the Atlantic, looms a majestic, polished desk in the darkest, reddest wood I've ever seen. I wonder what kind of tree it's made from. I don't ask him.

"School is fine," I answer, remembering from our conversation last year what he means by "studies." I stroke the arm of the leather chair, which is surprisingly cool against my skin, and wonder what my brother is doing.

"You're learning about American history? European history? Literature?" Grandpa asks, releasing a plume of smoke into the air between us. It shifts and reshapes and reminds me of the clouds in Arizona.

"Art class is my favorite," I mumble, and he draws on his pipe and assesses me with an unreadable expression. *Am I shrinking under his gaze?* I wonder if he's figured out magic.

Flecks of silver glisten in his hair. "At your age," he says, "you should be exposed to the very best thinkers, the most influential writing, and the ideas and the people who've shaped our civilization. Shaped humanity. Shaped how we live."

My mind flashes to last spring in science class when Peter Morgan fried ants on the windowsill using a magnifying glass and sunlight. The magnifying glasses used to be kept on the activities shelf, but after the mass scorching Mr. Donahue locked them in the cabinet. Peter shaped that.

"The more you know, the more you'll have," Grandpa says, upturning his palms and gesturing toward his office, or maybe the house, or maybe the entire galaxy.

I survey what's before me: rich, glossy matching furniture, shelves of hardcover books, wall paintings, ivory figurines, elegant lamps, *Smithsonian* magazines, a rack of pipes in a variety of shades and shapes, and a woven tapestry. The finale—the room's centerpiece—hangs prominently on the far wall, lit by silver dollar-sized spotlights: two framed pieces of paper with his name written in fancy script beneath the words Yale University on one and Columbia University on the other.

Not until my gaze returns to his cleanly shaven face do I realize there isn't a single photo of a human being in this room. Our eyes hold one another's. I crack my thumb knuckle. He sucks on his pipe.

"You have a slight lisp, Beatrice. When did that start?" he asks from behind a mask of smoke.

Shame, hot and ugly, crawls across my face and then swells over my neck and chest. It mutes me. I shrug while my skin burns.

"If you want people to listen to you—if you want to be a leader—you have to learn to enunciate." He stretches out the last word into four. Eee—nun—see—ate. "Consider holding a pencil in your mouth. Here, I'll demonstrate."

He places his pipe on the narrow table beside him, lifts the pencil from the *New York Times* crossword, and tucks it into his mouth, the way a dog would carry a long stick. He bends toward me and opens his mouth to give me an unobstructed view of where he places the pencil against his tongue.

He has metal fillings.

"Shee, it blox your tongue sho you can't lishp," he says.

I nod.

"Does your mother lisp?" he asks, setting the pencil on the newspaper, drawing a thin cloth from his pocket and dabbing at his lips.

Is this a trick question? "No?"

"No. She spent an entire summer with a pencil in her mouth. She retrained her tongue, so by the time she matriculated that fall, the lisp had been eradicated."

I try to imagine my mother, who forgets the bath water is running, refuses to follow recipes, and appears happiest when speeding in her Mercedes on dirt roads, putting a pencil in her mouth every day for a whole summer.

"The best things in life come from hard work," he adds.

His words make me tired; they make me want to go outside, lie in the sand, and wait for the tide to come in and lick my feet.

He crosses his legs and smooths the fabric on his thigh. "Are you being good for your mother?"

I have a vision of camping from a few days ago: Mom, knee-deep in a river, washing peas she'd bought at a roadside stand and then later, the four of us eating dinner and me secretly feeding my peas to a squirrel under the table.

"Yes, I'm being good," I say and force a small smile.

He puts on slender glasses and the frames practically disappear on his face. Our eyes meet. His eyeballs appear larger now.

"Beatrice, I believe it's time for you to grow up and leave the childish behaviors behind."

My face burns again. I expand like a balloon and squeeze the arms of the fine leather chair while the words, "Why are you so mean?" gather on my tongue. But another part of me wonders if he's right . . . wonders if my imagination and all the parts of me that I like are exactly what's wrong with me.

The leather squeaks as I deflate.

A black-and-white photograph on the wall draws my attention. A leopard in the wild stretches out in the sun, its head high but relaxed, its hind legs sprawling, and its long tail unfurled except for the very tip, which sticks up in a rebellious curl.

I wish I was a wild animal. I wish I didn't have to be human anymore.

Grandpa rises, slides open a small drawer in his desk, and removes a multipack of LifeSavers. He tears off a roll from the end of the line and returns the remaining rolls to the drawer. His short nails fail him. He has to pick repeatedly at the metallic foil to open it, but once he does, he dislodges a candy with his thumb and pops it in his mouth. He sucks on it for a moment, knocks it against his teeth, and then extends the pack toward me. He hasn't moved closer, so if I want one, I will have to get out of my chair and go to him.

I stare at the pack while it hangs there, taunting me, then I shuffle over and peel a candy from the roll, cursing myself for being weak.

Peppermint. *My favorite.*

"Thank you," I say to his sheepskin slippers. I'm pretty sure I just lost something. I'm pretty sure he just won.

Grandpa returns the LifeSavers to the drawer and calls out toward the hallway. "Sherry?"

I don't know who Sherry is. His wife, my grandmother, is named Helen.

"Sherry?" he calls again more loudly.

"Ready, Edward!" My grandmother promises from the kitchen.

Grandpa glides past me and out into the hall. He pauses at

the doorway to the kitchen and a slender arm with a gold wrist bangle passes him a short-stemmed, V-shaped glass filled to the rim with dark liquid. He takes the glass from her and sips, but instead of stepping into the kitchen and joining his wife while she prepares dinner, he strides through the long hall—wallpapered with maps of the world—to the empty sunroom and *The Evening News.*

I open his desk drawer, pull out the roll of peppermint LifeSavers, and shove it in my pocket.

CHAPTER 11

There's no reply when I knock on the bedroom door. "Mom?" I whisper.

I knock again and press my ear to the wood. The door falls opens. Inside, the blinds are half-drawn against the setting sun, casting stripes of muted, golden light into the darkness. My mother faces away from me, on her side. I tiptoe to the bed.

"Mom?" I whisper.

"Hmm," she answers.

"I think we're having dinner soon."

"Hmm."

I touch her shoulder. Her skin is warm.

"Mom . . ."

She rolls toward me and flicks on the ornate bedside lamp. I want to ask her about the summer she had a pencil in her mouth. I want to ask her if she was lonely living here. I want to ask her if there's something wrong with me. Her bloodshot eyes stop me. I can't remember the last time she didn't look depleted.

With surprising strength, she pulls me onto the bed, tucks me into the crook of her arm, then drags me close so I'm snug alongside her body. She strokes my face and my hairline, soothing me like no one else can.

"Are you okay?" I ask in a small voice.

"I'm okay," she says, her skin warm against my cheek. "Are you okay?" she asks.

I think about what Cowboy said about horses . . . powerful, brave, and full of fear. "I'm okay."

A series of quick taps strike the doorframe. My grandmother steps in. With high cheekbones, icy blue eyes, and chin-length gray hair, she appears at once mesmerizing and untouchable. A single pearl hangs from a delicate gold rope around her neck. A stylish coral dress hugs her slender body, while matching pumps offer an extra inch of height to her straight-up frame.

In her presence, I'm keenly aware of the vast difference in our appearance. We are book ends, not meant to join but to be linked by others. I'm grateful for Mom's arm slung across my body and the miniscule shield it offers for my frayed, cut-off jean shorts and the tank top Mom made for me from a Martha Stewart tablecloth. I have still never worn a dress, but my clothes are far cleaner than when I was younger.

Grandma's face warms, unexpectedly, at the sight of us snuggling. "Dinner will be ready shortly. I thought I'd check to see if you found the towels for your showers."

A shower had not occurred to me. Maybe I'm not any cleaner than when I was younger.

"Yes, we saw them. Thank you, Mother."

Mom's fingers idly comb my hair.

Grandma's eyes cut to me then to Mom. "Darling, why do you sew your daughter's clothes when you can buy them?" She leans against the elegant, scalloped wallpaper and slips her slender hands into square front pockets.

"I guess so I can be creative. And Harold gets squirrely if he sees too many shopping bags."

"So hide them," Grandma says with a hint of a smile.

"She does," I say.

Mom pinches my arm teasingly.

"You and Harold are happy?" Grandma asks. As she crosses her arms the spray of tiny diamonds on her wedding band throw sparks.

"Are we happy? Yes. More or less."

"Is it more or less?" Grandma says.

I expect tension in my mother's body, but I sense none. I wonder which is the familiar territory—the subject matter or her mother. "We're happy," Mom says.

"It's your job to make it happy."

I lie perfectly still while my mother's fingers burrow in my curls. I want my mother to stand up for herself. I want her to fight.

"I know, Mother. I'm doing the best I can," she says.

Grandma nods. "Have you resumed your painting?"

Mom's hand falls away.

"What's stopping you?" Grandma asks.

After a few beats, she answers. "I guess I'm uninspired."

"People would kill for your talent, Lily."

Mom sits up against the headboard. "Can we help you in the kitchen?"

Grandma pauses as if she's deciding whether to accept the subject change. "I'm all set."

I've been watching Grandma intently the whole time she and Mom have been talking, so now, when her gaze falls on me, I wonder if I've inadvertently summoned it. I'm afraid she'll see in my eyes that I don't like her, so I pretend to admire the frosted wallpaper behind her.

"Beatrice will change and get cleaned up for dinner?" she says to my mother.

"We only have camping clothes. Nothing fancy."

"Perhaps an old dress of yours will fit her. And one will fit you too?"

Mom caves without a fight. "Yes, of course," she says.

Moments later I'm standing beside my mother before a full-length mirror in a vast walk-in closet with recessed lighting, deep-pile carpet, and scented hangers. A flouncy navy dress with a flared crinoline tutu-style skirt hangs from my shocked body. Mom wears a sleeveless crème blouse and flowing wide-leg culottes in a delicate daisy print.

"Why does Grandma want me in this?"

"Because it's how she keeps her world together. If you're pretty on the outside, no one will notice how you truly feel on the inside."

"How does she truly feel on the inside?"

"I've never known for sure, Beatrice."

I watch us in the mirror as she coerces my hair into a cute, stubby ponytail.

"Mom?"

"Yes, honey."

"You look like the old you . . . and I look like a tortured doll."

She laughs out loud.

CHAPTER 12

We gather for dinner in the sunroom instead of the formal dining room, but I know from experience that the meal won't be informal. The men are stationed at the ends of the table, the women and children at the sides.

Everyone is seated except for Grandma who floats in and out of the kitchen carrying steaming pots to the heated cart beside my grandfather. Lukewarm food isn't eaten in this house. Two nights ago, our last dinner while camping, I ate Chef Boyardee Spaghettios with a plastic spoon straight out of the can.

Grandpa serves from the head of the table and passes each of us our plate. Mine has moderate portions of sweet potatoes, green beans, Brussels sprouts, and mystery meat.

"What kind of meat is this?" I whisper to Dad, sitting beside me at the foot of the table.

"That's lamb," he says quietly and Oliver, seated opposite me, his eyes dancing, cries out "Baa!"

Mom touches Oli's forearm, and he stops bleating but he grins at me and I grin at him and it's as if the water's been turned on, but the spigot is still closed.

The patchwork of scrapes on Oliver's face is healing well, but a stubborn one above his upper lip gives him a mustache. I smile wider. He smiles wider with teeth. The water pressure builds.

Oliver lifts a wedge of sweet potato from his plate with his fingers, pops it into his mouth, and challenges me with his stare.

Mom whips her head around. "Oliver, wait for grace." Dad scowls at Oliver, but it's quick and thin. We both know Dad's face when he's truly angry. I glance over at Mom who is watching Dad, and I understand that Dad's scowl was more to show Mom that he's on her side than it was to reprimand Oliver. They must have argued recently.

"Some hae meat and cannae eat . . ." My grandfather begins the Scottish blessing, which cues us to bow our heads in silence while he speaks. I lower mine, but I can't shake Oliver's mischievous eyes taunting me from across the table. The corners of my mouth twitch and I clench my teeth to stave off laughter. *Whatever you do, don't make eye contact.* But Oli's call is too mighty. My eyes cut to his and in that nanosecond, he snaps open his mouth to reveal gnarled, half-chewed sweet potato clinging to his teeth and tongue.

I giggle and squeeze my eyes shut. Grandma's hand pats my thigh beneath the table. I'm startled and silenced. I slink low, heavy with embarrassment.

"Amen," Grandpa says, and passes my mother the linen-lined basket of homemade rolls after which Oliver and I have been pining for hours. I sip my milk as Mom sets a roll on her plate and offers the breadbasket to Oliver. But instead of taking the basket, Oliver digs in, pulls out a roll, and stuffs it into his mouth, using his index finger as a cramming device. He stares at me while his teeth overpower the bread, eyes wild with rebellion, skin flushed with glee. I choke on laughter, driving milk up into my nose and straight out my nostrils.

Grandpa slams his fork on his plate. The five of us jump.

Mom shuts her eyes and presses her fingertips to her temples. Dad clenches a fist and glares at my grandfather. Oliver and I examine the food on our plates, and Grandma straightens her silverware.

I carefully fanfold the cloth napkin in my lap while preparing myself for a tirade from Grandpa. Hunched and tense, I wait through the silence long enough for the call of the seagulls, the crash of the ocean, and the creak of the sunroom windows to sound loud. Not until Grandpa has speared the lamb with his fork and the bite has disappeared into his mouth, do any of us move.

I'm surprised at how much milk came out of my nose, but I say nothing, just eat around it. I don't dare face my brother until my plate is clean. When our eyes finally meet, his are bloodshot and teary.

After dinner, Oliver and I are allowed to watch an hour of TV in the sunroom while the adults gather in the living room and drink something they call "port." Oliver and I sit together in the leather recliner, our bodies fused from shoulder to thigh, and we hold hands under a hand-woven cashmere blanket with 'Made in Italy' on the label.

Oliver falls asleep within minutes, but I am restless. I slip off the recliner and tiptoe across the long hall into Grandpa's office, which is the closest I can get to the living room without being spotted. The leopard in the photograph catches my eye, so I lower onto my hands and knees and prowl across the rug like I am one. My knees catch in the tutu. I stop just outside the doorway.

My father is talking.

". . . the public schools in our district are excellent. We know several of the teachers. Some are spouses of faculty members at my university. There's no good reason for Beatrice to leave her classmates and enter the private system."

From the strain of his voice, I can tell he's attempting control but losing it. I envision his body language: legs crossed at the knee, foot bobbing, jaw clenched, hands restless in his lap. *He's no match for my grandfather.*

"Harold, the best public school in the country will deliver the equivalent of a fair-to-poor education compared to a private school," my grandfather counters smoothly. "Frankly, I'm surprised I'm being met with resistance on this. I'm offering to pay for Beatrice to attend private school from seventh to twelfth grade. Why aren't you saying 'yes' and thanking me?"

"Edward, we appreciate the offer, we do," my father says, "but there's more to—"

"Lilly's given up painting. Is that accurate?" Grandpa interjects. "And how much do you earn now, Harold? You're still an associate professor, so sixty? Seventy?"

"I don't think that's germane, I—"

"But it is, Harold. You enjoy your teaching. You enjoy Vermont. You enjoy the culture of the university there, but it's small-scale. It's a blip on the map. Don't you want more for Beatrice? Don't you want her to make a mark? Of course you do. And for that she needs an exceptional education." Grandpa's voice drops off as if to signal the official close of the conversation.

"There are many ways to contribute to society, Edward," my father asserts, his usual evenness and steadiness crumbling. "If you truly believe that only people with an elite education are improving the world, then I suggest—"

"Enough, Harold," my grandfather says. "You say whatever you have to say to yourself to justify your choices, but don't impose them on your daughter. I was flabbergasted when I learned that you declined the position at New York University. You could be earning six figures by now."

"It wasn't the right time for our family. Oliver was two months old. Lily was having trouble . . . the recovery from Oliver's birth has been much harder on her than with Beatrice."

"Your family would have adapted."

"How can you possibly know that Edward?"

"I must have more faith in their fortitude."

"Really? You think you know your daughter better than I do? You know about her depression? You know she needs pills in order to sleep at night? You know she—"

"Please," my mother whispers. With one word she ends the match. I give up my leopard stance and lower myself to the rug onto my stomach. The crinoline tutu rustles as I crush it. My nose buried in the silk Persian pile, I try to absorb their words. *Depression. Pills for sleeping. Leave my classmates.*

"I'll be fine," my mother says in the high-pitched voice that I know means she doesn't believe what she's saying. "My doctor says it will pass."

"It's been five years," my father mutters.

"Dad," my mother's voice is stronger now, but I know she's still faking. "We are touched by your generosity. Harold and I are just tired. It's been a long three weeks of driving and camping."

Mom, what are you doing?

"We accept," she continues. "Westerly is the best private school in Vermont and it's only thirty minutes away. Beatrice has one more year of elementary school, but next year, for seventh grade, I think enrolling her at Westerly will be a wonderful experience for her. Life-changing. Thank you."

I hold out for a reversal from my father, but in his silence, I grow weary. I roll over and inspect the ceiling. Outside, the fierce Atlantic Ocean strikes the shore, but every time, it loses. The majestic water protests with its crashing and foaming, but in the end, it gives in.

The last words spoken are my grandfather's.

"You won't regret this," he says.

CHAPTER 13

Bam. Bas. Bat. Bamus. Batis. Bant.

Pigeons rustle and coo on the balcony while I silently conjugate verbs in Latin. All first-semester students at Westerly, like me, are required to take a year of Latin. We discover early there are no native speakers of Latin and the language is considered "dead," but Westerly's guidance counselors report that America's elite universities have begun to give high marks to applicants with Latin on their transcripts. Many of my classmates say they'll take Latin for all four years if it will get them into Brown. I'm just hoping to survive high school.

Miss Frank chalks *Eram* on the blackboard in efficient, block letters. In a blue-gray knit pantsuit the same color as her hair, Miss Frank appears to be about the same age as my grandmother—both stylish, ramrod straight, and wiry—but Miss Frank's fingertips are perpetually stained with chalk dust, and the only writing instrument I've ever seen my grandmother use is a Mont Blanc.

Miss Frank aims her index finger at Libby, whose been whispering throughout class. "Libby, *Eram*," Miss Frank commands. Her voice isn't loud and her words aren't harsh; it's her delivery that corrals us.

Libby drags her hand through her hair and dislodges a single ash blonde strand. I track it as it floats to the floor and lands on the toe of my shabby sneaker.

Libby glances over at Becky. Becky shrugs. Libby stretches then flicks up her collar, which also flips out the label on her sweater: *Talbots*. I hear girls talking about *Talbots* in the halls. I've never been there.

"*Eram. Eras,*" Miss Frank prompts.

"Right. *Eram. Eras*, Errr," Libby slurs the "r," then chortles and rolls her eyes at Becky who mirrors both actions to perfection.

"The verb 'to be,'" Miss Frank says, addressing the entire classroom. "Conjugate!" And like well-trained seals, a cohort of us heartily reply: "*Eram. Eras. Erat. Eramus. Eratis. Erant.*"

Becky crosses her eyes at Libby and I shrink in my seat, regretting having joined the chorus so exuberantly.

"Are we unable to concentrate because lunch period is next?" Miss Frank asks.

The correct answer is "no."

Libby and Becky together say, "Yes."

"Jinx," Becky says, and they giggle.

A few students gaze at Becky and Libby with what I think is awe, but in my discomfort, I shift away and watch the pigeons on the balcony instead.

"Miss West, I expect your full attention in this class, and I expect you to come prepared," Miss Frank says flatly.

"I'm just hungry, Miss Frank," Libby whines.

The wall clock strikes 12:10. In five minutes, we'll be released. My head swims in a pool of anxiety and low blood sugar. I suspect I'm the only student in the entire school who prefers Latin conjugations in this attic classroom alongside a pigeon commune to eating in the cafeteria.

The dreaded hallway bell rings, reverberating off the grand Tudor home's 100-year-old timber and stucco, crown moldings, and wide-plank hardwood floors. Students shove their books into knapsacks and rush out of the classroom in pairs, like duos disembarking Noah's Ark. I slowly push my textbook into my backpack and nod farewell to the pigeons. Miss Frank has already finished erasing the blackboard when I exit the classroom with no partner beside me.

The lunch line moves quickly. We slide our trays along a waist-high metal track while the women in hairnets on the other side of a plexiglass barrier overload our plates. The food always tastes delicious. They smother the vegetables in butter, the meat in gravy, and the chocolate chip cookies are the same size as our salad plates at home. I wonder if Westerly allows the women in hairnets to eat the food, too.

I fill a glass with milk from the self-serve beverage station, then stand before the mass of chattering students, willing my knees not to buckle. I spot a table with Libby, Becky, and three other girls. A chair is empty beside Becky, who, like me, went to Noah Webster, my town's public elementary school. We weren't friends, but we knew each other.

I catch her eye and lift my tray as a way of asking if I may sit with her. She blocks the empty chair with her knapsack and rejoins the others in conversation.

My face burns as I walk through the minefield of animated students—laughing, eating, and bumping shoulders aff-ectionately. The packed tables, rarely an open seat among them, declare their private network, their not-so-secret society. *Are they staring at me?* I spot an empty table by the exit, but as I lower my tray, a man's voice intervenes.

"Beatrice."

Mr. Whitaker, my American history teacher and Westerly's

only Black teacher, signals to me from one of the few tables with a window. Trays with plates of half-eaten food, scrunched paper napkins, and overturned plastic cups mark the seats where others once ate but have since left.

"Don't teachers have their own cafeteria?" I ask, standing by his table, tray in hand.

"We do," he answers, with an air of amusement. He straightens and simultaneously tugs on the hem of his sweater vest which has creeped up. Like most of the male professors, Mr. Whitaker wears striped Oxford shirts and ties, but none of his ties feature miniature whales, alligators, or polo players. They're solid or striped, like my father's.

"I heard that teachers eat lunch on china plates with real silverware and get served by waiters," I say.

"Not waiters. Just students who are in violation of the dress code."

I know he's kidding, although it's true we are allowed to wear only gray, navy, or white. I own two navy skirts, three gray skirts, and five white blouses. I do my laundry on Sundays.

"Why are you out here?" I ask.

He surveys the room as if to be sure none of the other students will overhear what he's about to say. "Sometimes I prefer to eat with plastic forks on plastic trays at tables with hardened wads of gum underneath, so I can chat with students like you."

It takes a moment for my brain to register his compliment.

"Please sit," he says, and gestures to the chair in front of me.

I'm not sure what we're going to talk about. *Is the polite thing for me to start the conversation?* "Did you have the meatloaf?" I ask.

"Two servings. Plus an extra helping of mashed potatoes."

He presses a hand against his protruding stomach.

I wait for him to ask me why I'm not sitting with my friends. I quickly test out answers in my mind. *Because they ate already. Because they are out sick today. Because I don't have any.*

"Most of Westerly's students know each other from Connors, the K-6 private school. You didn't attend Connors, did you?"

"No. I went to Noah Webster."

"Is Miss McCallum still teaching sixth grade?"

I perk up at the sound of a familiar name. "I had her last year. She used to give us an extra-long recess if we made it through the science lesson without breaking a beaker."

"She taught my nephew. He's older than you; you wouldn't have known him."

He sets his napkin aside and surveys the cafeteria.

"You're an excellent student, Beatrice. One of the best in my class and I suspect you are the same in your other classes," he says.

"Thank you."

He slides his tray and empty dishes out of the way and leans forward with his elbows on the table. Up close like this, I marvel at the smoothness of his skin and the absence of a freckle or a blemish. Although his gaze is a bit intimidating, it's his smile lines that I am most aware of. Even now, with his neutral expression, wispy threads at the corners of his mouth and eyes expose his nature; on him, a smile is ever ready, ever eager to show itself.

He rubs his palms together like he does in American history after he's asked us a question. In class, the action produces a click each time the chalk strikes the bulky ring he wears on his right hand. I see now that embedded on the ring's surface is a scattering of small blue stones. They remind me of a night sky.

"How are you settling in otherwise?" he asks.

I fiddle with my plastic fork. "I don't belong here," I announce. Only my father has heard this confession.

"You belong wherever you choose to be," Mr. Whitaker counters.

"I don't have their clothes. I don't know the places where they hang out. We don't travel where they do. Well, my grandfather does, but we don't. Our last vacation we went camping. We slept on the ground in tents. We don't eat takeout food or go to restaurants. I don't go to summer camp. We shop at used clothing stores. And my Dad doesn't golf. He makes stuff with wood."

"Sounds like a nice way to grow up," Mr. Whitaker says.

"I guess. I thought we had plenty until I got here and found out that we don't have enough."

"Enough what?"

"Stuff. Money."

He nods. "Seems like money might be the point of all of this," he says, waving his hand, as if to include the building and the campus.

I wonder what else. "Is that true?"

"No," he says. "But easy to believe if you decide who you are based on how the people around you behave."

"I'm not like them." I wait for him to say something reassuring.

"Get comfortable not being like other people," he says.

"Unless I figure out how to be more like them, I'll be alone." I'm embarrassed by the rise in my voice, but he appears unphased by my emotion.

"It's a bigger world than what you see here, Beatrice," he says evenly. "You might perceive that you're the only one, but in truth, there are others." He signals the room with his hand

and light catches the spray of multifaceted stones in his ring.

"The night sky," I say, transfixed by the twinkling gems.

He chuckles. "I suppose you could liken it to that. One night you might gaze up and see only a few solitary stars, but then on another night when the circumstances have changed, the sky appears blanketed with stars, trillions of them. And the truth is that even on those nights when you can only discern a few, it's an illusion, a trick of light, because those other trillions are there as well."

I consider my untouched plate of mashed potatoes and meatloaf, which moments ago I couldn't wait to dig into.

"What do I do with myself when I believe I'm the only one?"

He sweeps crumbs from the table into his open hand and drops them onto his plate. At last, our eyes meet. "Find something to enjoy," he says. "Something you're good at." He twists his ring as if sensing the part it played in our conversation. "And remember . . . it's just an illusion."

CHAPTER 14

"Your best transition so far," Dad says. "Now put her into fourth."

The clutch is spongy, but the gearshift slides smoothly into fourth as we crest Eagles Notch, the highest elevation in the state park. The pickup's engine rewards me with a contented purr while the Notch unveils a breathtaking view of Lake Champlain and New York's Adirondack Mountains.

My favorite hours practicing for my driving learner's permit have been spent here on the single paved road through this majestic state park, one of the last remaining undeveloped forests in the county. The roadway is the only blemish amidst a lush landscape exploding with foliage and new growth after July's heavy rains. Dad prefers we drive the park mid-day when the wildlife is more likely to be hunkered down in the shade than roaming in search of water or food. For miles we've driven through a hushed tunnel of green beneath a towering tree canopy. Without the overhead shield, the turgid August heat would be intolerable.

"Let's head home," Dad says. "The pullout is about a quarter mile up on the right."

After maneuvering the turnaround and shifting up to cruising speed, a sense of freedom and possibility opens in me.

As if my life is somehow about to get bigger.

"When does pre-season soccer start?" says my father.

"Three weeks. Coach Whitaker wants us seniors there a day before the first official practice. He's re-configured the lineup and wants to run through it with us before the juniors and underclassmen arrive. I think he's going to move me from left wing to center halfback."

"That's a good place for you. At center half you can make the most of your athleticism."

His astute comment surprises me. He and Mom have only attended two games in the three years I've been playing.

"We should start talking about which colleges you want to visit. And since your grandfather will be paying for your education, you should probably write and let him know where you plan to apply."

"I wish it was easier to balance my dislike of him with my gratitude for his financial support."

"Money has warped him," Dad says and starts re-organizing his well-kept glove box. I've never elicited more than a sentence out of my father on the subject of Grandpa.

Mom is sitting on the rear steps as we pull up our gravel driveway. Her striped capris pants and scarlet halter top pop against our farmhouse's fading white clapboard. She jumps to her feet as I kill the engine.

"She has seemed better lately," I say.

"Yes," Dad says. "Has she told you why?"

I whip around. "No. Why?"

Mom crosses the lawn like a fast-moving storm cloud, her loose hair flying. My question drops away. Our eyes fix on her. She halts mid-lawn and glares.

"It was my turn to take Beatrice driving, Harold."

"You weren't around," Dad says as he exits the cab. "I

thought you were taking a nap."

Her skin flares. "I was in plain sight weeding in the garden."

Dad pauses by the truck's grille. "Why are you so mad?" he says in the same level tone that he uses when he helps Oliver with his math homework.

Mom ratchets up. The storm cloud crackles with electricity.

"I've been off the sleeping pills for two months and you're still cutting me out," she says.

That's what's been different about her. She's been more present.

"I'm not cutting you out," Dad says.

"Yes, you are. When are you going to let me off the hook?" Her voice quavers. She plants her fisted hands on her hips. She is at once vulnerable and imposing.

Oliver busts out of the screen door in his pajamas, gripping his guitar. Wide-eyed with pillow head, he resembles a child more than a pre-teen as he anxiously searches our faces.

Dad reads my brother adeptly. "We should have this conversation in private, Lily."

The storm cloud darkens. "I'm not speaking with you in private. No more secrets in this family."

All eyes cut to her.

"Secrets . . . what are you talking about?" Dad says and goes still. Oli freezes by the rear step. I sit paralyzed in the truck. Mom sways faintly. *This is us.* My parents, my brother and me. Four corners with no center. Held together by a thread. And the thread is about to break.

She lowers her arms to her sides. The storm cloud disbands. "I've been lying to you," she says. "My pregnancy wasn't an accident."

"I never thought it was," Dad says.

"Not Oliver . . . Beatrice."

All eyes cut to me.

"What?" Dad says.

"In college. My pregnancy wasn't an accident." She clears her throat. "I stopped taking birth control pills soon after we started dating."

Her confession hangs in the air like a swarm of bees, a dense orb of humming, vibrating intensity.

"Why?" Dad steadies himself with a hand on the hood.

"I wanted to be a mother," she says.

"Right that second?"

I'm the product of her deception. I'm the sole reason they are married.

"It was after my show and Mitch Markwell's scathing review. I lost confidence. I lost faith in my ability as an artist."

"So you intentionally got pregnant? You forced the direction of our lives because of some arrogant critic's review?"

Oliver hugs his guitar to his chest. *He was planned. Conceived in full consent. Normal.* I feel myself retreat, carried away by a slow-moving escalator. *I'm not part of this family in the way I thought I was. Even here, I am an outsider.*

"I was twenty," my mother says. "I was confused and scared and, as you know, my parents wouldn't have tolerated failure."

"You don't know that you would have failed," Dad says.

"Even the possibility of failing was too much for me."

Dad presses his temples, his face slack, his shoulders sagging. A flock of geese pass overhead, honking and flapping with raucous abandon. Their joy is almost unbearable.

As their clamor fades, he speaks. "Lily, you can only see yourself."

"That's not true."

"I'm invisible to you."

"No, you're my foundation."

He shakes his head. "If a man doesn't rule over you like your father, he's invisible."

"I see you, Harold."

"No, you don't."

Mom inches closer. Her eyes travel over him as if she's replaying their history together.

"You sleep most soundly on your right side," she says. Her voice is nearly a whisper. "You don't like my crustless tuna quiche but you eat it anyway. You felt relief after your mother's long battle with cancer finally ended, but you'd never admit it out loud. You like domestic beer in a can. You graduated in the top 5% of our class at Cornell. You uncover the beauty in every piece of wood you touch. You are a faithful provider and a loving father, and I don't deserve you."

My father takes a deep breath, then tilts his face to the sky. He spreads his arms wide and arches backward as if he's free falling from great heights. The grace and surrender in his movement stuns me. *He's going to hug her. He's going to forgive her.*

He straightens. "I want you to leave."

"Dad?" Oliver's voice startles us. My father extends his hand. Oliver lays his guitar on the grass and pads over. Dad wraps an arm around his shoulder. Side by side, they have the same dark hair and kind eyes, the same air of intelligence and depth, but Dad is all neat, clean lines while Oli's pajama top isn't even buttoned correctly.

"Please go," he says to my mother.

I slide out of the truck and close the door behind me.

"Ginny offered us her cabin across the lake for the next two weeks," Mom says.

"Ginny knows?" Dad says.

"She knows now."

"You arranged for the cabin knowing I'd ask you to leave?"

"No. I arranged for the cabin hoping the four of us would go there together and have time and space as a family to talk about what happened."

"To talk about what you did," Dad says.

Mom holds his eyes for a moment. "To talk about what I did."

Dad pulls his arm from around Oliver's shoulder and grips his hand instead. "I'm not going with you and neither are the kids."

Oliver's and my eyes ping pong from parent to parent.

"Harold, I'm asking for your compassion. Please let me begin to make amends."

"Did you ever love me?" he says.

Her words rush forth. "Yes. Unequivocally yes."

"You love me yet you've been lying. What kind of love is that?"

"I made a terrible mistake. Let me make things right. Let me prove myself."

"Why now? Why are you suddenly telling me the truth now?"

She doesn't hesitate. "As the effects of the pills wore off and the constant undertow and disorientation began to release me, I realized I would do anything—face anything—to ensure I never had to feel that way again."

Fatigue envelopes me. I lower to the rough gravel. Away from my family. Apart. Mom comes over and squats at my side. She smells of lavender and summer rain.

"Trust me," she says as she smooths my hair. "Come with me to Ginny's."

Dad's eyes find mine. Maybe he sees something in them that worries him, or maybe he's just not up to losing another argument.

"You kids can go with your mom," he says.

"Are you sure?" Oli says.

Dad kisses Oliver's crown. "It's okay. I'm okay."

His words sound true. Rock solid. On pitch. But he spins away too quickly for me to see his expression and as he disappears into his shop, I think about the wood, the graceful twisted limbs and stoic barrel-shaped trunks that get to be in his care.

In his trustworthy hands.

With his hopeful heart.

CHAPTER 15

My toes curl over the end board on Ginny's dock, a slatted finger that juts from the grassy shore about fifteen feet into the glistening lake. A breeze rolls at me from the north, lapping against my face and tugging at my heavy thoughts. Loosening. Soothing. I let my beach towel slip off my shoulders.

The lake appears to be about a mile long and half a mile wide. Dense woodlands hug its shoreline and rise sharply into foothills. The lake has a glacier feel, as if it slid from the mountains a million years ago to settle in this basin, tucked out of sight. No homes or buildings mar the water's edge, just an occasional floating dock marks the human dwellings. Treetops sway in unison. Clear water taps the shore. A lone hawk rides the air stream. My eyelids close. Peace engulfs me.

Yesterday's turmoil invades my thoughts: Dad disappearing to his wood shop. Mom, Oliver, and I shoving clothes and food into the Mercedes. Arriving at the breathtaking cabin. Eating a solemn meal on the deck. I couldn't talk to her. I feel betrayed. Less whole. Less *here*.

I squat and run my hand through the chill water while reliving my morning. The sun had roused me as it broke the horizon. Although disoriented in the unfamiliar bedroom, my first coherent thought had been to avoid my mother. I had pulled on my bathing suit, found a beach towel in the linen closet, and left. The trail had been easy to spot and as the shimmering water became visible, I had felt its call in my solar plexus.

My reflection undulates in the leisurely current. A halo of curls. Searching eyes.

To my right a fish jumps and I notice a short dock a few hundred feet away. It's the only other dock in the cove. A folding chair sits empty and a small fiberglass boat with a furled sail swings from a mooring.

Another fish flips on the surface in front of me, launching a succession of ripples that build into widening symmetrical rings. I dive over them and welcome the jolt the cold water delivers. Soon I get lost in a patch of slimy weeds that seem to want me to stay and play with them. They loop around my calves and ankles, slithering, tugging. I burst into a freestyle stroke to break free.

My body quickly finds a steady rhythm: stroke, stroke, breathe, stroke, stroke, breathe. The flutter kick wakes up my legs and hips and loosens everything in me that felt stuck. My body lengthens. My heartbeat quickens.

Then yesterday's scene invades my mind.

Stop thinking.

I pound through the water, but the thoughts stubbornly hang on. Frustrated, I shift to breaststroke, but as soon as my head pops up out of the water, I see a small, old-fashioned wooden boat rowing across my path up ahead with a fishing line dragging off the stern. At the oars is a teenager, a male, rowing slowly but confidently, slicing through the calm water.

Given the boat's angle and mine, we are bound to collide. I keep swimming, but with my head above the water. After a few strokes, he breaks the silence.

"You're scaring my fish," he calls, his voice echoing around the cove. I recognize his accent. New York City. Like so many of the boarding students at school.

I slow but don't stop. "You're blocking my swim," I counter, assuming he's like the boys at Westerly: bold and arrogant.

I'm close enough now to see his features: thick, straight brown hair falling across dark eyes, a short, narrow nose fitting well on his oval face and full lips. He stops rowing and glides through the water, then he rotates the oars and drags them like skis. As the boat slows, his fishing line swings around toward me. When his bobber, a red plastic orb the size of a crabapple, reaches me, I stop and tread water.

"I've never seen you before. This is a private lake. You trespassin'?" he asks with a smile. His teeth are white and straight, with a narrow gap between the front two. He appears to be about my age.

"I'm staying at the cabin that's over there," I say and stretch an arm toward Ginny's dock.

"The Reno place?"

"Yeah."

"You a Reno?" The way he says it makes it sound as if Renos are rich and famous.

"No. My mom went to college with Ginny Reno. Ginny's letting my mom, my brother and me stay there for two weeks."

"Hmm," he grunts, assessing me. "What are you, some kind of triathlete? I'd have sunk by now treading water that long."

I blush.

"Where are you from?" he asks.

"Vermont."

"On the other side of Lake Champlain?"

"Yeah. You?"

"Can't you tell by my accent?" he says, opening his arms

dramatically.

"New York City."

"Born and raised," he says proudly.

"What's PS41?" I ask, reading the writing on his T-shirt.

"My old school," he says, tugging on the shirt. "Public School 41."

"Are you in public school now?"

"No. Private academy for boys."

"Ouch."

"You got that right. You?"

"Private." Then I admit, "Sometimes painfully private." Just thinking about school, which starts the week after we get home from Ginny's, triggers anxiety, so I change the subject. "You have a cabin here?"

"Yeah, my family. Parents. Four brothers. One sister."

"There are six kids in your family?"

"Yeah. How many you got?"

"Just my younger brother and me."

"Is he an Olympic athlete like you?"

"I'm not an Olympic . . ." *He's kidding.* "No, he's a musician. Guitar mostly. And ukulele. He's only eleven but he's like a — what do you call it a . . ."

"Child prodigy."

I nod. "One of those."

"Poor kid. The pressure." From him, the word sounds like "presh-ahh."

"Oliver has no idea how talented he is."

I tread water and watch him. He drifts in his rowboat and watches me.

"So how are we gonna resolve this situation?" he asks, fiddling with the oars.

He just wants to fish. Flustered, I answer, "It's okay, I'll just swim around your boat." But before I can get a stroke in, he says, "No!"

He winds in his fishing line, grabs the red bobber, and sets the rod beside him along the length of the boat. Then he fumbles at his feet, pulls off his PS41 T-shirt, and stands. His swimming trunks extend to his knees and are stylish, lime green with a bright yellow Adidas logo. His body is lean and tan but not muscular.

I start to swim. "Wait!" he yells. I'm as restless as a dog. He grasps the edge of the boat with one hand. "Is it cold?" he asks, crouching.

I smile. "Like ice."

"You're wicked!" he cries.

I start to add, "Don't do it!" but he's already midair, pivoting around his steadied hand and then splashing into the water. The empty boat rocks and drifts.

He surfaces and whips his head violently, which gets his wet hair off his face, but it sticks out from the sides of his head and a triangular peak rises like stiff egg whites above his forehead. He swims closer. His skin is flawless except for a tiny scar on his left cheek. His brown eyes are so dark I can't tell where the irises end and where the pupils begin. The effect is intensity. And warmth. My stomach flutters.

"Didn't expect that, huh?" he asks, nodding to the boat and then sinking so his mouth and chin disappear beneath the surface. He blows bubbles.

"Didn't expect that," I say.

"I'm Michael John," he says.

"Beatrice," I say.

"How far you swimming?"

"I don't know. Halfway across?"

"That's far," he says. It sounds like *fah*. "Want to go sailing instead?"

I shrug casually although my heart races. "Okay."

"We just gotta drag my fishing boat over to that dock there," *Theyah*, he says, pointing to the dock I noticed earlier.

"Are there two ropes?"

"No, just one. We can switch off," he says, and swims over to his rowboat, pulls himself up, digs around in the bow, then slips into the water with a thick rope in hand. With one end tied to the bow cleat, he slips the other between his teeth and swims like a happy Labrador.

"You're not!" I say, and he shakes his head "no," rolls over, and does the backstroke with one arm while the other clutches the rope.

I swim slowly beside him. Neither of us speaks. He sucks in a mouthful of water and spits it out in a high arc, like a fountain, all the while swimming casually, contentedly, while dragging a small boat alongside a girl he just met. Alongside me.

I've never met a boy like him.

CHAPTER 16

My mind kills my serenity. *Should I offer to help? Isn't that polite?* Just as the words start to form, Michael John rolls onto his stomach and ties the rope around his waist. With both arms free, he moves faster.

I can't stop myself. "Do you want me to take over?" I ask.

"I got it," he says.

Soon we can stand. The lake floor feels downy underfoot. Michael John pulls himself up on the dock and cleats the rope securely. Then he gets in the rowboat, grabs his fishing rod, and carefully untangles the soggy worm from the hook. He could just as easily leave it on the hook and let it shrivel in the sun—which seems cruel, even though the worm is likely dead—but he tosses it into the lake.

"Here, fishy fishy," he calls.

He grabs his sneakers and PS41 T-shirt from the boat and dumps them in a pile on the dock. "You wanna life jacket?" he asks.

"For sailing?"

He nods.

"No thanks."

"Good. Because the life vests are up at the cabin and I don't want to run into any of them."

"Your parents?"

"My brothers."

He jumps in the water. I follow as he swims over to the sailboat.

"Is this a Sunfish?" I ask. It resembles a boat my grandparents once owned. Twelve or thirteen feet long. Fiberglass.

"Sailfish," he answers.

"What's the difference?"

"You'll see."

When we reach the boat, I do see. There's no cockpit. It's a sailboat with a hull, a rudder, a mast, and a boom, but the surface is smooth, like a surfboard. You can't sit in it; you can only sit *on* it. Which means it will be faster, but harder to hang onto in choppy water or at high speeds.

I wonder how we're going to get in just as Michael John reaches up and grabs onto a narrow wooden runner along the outside edge of the deck. He pulls his torso up onto the deck, then swings his leg up and rolls onto his back. He closes his eyes, snores, and pretends to sleep beneath the slim metal boom hovering above him.

"You comin'?" he says, with his eyes still closed.

"I don't know if I can do it."

His kind eyes cut to mine. "You can." Is all he says. And I do.

The wind has picked up since I first stood at the end of Ginny's dock, but it doesn't seem like there's enough to sail. We sit on either side of the boat at the stern, cross-legged, facing the bow. Our knees bump into each other and we sit in a shared pool of water dripping from our wet bathing suits. He slides me the rudder.

"Drag the rudder side to side like this," he explains.

Sure enough, the motion gets us moving. He unravels the knot on the sheet, lets out the line, and the sail swings wide. We immediately pick up speed. He scoots closer and sets his hand on the rudder, over my hand. My arm lights up at his touch.

"Oh, sorry," he says, and retracts his hand then passes me the sheet.

As we leave the cove, the wind picks up and fills out more of the sail. Michael John adjusts the rudder, I let out the sheet, and wordlessly we make the most of what wind we've got. The boat responds well and we pick up speed. It's as if we've been sailing together for years.

The wind rises steadily and at about the middle of the lake, Michael John starts naming the empty docks visible from the shore. "McMahons," he says, pointing to one on the left. "Proctors," he says, to another on the right. "Cousins of McMahons,'" he says, at yet another farther up.

"Is everyone from New York City?"

"Mostly."

"They have kids?"

"All of them have kids."

"You like them?"

"The kids? Yes," he says.

"How many families have cabins here?"

"Eight."

A gust of wind jolts us and pushes all my wet hair forward into my face. I smooth it away, but it just flops forward again.

"Let's come about," he calls. "You know how? Just watch out for the boom. You ready?"

"Ready," I say over the hiss of the wind and the slap of waves against our hull.

"Get ready to let out the sheet. Okay?" I nod. He lifts his

chin and hollers, "Helms alee!" at the air, the lake, and the sail, then he drives the rudder hard to the left behind me and we duck as the boom swings just inches above our heads. We scurry to switch sides. His knees and elbows bump mine. I draw in the sheet, he slides the rudder over, and we tack in the opposite direction. *Now we're moving.*

The boat keels, putting me on the low side and Michael John up high. Water rushes by; it's right there—inches from me —roaring past, spilling over onto the deck and my fingers, which cling to the slim handhold of the runner. Michael John grips the rudder in one hand and the runner beside him with the other. Against the bright sun, I squint to grab a glimpse of his profile.

As if sensing my stare, he yells over the whipping wind and choppy water, "You good?"

"I'm great!" I shout, and we both laugh.

An excellent sailor, he understands the wind, and it shows itself in return. We tack east and west as the sun rises high overhead, at times talking, at times in comfortable silence. He tells me about his favorite places on the lake and up on the mountain he refers to as "Dunder." He offers me the rudder, but I refuse—too much pressure. No matter what the boat and the wind send his way, he responds calmly and skillfully.

But when two figures appear in the sandy area at the head of the lake, his body tenses. They jog past a fire pit and a picnic table then race into the water, leaping and splashing. Yards ahead, a sailboat floats on a mooring.

"Crap!" Michael John says.

In seconds, they have released the bow line and scrambled into the cockpit. I watch as the bigger figure hoists the sail.

"Who are they?" I ask over the wind and surf.

"Two of my older brothers," he says.

"Is that bad? What are they going to do?"

"They're going to capsize us."

CHAPTER 17

The sailboat comes about and Michael John chooses a tack aimed at the middle of the lake.

"Let's go straight to your dock."

He shakes his head. "And let them win? No way. If we cave, I'll never hear the end of it."

"Let's outrun them. Can we outrun them?"

"We can try," he says, "but it's gonna be hard to hang on."

"I don't care."

He nods and adjusts the rudder so that the sail swallows more wind. I tighten up the sheet and suddenly everything kicks up a notch. The boat heels with Michael John's side of the hull surging up out of the water and mine sinking under. Water sweeps over the low edge of the deck, rushing from bow to stern by me, *at* me, and I scramble for a foothold. I jam my toes against the runner and steal a glance at his brothers.

Michael John checks over his shoulder. "Dammit!" They've picked up the same tack we have and now that they're closer, it's obvious why they've gained on us so quickly. Bigger boat. Bigger sail. Faster.

"Dammit," I echo.

Within minutes they are sailing parallel to us, downwind, far enough away that we don't collide, but close enough for us to know we are trapped.

I brace myself for teasing and cruelty from them.

Nearer of the two is the bigger brother, muscular and broad, hand confidently on the rudder. "Who are you?" he shouts.

"Beatrice!" I reply.

The other brother, shorter and lanky but fit, ducks under the boom. "You got sisters?"

Caught off-guard, I smile. "No!"

In unison, they say, "Shit."

"Who are you?" I say.

The tall one touches his chest. "I'm Patrick!" then he shoves the lanky one and yells, "He's Aidan."

I nod and wave. *I'm such a dork. I just waved.*

They wave in return.

"They don't seem that bad," I say.

"Trust me."

"Michael John!" Patrick hollers.

"Patrick!" says Michael John.

"We are going to capsize you." Pause. "Because we can." Pause. "But we're not going to take your centerboard this time because of . . ." Pause. "What's your name again?"

"Beatrice!" Michael John and I shout in unison.

"Because of Beatrice," Patrick says. "We'll take your centerboard and leave you stranded in the middle of the lake another time." They laugh.

Michael John leans toward me and whispers, "Helms alee." I quickly duck and let the sheet out. He slides the rudder to the other side and the boom swings over our heads. We scramble to switch places and tack away from the brothers.

"Nice move, but you can't outrun us!" Patrick hollers from somewhere behind us.

Within minutes, they are beside us, upwind this time, on a

line close enough to block our wind with their larger sail. Each time we slow, they creep in and disable us a little more. Soon I can see the rash of light freckles across Aidan's face, chest, and shoulders. Patrick has the physique of Westerly's boys' varsity lacrosse team captain: square jaw, thick neck, giant hands, and ripped abdomen.

"Just let out the sheet," Michael John says in defeat. We level out and the sail flaps in its newfound freedom, our lines rattling against the mast and boom. At the mercy of the current, we drift, but Patrick and Aidan are upon us in no time. As Patrick's mitt of a hand grabs the runner beside Michael John, the air crackles with intensity. My fingers grab more tightly around the lip of the hull, even though we aren't moving.

"Get lost, Patrick," Michael John says. *Brave.* Michael John is shorter and lighter and clearly a few years younger than both of them.

"No," Patrick chirps, in the voice of a bratty child. Aidan prowls closer and kneels in the cockpit, his eyes trained on Michael John.

Am I safe? How far will these boys go?

"Jerk," Michael John says.

"How old are you?" Aidan asks me.

"Seventeen," I say.

"Where'd you come from?" Aidan asks, his accent pronounced.

"Who cares where she came from?" Michael John says. "Get lost!"

Aidan snaps. He leaps at us from the cockpit, tipping us into Patrick, while the hulls smack together and the masts cross like dueling swords. Aidan pulls Michael John by his foot, but Michael John kicks him in the sternum with his other foot.

"Asshole!" Aidan punches Michael John's shoulder.

"You're an asshole!" Michael John kicks out again, this time connecting with Aidan's thigh. I hustle away from them and nearly fall into the lake.

"Hey, hey, hey," Patrick says, and grabs Aidan's forearm and Michael John's ankle, all the while staring at me with a goofy, toothy smile. "Not in front of the young lady."

The corners of my mouth curl but it's more from nerves than amusement. I've never known a family who fights like this. Then again, I don't know any families with six children, or families with so many boys. I've never been to New York City. Maybe I'm naive.

Michael John untangles himself from Patrick's hold, scoots my way, then slips past me, off the deck, and into the white-capped water. Aidan claims Michael John's place beside me and assesses me with intensity. He sits close but doesn't touch me.

"Don't be scared," he says, reading my face accurately. "We've gotta flip the boat and then we'll be gone. Mom is grilling steak for lunch. Can't miss that," he says. "Want to come with us? We got potato salad."

The brothers' charm and magnetism lulls me into a fugue state, and I forget my unease from moments ago. Attractive boys talking to me? Inviting me to lunch? It's never happened before. Older boys don't acknowledge me at school. *Boys* don't acknowledge me at school. *Is this what it feels like to be a supermodel?*

I giggle nervously. The thought of being the object of their attention for a little while longer, for a meal, makes me giddy, until a splash yanks my focus away. Michael John floats on the choppy surface, his arms wide, his face to the sky, spitting water in a fountainlike arc. He kicks occasionally to steady himself but lets the driving current take him. The sailboat, his brothers, and the conflict appear forgotten. He's returned to his element. Alone. An island.

I release my grip and tumble into the lake to the sound of Aidan's disappointed, "Aww." I swim a short distance, then watch as Aidan and Patrick capsize the Sailfish, but as promised, Patrick doesn't allow Aidan to take the centerboard, which would make it impossible for us to sail to the dock . . . or anywhere.

Staying above the choppy water line is more difficult in the vigorous wind and I am suddenly struck by how hungry and thirsty I am. I don't know what time it is or how many hours I've been away from the cabin.

Aidan and Patrick sail away. Michael John bobs tranquilly and I realize I'm treading water in the middle of an unfamiliar lake with a stranger and a capsized boat.

There's nowhere I'd rather be.

I dive below the surface where the sail billowing in the open water presents an eerie sight—a ghost ship, helpless, abandoned. It's nothing I've seen before, a sailboat fully capsized. I can't fathom how we're going to get it upright.

I bubble up to the surface as Michael John swims to the hull, grabs hold and hangs there, motionless. The crippled boat is now our life raft. I swim over but keep my distance. I can sense a shift in him. I hug the hull and let my legs float out behind me.

"Those bastards turtled us," he says, facing me.

I realize I'm staring into his eyes. Two pools of dark chocolate. I wrench my gaze away. "Turtled us?" I ask.

"Yeah. When a boat capsizes and flips completely upside down, it's turtled. The hull becomes like a shell, a turtle on the water. It's hard to get it upright. Sometimes you can't."

He moves closer, only a foot or so away, and we hang side

by side in silence, our arms overhead on the hull, our legs long and loose. Water drips off his nose. He rests his head against the fiberglass hull. I do the same. With the noisy wind now blocked and the sun forcing us to squint, I find the courage to speak.

"Are your other brothers like that?" I ask.

"Sean isn't. He's the oldest. He's in college. And Brendan only beats up Aidan. Nobody touches my sister, Mollie. She's third after Brendan, a year older than Patrick."

I put them in order in my head: Sean, Brendan, Mollie, Patrick, Aidan.

"You're the youngest?" I ask. Something heavy passes across his face.

"I'm the youngest," Michael John answers and I realize what I'm seeing. Vulnerability. He knows what it is to be fragile in the world, but instead of retreating like I do, he fights back.

And the violence takes a toll on him.

"I should get you home," he says.

I don't want to go.

"Okay," I say.

We drag ourselves up onto the hull and he shows me where to stand beside him. Together, we grasp the centerboard and lean, leveraging all our body weight to get the boat into rotation. When it begins to roll, we jump on the centerboard—jutting like a dorsal fin—grab the runners on the deck, and lean as far back as we can to keep the revolution going. As the mast, shedding water, rises into the air, he yells, "now!" We both let go and leap out of range as the hull smacks the water and the boom swings wildly.

We sail to our cove in silence. It dawns on me that I may never see him again. Maybe I saw more today than he expected to reveal, more than he is comfortable with me knowing.

As we approach the weedy area off Ginny's dock, I expect

him to slow and ask me to swim the rest of the way so the centerboard and rudder don't get entangled in the weeds. Instead, he sails over the troubled section and maneuvers us so close that all I have to do is put my hand out to touch the dock.

Awkward and unsure, I search for words to reconnect us. None come. I don't want to go but my body doesn't listen. It slides away from him, off the Sailfish's deck and onto the dock. I wish I was a different kind of girl, the kind who knows the perfect thing to say to a boy.

Michael John scoots to the middle of the stern, into the space we used to share. With the line in one hand and the rudder in the other he says, "Give me a push?"

I roll onto my knees and shove the stern away with all my strength. He slides the rudder from side to side, then coasts patiently, a journeyman carving his path through the unknown.

I sit at the end of the dock, my feet swinging like a slow pendulum underwater, and watch as he crosses the cove to the mooring. The sail lowers easily and he cleats it with quick, sure loops. He vanishes beneath the surface, then emerges at the end of the dock, whipping his head to shake off the water. With his T-shirt and sneakers bundled under his armpit, he grabs his fishing rod, tucks the hook safely around the pole, and disappears into the woods.

My towel lies in a heap where I left it. I knot it around my waist like a sarong and retrace this morning's steps along the dock. I train my eyes on the trail to Ginny's cabin, but every other part of me aches to glance over at Michael John to see if he's truly gone. Not until my bare feet touch the earth do I hear, "See you tomorrow?"

I exhale, not realizing I'd been holding my breath. "See you tomorrow!"

And in an instant the turtled thing between us is upright again.

CHAPTER 18

On the sprawling shaded rear deck, Mom sits motionless in an Adirondack chair, holding a steaming mug and staring blankly into space. Behind her the cabin gives the impression of a cover spread from *Architectural Digest*, a vision of rich blonde wood, tinted windows, and peaked roofs dotted with skylights. Despite her melancholy, the cabin's grandeur suits her.

"Good swim?" she says as I approach.

"Yes." I've been gone for hours but I don't explain.

"Sit with me?"

I choose a seat two chairs away. Its steep "V" slant and high armrests hold me like scaffolding. The beach towel makes a nice blanket across my body. She watches me settle.

"I'm just going to jump right in," she says and clears her throat. "The choice I made in college was from a place of fear and insecurity and lack of faith, but the result of that choice was you, so I wouldn't change what I did."

They are the perfect words, but I can't feel them.

"I loved your father, and I told myself that once you were born my lie would shrivel up and disappear. But it didn't. It festered."

I hug my knees to my chest and watch a young woodpecker hop up a tree trunk.

"I got the idea that having another child might bring Harold and me closer—and he agreed—but after your brother was born, nothing changed inside me. My lie just got harder to ignore."

Questions form in my mind, but I don't ask them. Speaking seems like an olive branch. A bridge to me for her to cross. I imagine an invisible wall around my chair.

"Your grandmother knew about my lie and when I was having trouble after your brother was born, she let me try her sleeping pills."

I grow the wall thicker.

". . . somehow Dad got me a prescription of my own through a doctor friend or maybe just someone with whom he has influence . . ."

I locate a tiny spot in the trees, a spyhole through which I can see the roiling lake.

". . . trapped in a fog. I felt sluggish and emotional. I couldn't paint or garden . . ."

The whitecaps look like root beer foam.

". . . my mother's trust fund has always been my safety net . . ."

I snap into focus. "Your mother's trust fund? I thought the money was Grandpa's?"

"No, it's Mom's. He didn't grow up with money. Her grandfather had a logging company that made a fortune deforesting the Northeast. It was necessary to a degree, but some say it went too far and caused irreparable damage to the ecosystem."

I slip up and ask another question. "Is that why you painted trees?" A chipmunk dashes across the deck.

She swivels my way but I don't reciprocate. "The logging has always bothered me."

Her gaze penetrates my wall. I feel exposed, so I launch to

my feet. "I need to go for a walk," I say. Drawing my wall in closer, I spin away to avoid catching sight of her expression or reading her emotions.

A melody floats from an upstairs window. *Oliver.* His strumming is my beacon. I climb the stairs, change into shorts and a T-shirt, then find him in a bright sunroom with two plate glass walls.

He once appeared disproportionately small compared to his guitar, but now, lanky and lean at eleven, he's grown into it.

"Oliver," I say, settling against the door jamb.

"Beatrice," he says, without turning around. "I knew you were there. I felt you staring at me."

"Sorry."

"Creepy."

I smile.

"Am I up?" he asks.

"With Mom?"

"Uh huh."

"You didn't talk this morning?"

"No. Slept late."

"Then yes. You're up."

"Do I want to do this?" he asks, still facing the glass.

"I don't know. Yes?"

He stops playing and twists around. "That was helpful," he says.

I chuckle. "Sorry."

He strums the opening chords of Prince's, "When Doves Cry."

"I love you," I say.

"Love you, too," he says.

The dirt driveway snakes away from the cabin at a steep angle. Head lowered, I watch my own sneakers as I climb, then notice the indigo salvia shooting up from the midline. Soon my eyes lift to the golden forsythia bursting along the roadside, a stand of waving birches, and a trio of crawling milky clouds.

I'll think about my mother later. I'll talk to my mother later. The sailboat drops into my mind.

Michael John.

I smile.

CHAPTER 19

Mom is teaching Oliver how to make crêpes as I skulk downstairs and flop onto Ginny's overstuffed sofa. Blueberries and butter linger in the breeze through the open-air kitchen. Mom and Oli's shoulders touch and I try to remember how old I was when I grew taller than her. There are no pencil markings on a doorframe in our house to remind me.

"I heard you come in late. Did you have fun?" Mom says.

We haven't been alone together since our conversation the morning I met Michael John. I avoid her so that when I'm feeling weak and missing her and get the urge to tell her everything that's going on, I can't. By the time I do see her, the feelings have passed and my wall is once again in place.

"We went night sailing."

"Perfect, Oliver. Flip it now," she says. "When can we meet him? You've spent every day since we got here with Michael John, and I don't even know what he looks like."

"He's my height. Dark brown hair—"

Mom rolls her eyes. She has read me perfectly. My sarcasm, my resistance. "I'm happy for you," she says. "I just want some time with you."

"We have forty-eight hours left. Plenty of time," I say, knowing full well I won't introduce them.

"Now the blueberry filling. A little less. Perfect," she says to Oliver, who is apparently a culinary savant as well as a gifted musician. She steps away, swirls her hair into a bun, and secures it with two chopsticks. In a sleeveless dress and a golden tan, she appears twenty years younger than when we arrived here ten days ago.

She hooks an arm around my brother's waist. Oliver relaxes against her. I expected him to respond as I had, to maintain distance, wait for her to prove herself, but he has done the opposite.

"Let's spend the day together," she says. "Get ice cream at the place we found. Oliver, what was the name? It was clever."

"Ethel's Dew Drop Inn," he says with a flicker of amusement. "Just an ice cream stand. Not an Inn."

"I can't. We're riding the McMahons' horses up Dunder Ridge."

They go stock-still.

"Horses?" Mom says.

"Yeah. The horse pasture is behind the barn where the tractors and plow are parked."

Oliver stares at me, spatula in hand, crêpes sizzling and forgotten, grayish smoke spiraling up from the pan.

"They're burning," I say flatly, fully aware horses are a touchy subject in our family, particularly for Mom and Oliver. Understandably.

"Horses are dangerous," my mother says. Oliver's attention returns to the searing pan but he makes no move to rescue the charred crêpe. I think I know what he is reliving.

"So are cars," I say curtly. "I'm sorry. I'm just—it's just— Mom, you and I are going to have the rest of our lives to spend time together, but we're only here for two more days. I may never be here again. I may never—"

Oliver slings an inky blob onto a plate and slides it in my direction. "Crêpe?" he asks.

"Are you pissed at me, too?"

"I don't care what you do."

By avoiding Mom, I've essentially avoided him too. His hurt registers. "Tomorrow. The three of us."

They stare unconvinced.

"I mean it."

"Okay," says my mother.

"Whatever," says my brother.

"Tomorrow," I say, fully believing I will keep my word.

"Fine, then you can have this one," Oliver says. He takes a plate from the warming oven and slides it across the island counter to me. On it lies a perfectly rolled crepe beneath a swirl of whipped cream. Blueberry juice oozes from each end like blood from a wound.

‡‡

Low-hanging branches make the dirt road to Dunder Ridge nearly unpassable. It's as if the forest is eager to reclaim it.

Our horses smell like a beauty salon. I marveled at the tack and supplies in the barn: shampoos, mane and tail conditioners, insect sprays, and wound salves plus brushes, hoof picks, nutritional supplements, and a five-pound bag of organic carrots. Built-in brackets held pristine Western and English saddles, saddle pads, crops, bridles, and a lunging line.

Michael John leads the way on Zappata, the taller of the two Morgan horses, whose rich, chestnut coat has already darkened from sweat. Beneath me, Pete, black from nose to tail, ambles congenially. Birds, rabbits, chipmunks, and squirrels bring the woods to life all around us, but we ride in silence. It's our last day together.

"What are your parents like?" he asks, as the road clears. He slows Zappata so I can catch up and ride beside him.

"My dad is a university professor. He's quiet. He loves to build things in his wood shop. Mom's creative, very beautiful. She used to be a painter. She did abstract human portraits in college, but now just mostly trees."

"Why didn't your father come on vacation with you?"

I struggle with how much to share. "My parents are in a rough patch. The whole family, really." I bury my fingers in Pete's mane. "This vacation was supposed to be about my mom rebuilding her relationship with my brother and me. I haven't been part of it. I've spent my time with you instead." My unplanned honesty hovers in the air. Embarrassment stirs in my stomach.

Suddenly, the fire road opens onto a breathtaking lookout over Lake Champlain and the Green Mountains. An osprey glides past. I watch in awe.

"I bet your mother loves you," he says.

I swallow. *I should speak to her. I shouldn't shut her out.*

We carve our initials in the legs of a rickety lookout tower while the horses graze in the shade. He gives me half of his mashed Snickers bar. I teach him how to whistle through a blade of grass.

Later, near the base of the mountain, Michael John leads us offroad onto an obscure trail through the thicket. Zappata and Pete perk up with the change in landscape and deftly navigate the uneven terrain.

Ahead, a partially fallen tree leans diagonally across the trail, its root bed unearthed, its crown tangled in the high branches of a sturdy spruce. Michael John flattens against Zappata who dips his head and strides confidently through the narrow, triangular opening. But Pete halts, bobs his head, and nearly tears the reins from my hands. I encourage him with a tap of my sneakers, expecting him to saunter forward. Instead, he explodes through the triangular space before I can duck fully. A knifelike cut sears along my spine and when Pete and I emerge on the other side, my T-shirt and bra are in my lap.

Naked from the waist up, I shove my bra into my pocket, scoop up the remains of my T-shirt, and press the fabric against my bare breasts.

"Michael John?" I yell.

"Yeah," he says.

"Help."

Zappata halts with a single "Whoa," and Michael John pivots in the saddle.

Shock registers then a smile unfolds. He lowers his head while his shoulders jiggle with laughter.

"It's not funny!" I say while I laugh and frantically clutch at my T-shirt. Panic flushes my skin. "What am I going to do?"

He collects himself, but the corners of his mouth continue to twitch. "Are you okay?"

"Yeah. I don't feel blood, just a little burning."

"Take my shirt."

"Really?"

"Of course," he says, and his voice cracks. He slips off Zappata, pulls off his T-shirt, flips it right-side out, and hands it up to me with his eyes squeezed shut. Once he's in his saddle, he says over his shoulder, "Tell me when you're not naked."

His T-shirt, although sweaty, smells of lemony laundry detergent.

"Okay," I say.

"Okay?" he asks. He spins to face me, but keeps his hands clamped over his eyes.

"Okay," I say.

He peeks at me through spread fingers. I smile. He lowers his arms.

"My shirt looks good on you," he says. Then he clucks to Zappata who obediently resumes walking.

At the stable, an elegant woman sits on a bale of hay. I assume she is Mrs. McMahon, the owner of the horses, checking to be sure the animals are okay. In a white peasant blouse with a beautiful, embroidered yoke, a casual skirt, and flat shoes, she seems comfortable in the rural setting but at home some place grander. Salt-and-pepper curls frame her round face. Her skin is lightly powdered. Her nails are short and shapely but unpolished.

We dismount as the woman rises and approaches Michael John. He stuffs one hand into his jeans pocket and holds Zappata's reins with the other.

"Hi, Ma," he says, and she takes his face in her hands and kisses both of his cheeks. The gesture is so loving, it stops my breath. I haven't let my mother touch me since we left Vermont.

"Is this a new thing? Riding half naked?" she asks, patting his cheeks affectionately and shooting me a wink, as if I'm in on the joke, as if I'm already a member of her inner circle. Without waiting for an explanation, she glides over to me. "You must be Beatrice."

Mesmerized by her warmth, all I can come up with is, "Yes."

"We barely see Michael John anymore. I hear the two of you have been all over this property." On her, the New York City accent sounds regal.

I extend my hand. "Nice to meet you, Mrs.—"

Before I can finish, she takes my hand in both of hers and steps in close, so close I can see where Michael John got his eyes. "Mary. Call me Mary," she says, and despite my filthy T-shirt, damp with sweat, horsehair, and presumably a little blood, she hugs me.

Pete shifts his weight, lets out a snort, and Mary straightens but doesn't let me go.

"Come to the cabin tonight and have dinner. It'll be just the three of us. My husband and my other children leave for Manhattan this afternoon." Skyward she adds, "A little peace and quiet at last . . . thank you."

I glance at Michael John to see if he approves, but Mary gently guides my face to meet hers. "Come to dinner," she says, her eyes holding mine.

I wobble a little as I beam at her.

"Okay."

‡‡

I stealthily slip inside Ginny's cabin to shower, get my bathing suit, and search for clean clothes for dinner. Mom paints on her easel on the rear deck. She is enrapt by what she's creating, and unaware of me or presumably of the smudge of paint on her cheek where she must have had an itch. A breeze pushes her hair off her face. She taps her foot like she did when she painted my portrait, the winter she was pregnant with Oliver. Her yellow smock billows out from her thin form. It's the smock Dad gave her after Oliver was born. Two springs later Oli spilled grape juice on it.

My radiant mother has returned. Relaxed and clear. Joyous and present. I could race to her right now and instantly her arms would pull me in; she'd whisper something clever against my cheek; and she'd rock me back and forth, drawing out my words and my worries and soothing me, lulling me, and welcoming me home to her.

I turn away and drag my body and my shredded T-shirt and bra upstairs to the bathroom, strip, and stand under steaming hot water in Ginny's shower, hoping her lavender soap, loofa pad, and pricey shampoo will scrub away the nagging sense that I am about to lose something. Or worse, that I have already lost it.

CHAPTER 20

From where we stand at the cliff's edge, our line of sight corresponds with the treetops on the opposite bank of the lake.

"Don't look down," Michael John warns.

Shadows in the water below undulate in the lake's current. "Too late," I confess. With a shelf-like rock jutting out on the left and a buffer strip of hearty trees and shrubs thrusting out from the shoreline to the right, the target is unmistakable. "You've done this before?"

"A thousand times. A trillion times. My brothers and I have been jumping off this cliff since . . . forever. Aidan's even been thrown off this cliff," he adds, as if to guarantee its safety.

"What did he do to earn that?" I ask. The best stories in their family seem to be ignited by Aidan.

"I don't remember. Something annoying."

A fish flips in the bullseye below. "Do all the kids jump off these cliffs?"

"Only if they're with us. The cliffs are kind of in our front yard."

As if on cue, the smell of honey barbecue finds us. On their front deck, Mary has clearly begun grilling dinner.

"You're the first girl, though."

I smile proudly.

A flock of birds swoop over the water, then shoot high and change direction, like an airborne school of fish.

"Hello, birds," I say, admiring their performance.

"Hello, birds," Michael John echoes as his fingers interlace with mine. Surprised by his touch, I turn and discover him watching me. A hidden-away part of me expands tenfold.

He leans in.

"I'm shy," I blurt, and he nods with mock interest, then kisses me. His lips are salty, soft, and perfect. When we pull apart, we smile at each other. A thousand thoughts scurry forward but none get past my mouth.

"Ready?" he asks, squeezing my hand.

"Ready."

"One, two, three, go!" And we leap.

Clutching his hand, air flooding my nostrils, I freefall beside him in a dizzying, euphoric blur. Slam! We strike the water and are ripped apart. Jolted and shocked, I struggle to orient myself. Underwater. Underworld. Panic drums in my chest. It's piercing cold. A single word enters my head.

Up.

Michael John hangs above me, suspended in inky stillness, his lemony swim trunks ballooning around his thighs and tiny bubbles peeling off his skin. In muffled silence, the lake holds us affectionately for a beat.

He explodes into action, kicking, driving upward through the water with confident strokes. My body sparks to life. Heart bounding, eyes wide, I follow his lead and together we swim toward the kaleidoscopic surface.

He holds my hand on the way to his cabin and the three of us eat outside in rocking chairs with plates in our laps and citronella fly-repellent candles and Diet Cokes on the railing. We face the woods and, in the distance, the cliffs and the lake.

Mary tells stories of Michael John when he was younger and while he blushes and begs her to stop, I ask questions to keep her talking.

Not until Michael John brings the last barbecue rib to his lips, do I hear the siren. It's nearby, near enough for Mary to launch out of her chair and race to the rear of the cabin. Michael John drops the rib to his plate and twists around southwest. I'm not sure exactly where the noise is coming from, but there are only two cabins at this end of the lake.

I fly out of my chair and join Mary at the base of their driveway, which zigzags up the hill and out of sight. The siren moves past us. South of us. Southwest. Where there's only one other home.

"There's only one other home," I say.

Mary puts an arm around my shoulder. "We don't know what's happening. Try not to think the worst."

But the worst has already descended on me. "There's only one other home," I repeat, and she holds my face in her hands, like she did to her son hours earlier.

"What if it's my brother?" I ask, my voice cracking. But I know it's not. Tears leak from my eyes. Mary wipes them away with her thumbs. I suck in my breath.

"Breathe," she says, and shows me.

Nodding, I suck in air. It whistles through my teeth.

"Exhale," she says, and a thin stream escapes my lips.

Michael John stands silently behind his mother, but I can't meet his gaze. I peer up at the oscillating tree canopy and the darkening sky beyond.

Mary gently guides my face toward hers. "You're not alone."

I nod and start to tremble.

"Michael John, take Beatrice on the lake trail to Ginny's.

Your father has the car, so I'll call the Richardsons and see if I can borrow theirs. I'll get my kit." Her voice is calm and clear.

Neither of us moves.

"Now, please," she says. He grabs my hand, and we bolt.

Dusk has fallen. We push through the trail's overgrowth. Michael John is sure-footed. I stumble twice. Frogs sing from the shoreline reeds but they offer no solace.

Ginny's dock comes into view, then the trailhead to her cabin. Lights blaze through the spyholes in the forest and in my thickening panic, I sprint past Michael John. Sweat drips into my eyes. I take the stairs two at a time. The deck is empty.

I spot movement on the other side and race through the kitchen and living room. Oliver sits on the front steps, his back to me, talking to a Trooper with a wide-brimmed hat, a crisp uniform and a holstered gun. A short pad of paper and a stubby pencil all but disappear in his thick hands. His sedan, lights flashing, idles in the roundabout where the Mercedes should be.

Oliver pops up off the steps and we meet in a hug. He buries his face against my shoulder while I search the Trooper's face for answers.

"Is your father here?" he asks.

"No. He's at home. Where's my mother?" I ask.

"You are the daughter, miss?"

"Yes. I'm his sister. I'm the daughter. Where's my mother?" Oliver's hold on me tightens.

"Miss, your mother was in an accident. We found this cabin's address on a scrap of paper in the glove compartment, but the vehicle is registered in Vermont."

"Yes. We live there. We live in Vermont. Where is she?"

A Land Rover barrels toward us. Michael John says to the Trooper or maybe to me, "My mother is here. She's an ER nurse."

The Rover halts, awash in the Trooper's bouncing strobe lights.

"Please just tell me."

Mary walks around the Trooper and up the steps. She stands behind me and rests a hand between my shoulder blades, as if she knows that somebody needs to prop me up.

"Your mother was involved in an automobile accident on Route 42. A witness claims she swerved to avoid a deer and was unable to correct her vehicle. She crashed into a tree."

It's quiet. So quiet. The wind. The critters. The trees. All gone. Nothing remains but my heartbeat. Thump, thump.

"I'm sorry to tell you she did not survive the collision."

I'm falling. Oliver with me. Mary's hand pulls away. The deck is hard and smooth, and my legs and arms become Oliver's legs and arms and our heads touch and our eyes close and together we cross the line that should take longer—if it was fair or humane, it would take longer—but it's an instant. By the time my brother and I tangle in a heap on Ginny Reno's deck, we have passed from "before" when Mom was alive to "after" when she is dead.

CHAPTER 21

The threadbare bathmat offers little protection from the frigid tile. *How long have I been sitting here?*

Earlier, Dad had come to my room and then to Oliver's, as he had every night since Mom died three months ago, to say goodnight, kiss our foreheads, evaluate our condition with sympathetic eyes, and then back-step out of the room, as if he knew turning around and walking away would be too harsh. I pretended I was asleep. I couldn't bear to not hear the perfect words, to not feel better.

My father is there, is here, much more often now. Or maybe he always was, but my attention was on my mother. I don't know. Time has grown muddy, as have my memories.

A piece of graph paper on the refrigerator keeps our house running. Each week, a new one goes up, held in place by refrigerator magnets. One magnet says, "Eat More Kale," and the other lists the telephone number for Poison Control.

The chart defines the week: who's cooking, who's doing dishes, who's cleaning bathrooms, who's filling humidifiers, who's bringing in firewood. We do the food shopping together, but nobody dusts or vacuums or mops. It's about getting through the week, not foolish luxuries.

We have been visiting colleges around New England. I try

to pay attention to the student tour guides and their clever stories about campus life, but every tour, no matter how impressive the facilities, no matter how limitless the opportunities, I find myself watching the mothers and noticing, on the rare occasion, when a prospective student like me is touring without one.

"With" or "without" marks the dividing line in my new reality, and I fall on the same side every time and wonder if there will ever be a day when I'm not losing that game.

I hear the sound that is the reason I sit in the dark in this bathroom between Oliver's room and mine. The bathroom has two doors, one to my room and one to his. The number of times we've caught each other peeing can't be counted. We used to retreat, but now? Now if I'm taking a shower, he'll come in and pee anyway, and if he's brushing his teeth, I'll come in and pee anyway.

Without a spoken agreement, we leave both doors ajar at night. Maybe for him, it's about maintaining our connection. For me, it's so I can hear him crying, like he is now. I can't go to him. I can't fathom the pain of curling up with him and experiencing our loss together, so I get as close as I can, as close as I dare.

Oliver's sobs aren't loud enough to summon my father, but they wake me from sleep every time. I've become tuned to grief. Like a dog, I can hear the high whistle that other humans can't.

The memorial service is tomorrow. It's been twelve weeks since the accident. Dad wanted to wait so we could all have time to process her death. I feel today the same as I felt the night she died.

I draw the quilt around my shoulders and rest my head against the wall between the toilet and the shower, listening to Oliver and trying, but failing, to forget the lake, the sailboat, and the boy with the fishing rod.

As Oli's cries give way to sleep, I try, but fail, to feel my mother.

‡‡

Grandpa and Grandma won't sit. The rest of us—Dad, Oliver, Ginny, and me—assemble around the kitchen table with Mom as the centerpiece in a black urn with gold trim. Apparently, she wanted to be cremated and scattered from Eagles Notch rather than go full-bodied into the ground to spend eternity beside her father's churlish relatives. Grandpa had puffed and protested, but fell silent once he saw the will. Mom knew he'd yield to the letterhead of a prestigious law firm.

Dad and Oliver pick at a meat platter, Ginny nurses her second gin and tonic, and I make soup out of a bowl of fudge brownie ice cream while Grandma and Grandpa—buttoned up in their overcoats—watch us as if we're zoo animals.

"How's the bed and breakfast?" Ginny asks them.

"We're at the Hilton," Grandpa says.

Oliver stabs meatballs with a toothpick.

"The memorial service was lovely," Ginny says.

"Indeed," Grandpa says.

Ginny won't accept defeat. "You're in town through the weekend?"

"No, we're leaving in the morning," Grandma says.

Grandpa comes to stand behind the empty chair at the head of the table. "Harold, I want to assure you that I intend to continue funding Beatrice and Oliver's educations through college. It's what Lily would have wanted for them."

Knowing that the trust fund is Grandma's, I survey her for signs of irritation at his use of a singular pronoun. She meets my gaze with keen eyes. I return to massacring my ice cream.

"Thank you, Edward. The kids and I are grateful for your support," Dad says, then bows his head. All fight has obviously left him.

"May I be excused?" I ask.

"Sure," Dad says and gives me a joyless smile hedged by stubble. In my entire life I've only ever seen him clean shaven.

At the sink, as the hot water whisks away all remnants of my ice cream, a hand lies on the curve of my shoulder and a faint brume of Chanel No. 5 sails in. I stand stock-still, alarmed by how good the female contact feels. As if she's read my mind, Grandma shuts off the water but leaves her hand on me.

"We need to get you a haircut," she says. "And new clothes. You can't look like a farmhand when you go to college next fall."

"Hear hear," Ginny says and lifts her gin and tonic.

"Okay," I say. All fight has left me too.

Mom's fleece hangs from a hook by the door and I pull it on even though the sleeves are too short. With one hand on the knob, I twist around and glance at my family. Dad selects a Vienna sausage from the platter and dunks it in mustard sauce. Oliver lowers his forehead to the table. Ginny asks my grandfather about real estate in Martha's Vineyard. Grandma dries my ice cream bowl.

Outside, the brisk, starlit night offers me respite. I can see my breath. My body registers the cold with a shudder. *I'm still alive.* Behind me, the door opens and for a moment Grandpa's lordly voice engulfs me. Grandma steps from the house and tugs the door shut. She draws her cloche hat snugly over her ears and with a slender gloved hand holds the collar of her cashmere coat closed over her throat. Her perfume finds me. We stand shoulder to shoulder and face the darkened lawn and Mom's art barn.

"Your mother couldn't leave well enough alone," she says.

I don't want to talk about my mother.

"I told her to let things be, but she wouldn't," she says.

I scan Grandma's profile. She has Mom's nose.

"You don't always have to be on the outside struggling, Beatrice. Just join the circle. Play along."

Fatigue pours over me.

"Life can be easy," she says.

Then I'm doing something wrong.

The steely November moon disappears behind a bank of streaky clouds. The frosty air nips at my cheeks. I decide to speak. "May I ask you something?"

"Yes," she says.

"Why do you pretend the money is Grandpa's?"

She turns toward me, but in the absence of moonlight her expression is indiscernible. "It's easier that way," she says.

"Easier for whom?"

"For your grandfather," she says and gathers her coat more tightly over her throat. "He married above his station."

I pause, sensing there's more to come.

"Anyway, I don't mind. What's easier on him is easier on me," she says, but the words flow too evenly, as if she repeats them often. Like a mantra.

Commotion at the kitchen door drives me away. Under the camouflage of dark I leave my grandmother and the farmhouse and wander out to the corral and stable. We've neglected the structures horribly, but they were built soundly. The corral fence doesn't even groan as I throw my legs over and sit. Minutes later, footfall approaches and the searching beam of a flashlight sweeps wildly.

"Your grandparents are intense," Ginny says and maneuvers herself onto the fence beside me.

"I don't know how Mom did it," I say.

"She did it because she had to. A girl needs a mother so she can learn how to be a woman," she says.

"Thanks, Ginny."

"Oh god, I didn't think. I'm sorry," she says then rustles in her coat pocket. Seconds later the tip of her cigarette glows.

Join the circle. Play along. Grandma's words.

"May I have one?"

Ginny hands me the pack and the monogrammed gold cigarette lighter that she used to let me hold when I was a kid. It still fits well in my palm.

CHAPTER 22

My fingers prickle with numbness. Tobacco's bitterness sours my mouth. Ginny hugs me beside her rental car and disappears out the driveway. My grandparents' car is already gone, but my father's pickup truck remains. Amidst the frigid blankness, gilded light spills from our kitchen. Its soothing glow should lure me, but instead I linger in the cold, contemplating the farmhouse.

This is us.

Dad. Oliver. Me.

The doorknob feels sub-zero against my flesh. The kitchen floods me with heat. All the food's been put away. Mom's urn hasn't moved. My father hunches over the sink with soapy bubbles up to his elbows, scrubbing a plate.

Oliver slumps at the kitchen table wearing a bath towel like a cape. His hair is wet.

"Where've you been?" Oliver says.

"I was sitting with Ginny by the corral," I say.

"You missed Grandpa's recap of world events."

"Lucky me."

"I don't think I'll ever leave Vermont again. Or this house," he says and hugs the table.

I'm here but not here. Speaking but not engaged. Sleep

talking. Sleep walking. *Now is the time to tell them that I'm crushed. Tell them how much I hurt. Ask them how to make it stop.*

"Were you smoking?" my father asks. His eyes are red-rimmed, his skin sallow.

A wall forms around me. Invisible. Impermeable. "Yes."

"Why would you do that? You're an athlete," he says, rinsing the plate. He goes still then suddenly flings the plate into the soapy water. Suds spatter the backsplash and the front of his shirt. "We don't smoke in this family!" he shouts.

My body pulses with adrenalin.

Push off. Push away from the shore. It's safer alone.

"Oh, I see. We don't smoke but sleeping pills are okay," I say.

He pales. Suds drip from his elbows onto the linoleum. My heart rate spikes. I feel jittery and light-headed and slightly sick to my stomach.

"I can't believe you said that," he says in nearly a whisper.

My voice rises. "You let Mom take sleeping pills all these years. How could you do that?"

"It was complicated," he says.

"You let her self-destruct."

"Beatrice, she died in a car accident."

"Can we stop this?" Oliver says.

"You should have done more for her, Dad. You should have tried harder."

My father flinches. Oliver pulls the towel over his head.

"You have no right to say these things," Dad says.

I can't tell what's true anymore. I don't know who I am without her. Help me.

"I blame you," I say, then cross the soundless room on shaky legs.

I climb the stairs. Reach my bedroom. Close the door.

Impenetrable. *This is me.*

Part II

CHAPTER 23

I'm dragged awake by forces I don't recognize. I listen for the footfall of my upstairs neighbor or music from a passing car. Slowly, cautiously, I open my eyes. Red-orange morning light dances across my bureau against the far wall. My body and my bed harmoniously meld.

Nicholas lies on his side away from me. The curve of his shoulder rises rhythmically with each breath. His spine tracks gracefully along his lengthy torso. His upper body shows no signs of physical labor. No overworked muscles. No scars or wounds. His skin is unblemished and evenly tanned. Not even shirt lines mar his upper arm or the base of his neck. Nicholas would never tolerate a farmer's tan.

Would my father like him? Would Oliver? STOP. You haven't spoken to them in ages.

I clamp down the hollowness that still rises at the thought of them. *Don't let it take hold.*

I roll over. My seventy-pound silver Labrador stares at me from his fleece bed, his head lowered on front legs that stretch straight out like a diver's. Tawny eyes bore into mine. He lifts his ears but his body lies motionless except for the last three inches of his tail which flutter hopefully.

Unmistakably Labrador but wrapped in a coat similar to a

Weimaraner's, Lobo's robust health and equanimity reflect a raw food diet, daily exercise, and boundless affection. His confidence registers above the curve, thanks to daily infusions of wonder and delight from strangers who ogle him and say, "He's beautiful. What is he?"

I resist Lobo's telepathic appeal for breakfast, but within moments a new intruder descends. From my bedroom window in San Francisco's Polk Gulch neighborhood, only one tree is visible, but it sounds as if every bird within a ten-mile radius has just landed on it.

With practiced skill, I slip out of bed without waking Nicholas. The window closes soundlessly and I lower the shade. In six steps I'm in my kitchen where Lobo, having nearly mastered teleportation, sits on his haunches by the island counter drooling. While loading his bowl with raw chicken necks and steamed collard greens, I whisper words of appreciation to my apartment, which despite being tiny, is quiet, affordable, and within walking distance of work.

By the time I load the coffee machine with fresh grounds and water, Lobo has finished eating and stands by the sliding glass door ready to pee in my "yard," a 10 x 15-foot fenced-in rectangle where nature has found a way up through the concrete. Lobo does his business on a brownish clump of grass and races into the kitchen.

"Hey," Nicholas says groggily, from my bed.

"Hi." I walk over and sit beside him. He stretches, bare-chested, hands behind his head and one bronzed leg protruding from a sheet that scarcely covers his groin.

He lifts his eyebrows suggestively and I glance at the clock. "It's quarter to nine! Oh my god, it's quarter to nine!" I spring up, pluck clean underwear and a bra from my dresser, pull a blouse and miniskirt from my closet, grab my knee-high black boots, and run into the bathroom to change.

"Don't stress," Nicholas calls in a tone fitting a handsome man wearing a half toga while reclining in a woman's bed.

"It's the first of the month. Morning meeting. The new account assignments are today," I explain frantically through the closed bathroom door.

"You brought your boots in there? You won't even let me see you put your boots on?"

My face burns hot. We had sex last night and hours later I can't even change in front of him. We've been dating for over a year.

"I don't want to be late to this meeting, Nicholas," I deflect.

It's what I do. I deflect. Jiu Jitsu without the spiritual practice.

I brush my teeth, gargle with mouthwash, then burst out of the bathroom fully clothed to find Nicholas naked, pouring himself a cup of coffee in my kitchen. Well over six feet, broad-shouldered and thin, but not muscular, I wonder if the feature that makes Nicholas's body so beautiful is the fact that he likes it so much.

I tuck my blouse into my skirt, then untuck it, thinking the loose fabric will better conceal my curvy hips or compliment them or just cover them so I don't have to think about whether the curves are a good thing or a bad thing.

Nicholas faces me with everything just . . . dangling as he sips Fair Trade Wicked Jim dark roast coffee from my Cornell University mug. The image is not what I imagined when I had grabbed the mug off the bookstore shelf—my last purchase before graduation five years ago. I wonder if the mug will now, in perpetuity, conjure images of Nicholas's naked glory.

Lobo lies by the front door. Quiet. Still. Hopeful.

I grab my Kate Spade mini-backpack, pull out my phone,

and text Scottie, my upstairs neighbor and professional dog walker—another perk of living in this apartment.

Can you walk Lobo? Long walk?

I scratch Lobo's head, slide my hand over his silky ears, then reach for the doorknob.

"What about me?" Nicholas asks, and sets the coffee mug on the counter, his arms stretched out and everything else still . . . out.

I walk to him and tilt my head for a quick kiss, but he gathers me up and kisses me deeply, passionately, with one hand gently holding the base of my neck and the other pressing into my lower spine. For a moment, I give in. I let go.

When at last I pull away, I'm breathless. My phone dings.

Sure. Lobo is my boy. Javier says hi.

Javier is Scottie's partner, my landlord, and a successful immigration lawyer, which is why Scottie gets to walk dogs for a living. Thank god for Javier.

Hi to Javier. Thanks!

Instead of walking, I cheat and hop on the Post Street bus, making me only ten minutes late when I arrive at the brick, three-story building on Market Street just off Union Square. The agency where I work occupies the third floor, but rather than waste time waiting for the overburdened elevator, I race up the stairs. By the time I've taken a seat in the crowded meeting room, the climate beneath my clothes has gone tropical.

As usual, I join the small creative team on the window side of the classic rectangular boardroom table, while the account executives claim the remaining six seats. The head chair, the only one in the room with armrests and access to the digital blackboard, remains empty.

The male account executives wear ties and slacks, while the

female ones are poured into stylish dresses and, no doubt, spiked heels. We three creatives get away with more casual clothing, but leadership's expectations of our performance are equally high. This morning, the account executives, puffy and bleary-eyed, each hold some version of a venti Starbucks beverage in hand. I wonder where they got drunk last night.

"Today's the day," Marlene, the veteran among the creatives, whispers to me.

"I don't know, Marlene. I think Erica's going to get the PharmFresh account assignment. I mean just look at her . . . not an ounce of body fat. She probably *uses* fat-free, low-calorie butter replacement spray."

Marlene shakes her head. "PharmFresh will be yours. You're a better writer. Plus, you're the master of kitsch," she adds, as if it's a high compliment.

A form strides through the hall outside the meeting room, but I can't see past the interns who stand shoulder to shoulder, nervous but well-funded, like suspects in a police lineup somewhere swanky. Nantucket or Greenwich.

As unpaid employees, the interns tend to disappear after a month, but new ones quickly replace them. A revolving door. Eager in, disappointed out. It's tough to get a foothold in our business.

Fiddling excitedly with my pen, it slips out of my grasp and missiles into my lap. While retrieving it, I realize that my skirt is on backward and a dot of mint toothpaste clings to the hem of my blouse. As I rub at the stain with a moistened thumb, the boardroom door flies open and our boss glides in.

"Big day, today," he announces in greeting and quickly scans our faces so that we each receive an equal helping of acknowledgement. "One new account to announce this morning, which means two of you will have a hot new assignment. This client's a biggie; if we get this first product right, they've promised us the rest of the product line within six months." Heads nod around the table. Everyone smells money.

"The potential here is for a multichannel campaign for the complete line, but it starts with a single compelling slogan. The client has given us their best-selling product as our inspiration. I know you're all excited. I'm excited, too. We have a great team. Let's show our new client why we are the best boutique ad agency in the Bay Area."

"Woo hoo!" The account executive directly across from me ceremoniously raises his venti drip. His name is Derek, but the name written on his Starbucks cup is Tabatha, which is not the name of his girlfriend.

The boss nods and raises an empty hand to join Derek's toast. Our boss is the kind of guy who doesn't leave another guy hanging.

My body registers his presence with a lustful tremor of electricity. While he stands confidently at the head of the table, I marvel at how he presents himself: jeans baggy enough to be casual but pressed enough to appear elegant; a magenta dress shirt with offsetting white cuffs and collar—hip, but credible; curly hair, not unruly; and manicured hands large enough to throw a football. I drink in his masculine radiance and wonder how this man, naked in my kitchen just minutes ago, could so quickly transform into a composed and seemingly well-rested vice president, prepared to lead a team of twenty or so twenty-somethings, most of whom are preoccupied with beating one another up the proverbial ladder.

At thirty-seven, ten years my senior, Nicholas has held the agency's VP spot since he was my age. None of us have ever met Carlos, the owner, and Nicholas's sole supervisor, in person. A recluse who reputedly resides in a castle in Tiburon, just north of San Francisco past the Golden Gate Bridge, Carlos suffers from agoraphobia, claustrophobia, and germaphobia. He's also a creative genius and a multimillionaire.

I rise up slightly off my swivel chair and give my skirt a tug, hoping to spin it around, front first. In a single attempt, I've drawn several sets of eyes upon me, and I calculate that at least two more tugs are required to correct the skirt, so I leave it and run a hand through my tangled hair.

"PharmFresh has been in my sights for months. Lots of competition for this one. But we landed them over several bottles of a fine Napa Valley pinot noir. And a Bordeaux. Gosh, I hope they remember they signed the contract."

Chuckles ripple around the room. Derek raises his venti drip again. This time he toasts, "That's what I'm talkin' about!"

Nicholas smiles and again joins the toast, but this time, instead of an empty hand, he raises the stylus pen for the digital blackboard.

"We're taking on the top bestseller in a food product line of fat-free, low calorie—wait for it—*spray* offerings. The leader of the pack? B'udder, a butter-flavored spray for anything you'd use regular butter for—except baking—but without the fat and calories."

He flashes us a wide toothy smile that reaches all the way up to his eyes. Landing new clients and promoting products, even nondairy butter replacement in a spray bottle, lights him up. He loves his job.

Do I love mine?

The question triggers a warning light in my system, which sets off a chain reaction. I lower my eyes as a wave of awareness, a truth, tries to rise. Unwilling to acknowledge it, I dig blindly into the pink pastry box that sits untouched in the center of the meeting room table. I root around and grab the first thing I touch. *Please not a cheese danish.* It's a blueberry muffin. I break it in half on a napkin, tear off a chunk, and eat it. Immediately, my body relaxes.

"Given their success working together on the Randy Brothers Hot Sauce account, I'm pleased to announce that Derek and Beatrice will be lead account exec and creative, respectively, for B'udder and PharmFresh." All eyes fall on Derek and me, which isn't a problem for Derek, but I've got a mouth full of blueberry muffin.

Marlene squeezes my upper arm and I nod at Derek who counters with a raucous, "Beaaaaa," and Erica, the newest on our creative team, stares off toward the wall. I sympathize. It's hard to be in this room when you don't win.

CHAPTER 24

It always starts like this, with the product on my desk before me, asking me to understand it, to speak for it. I pick up the spray B'udder and examine the canary yellow bottle. The label depicts a cartoon cow and a chicken standing side by side in front of a barn and staring blankly—a takeoff on Grant Wood's *American Gothic* painting, but surprisingly the chicken holds the pitchfork.

Across the hallway, Derek talks animatedly into a headset, gesturing with the hand that doesn't have the venti drip. The account executive team has the interior, windowless offices because they're supposed to be out on the road visiting clients and cultivating prospects. The creative team each has an office with a coveted, street-facing glass wall. My office, though cramped, gets the most light because it shares a glass wall with Nicholas's, the corner office, where light floods in from multiple directions.

Well, it doesn't flood. Our building is tucked between two tall office buildings, so one of Nicholas's glass walls soaks in afternoon sun while the other affords an unobstructed view of the offices next door—a hive of cubicles and fluorescent tube lighting, mismatched lateral filing cabinets, and people slumped in rolling chairs, fixated on double monitors.

I contemplate the B'udder spray from all angles, then I swivel around to the window. The six-story stone building directly across Market Street is the home office of Wells & Menklin, one of the biggest law firms in the Bay Area. No matter how late I leave at night, there are lights on in the smaller offices on the lower floors, and no matter how early I arrive in the morning, the same is true. Seems the higher the floor, the bigger the office and the less time the lawyer spends in it.

I spritz B'udder onto my index finger. It doesn't smell buttery, and the color is slightly orange. Nicholas rolls into my office. I lick my finger.

"Got a minute?" he asks, his face radiant and expectant.

I nod and he closes the door, but instead of sitting in my guest chair he hovers by my plastic Ficus tree and fiddles with one of its stiff, textured leaves.

"Are you excited?" he asks.

"About?"

He throws open his hands as if to receive a huge beach ball. "PharmFresh?"

"Yes. B'udder. Of course, I'm excited. I was having a little trouble finding the heartbeat, you know, the sweet spot, in a dairy product that contains no dairy."

He starts to speak but I quickly raise my hand to stop him.

"But now that I've tasted it and experienced its . . . buttery essence . . . I know I will. Every product, no matter what it's made of or what it does to our bodies, deserves a compelling slogan." I smile, with teeth, to squelch any doubts about my enthusiasm and to distract myself from more closely examining what I just said.

Next door, Marlene's chair is empty and although Nicholas's back is to the account executive's office across the hall, he maintains a neutral expression when he asks, "Dinner at your place? Pad Thai? Caribbean jerk? Al Pastor burritos from that new El Salvadorian restaurant on 24th Street? We should celebrate your landing the PharmFresh account," he adds and allows himself the smallest of smiles.

"I don't know if I landed it so much as you gave it to me," I say. It's a conversation we have had before.

"Bea, you are the best damned creative in this office, and everyone seems to know it but you."

"Thank you. It's just—I would die if our personal relationship—"

"Oh god, kill me right now. Please, just kill me. It's my neck on the line. I'm the one who reports to Carlos. I'm the one who'd have to stand in front of him and explain why a client isn't happy. Well, not stand in front of him. He doesn't do that. I'd have to call him or video chat him or—"

"I get it. I won't bring it up again. Thank you for PharmFresh. I'm gonna nail it."

"I know you will. What about dinner?"

Tempted to once again retreat into his company and into his body, I force myself to silently admit he's stayed over the last six nights in a row, and I don't sleep soundly when he's there.

"I can't tonight. I've got to do laundry. Go food shopping. My dog probably thinks Scottie is his owner. I should really call my brother. I need a good night's sleep."

He mimics being pummeled with bullets, each statement ripping a new hole in his chest. It's silly and such a contrast to the guy who led the morning meeting. I giggle, which seems to be what he was hoping for.

"Boring," he says.

I search his eyes for evidence that he's hurt. I find none.

"Do your magic," he says, pointing to the B'udder, then he winks and leaves.

Addressing the B'udder as a girl might her favorite doll, I hold the bottle in my palm and affectionately say,

B'udder: The udder butter.

B'udder: Big on taste, not on your butt—er.

B'udder: Because some of the best things to eat don't come from a cow.

B'udder: Because real butter is just too damn delicious.

"Crap!" I say aloud.

By the time I leave at five, I have amassed nearly twenty awful slogans, but I know I'm onto something. Often my best ideas come when I'm walking Lobo or ascending to consciousness after a vivid dream. It's as if the answer has to be slipped to me when my analytical mind is off duty.

I'm almost at Union Square when my phone dings. It's Scottie.

Just let Lobo out to pee. You want me to walk him?

No thanks. I will. Be home soon.

BTW you have no food in your refrigerator.

No worries. Bringing home spray butter.

Is nothing sacred?

It pays the rent.

I'm about to send Scottie an angel emoji when my phone dings. It's Oliver. What I told Nicholas was a lie . . . I had no plans to talk to Oliver. Last time Oliver called—a year ago or so—it was to tell me about the woman he'd started dating and to encourage me to call our father.

Bea, can we talk tonight?

Mid-sidewalk I stop, too flustered to care about the grumblings of the people who walk behind me.

Sorry, Oli. Can't tonight. I have to

Have to what? I stare at my phone then shake it, remembering the Magic 8-Ball I once found in the guest cottage at my grandparents' house.

It resembled an oversize 8 ball from a pool table, but if I shook the ball then asked a question, the ball would give me guidance. "Outlook good." Or "Don't count on it." I must have overdone it with the shaking and asking because by the time we left, the only answer the Magic 8-Ball gave me was, "Reply hazy, try again." *What would it tell me now?*

I delete what I'd written, and phone in hand, I allow the river of multinational tourists to sweep me up. We flow across Union Square, a one-block plaza hosting department stores, salons, and the towering Westin St. Francis Hotel. Cars, taxis, and cyclists whiz by as I leave the Square at the north end by Powell Street. Unphased by incessant honking, a whirring of electric buses, and a jangle of trollies, I concoct rationalizations for rejecting my brother's outreach. I am sure I'm only thinking them, but when a goth teen eyes me curiously, I realize I've been muttering aloud.

The surge of tourists ebb as I walk up Sutter Street past galleries and restaurants and then vanish when I reach the high-end apartments near Van Ness Avenue. Surprised by a sense of urgency, my fingers clutch my phone in a death grip.

While cresting the steep Sacramento Street hill, it hits me. I'm an adult living in an exciting, thriving city. Three thousand miles separate me from Vermont, my father, and my brother, but with one text—a pinprick—my world deflates. I lose altitude. I—

Whoosh.

A speeding vehicle misses me by inches. I leap for my life onto the sidewalk outside my building.

Then a *whoop* from a police siren spins me around.

And there in front of me, directly across the street, is a horse.

CHAPTER 25

Tall and gray, with a glossy, black mane and tail, the motionless Thoroughbred looms over the southeast corner of Sacramento and Gough Streets in the small, sloping Lafayette Park. The animal is impeccably groomed with pink fetlock wraps and a matching saddle pad that detracts little from its dignified comportment. Its rider, an armed, uniformed Hispanic police officer, sits stock-still with her forearms resting on her thighs, her reins slack but not sloppy.

The only horses I've ever seen in downtown San Francisco were in the background at rallies at the Civic Center or marches in the Castro. I've never seen horses in our residential neighborhood nor a solo horse anywhere within city limits. But that's not what has my attention. What's more alarming than the presence of this grand animal, practically outside my bedroom window, is that the horse is staring at me. Not the police officer. Just the horse.

Vividly, I'm flooded with memories: Topaz's earthy smell and rolling gait, his sweat soaking through my jeans, the sensation of well-being. Riding Pete up Dunder Ridge, bolting through that fallen tree, shredding my T-shirt and Michael John loaning me his. It was the same day Mom . . .

I wrench my mind away and pull my keys from my

backpack. My fingers clamp the building's front door handle and my key slides into the lock, but instead of forging into the building, into my usual routine, I find myself twisting around for one more eyeful. The horse continues to stare at me. A breeze lifts its mane and tail. The backside of my neck tingles. I let go of the key and dig out my phone. I glance over at the horse. Then I send the message I was incapable of sending an hour ago.

Hi Oliver. Just getting home now. Call anytime.

Lobo has eaten but hasn't yet walked and my dirty clothes have been consolidated in a laundry basket but not yet stuffed into my washing machine when my phone rings.

"Hey," Oliver says.

"Hi, Oliver," I answer.

"How are you?"

"Good. I'm good. Things are really good. How are you?" I can't even remember what he knows about my life; it's been so long. So superficial.

"I'm well," he chuckles. "I'm . . . I guess I'll just come out and say it. Rachel is pregnant. And we're getting married."

I instantly need a chair, but the stool in front of me seems too far away, so I tip against the wall and slide to the floor.

Say something positive.

"Oliver, that's incredible. Amazing. Congratulations."

"Yeah, thanks. We've been together for two years."

"Two years? That long?" *I haven't spoken to my brother in two years?*

"Crazy, right? I'm sure I told you. We met at the restaurant. She's the front-of-house manager. Our schedules aren't the same. As head chef I have to be there for the dinner shifts and she's usually managing lunch. Well, anyway. That's just . . . yes, we've been together for two years."

"And you're ready for marriage?" *And a baby?*

"I am. I mean, I'm only twenty-one, but it's right. All of it. The baby. Rachel. And Dad loves her. She went to The University of Vermont, so they know a few of the same faculty members and they share that pride. You know how the UVM campus is."

"Those darn Catamounts." The words sound fake even as I'm saying them. *Maybe it's just me who's been superficial.*

"I think Dad's grateful for the company and for the chance to have some new projects. You know he's renovating the walk-in closet by my bedroom so we can use it as a nursery?"

"At our house? I mean, his house?"

"Well, yeah. Rachel and I live there with him. We've been there six months. I thought you knew."

My stomach rolls. My head thunders. Lobo leaves the comfort of his bed and comes to me, as if sensing my shift. I caress his head and scratch him beneath his chin. *Breathe.* I tell myself.

"I don't know. Maybe. I . . . so you're all there *together*?" I haven't spoken to my father since I moved to California, since the day he called and asked if I wanted anything from Mom's studio before he cleared it out. Our interactions had been strained for years by then—ever since our argument in the kitchen after Mom's memorial service. During college I had made a point to find summer jobs on campus so I'd only have to go home for occasional holidays. The news that he was clearing out Mom's studio was the last straw for me. He continues to send me a card every birthday and every Valentine's Day, and he puts a $50 bill in every Christmas card, but I send nothing. I do nothing.

"Yeah, it works. It works well, in fact. It's not like the old days with the ominous chart on the fridge." He chuckles again. I can't believe he can even mention the chore chart and laugh in the same breath. Warning creeps across my skin. Lobo tucks closer.

"I don't want to keep you," Oliver says. "I know you're busy. I, well, it would be great if you came to the wedding. It's going to be a small ceremony in the backyard, nothing fancy, a minister, a few of our friends and one or two of Dad's. I know you and he aren't . . . I know you aren't really speaking to him, but it would mean a lot to me." He clears his throat. "It would mean a lot to me, Beatrice, if you were here."

No. Absolutely not.

He lets out a long breath. "Plus, we're grappling with some urgency because I'd really like for us to be married before the baby is born."

A light breeze pushes a tumbleweed of dog hair past my feet. Nicholas likes to say that there's enough dog hair on the floor for me to make a whole new puppy.

"When's the due date?" I ask.

"Three weeks."

And like an M.C. Escher drawing, the walls of my apartment tilt at angles, the ceiling dips, the floor stretches. Where there was order, there is now mayhem. Where there was control, there is now a freefall. I manage to push words out despite my breathlessness.

"When is the wedding?"

"Two weeks. The Saturday of Labor Day weekend."

I rest my head on the wall as my litany of excuses and rationalizations march into my skull, each one more self-righteousness than the last. None emerge from my lips. Instead, my mind goes to the horse across the street in Lafayette Park.

His glistening coat. The flutter of his mane.

His unlikely presence. His ease. His grace.

Cowboy. Winter. Oliver.

Miracles.

What follows is a whisper. No, smaller. A flicker.

But it's enough.

I hear myself speaking before the words are fully formed in my mind.

"I can't imagine how this is going to work—being in that house with Dad, being in Vermont after so many years." My throat tightens. "But you're my brother and I want to meet the woman who has become so important to you. So I guess—I guess I'll just have to show up and see what happens with Dad."

Are you insane?

He draws in a deep breath. "Thank you, Beatrice. I can't wait for you to meet her. I can't wait to see you. It's been way too long."

"It has," I say, anxious to sever the connection to my family. To the past.

"I love you," he says.

"Me too."

Phone in hand, I scratch Lobo's hind leg, which sends his tail thwapping appreciatively against the laminate wood floor. The vaulted ceiling draws my eye with its superhighway of hairline cracks, and I realize I have no road map. Nothing to delineate a clear way forward. Like that frozen Magic 8-Ball. "Reply hazy, try again."

I text Nicholas.

Come over. Bring Thai. Bring Pinot.

CHAPTER 26

In every sense, the fog offers relief. The fog outside, low and gray, settles into the deepest corners of the city while the fog in my head, thick and dizzying, disrupts my flow of thoughts. Derails the train.

Too much pinot.

"Is there more wine?" I ask, my voice gravely.

Still nighttime, we sit on the plush carpet in my bedroom, beneath the window that overlooks The Tree. Bolstered by the wall, we face my bed and the candlelit apartment. Partially veiled in a whirl of shadows, Nicholas rests beside me, legs outstretched, a shoulder pressed against mine.

"Wine is gone," he says, sounding as drunk as I feel.

"We drank two bottles?"

"We did."

At this, I drag open my eyes and search his face for judgment or regret, but find his eyes closed, his body still. The high achiever. The boss. The boyfriend. All at rest.

I sense an opening, or maybe it's just that my filter has passed out.

"How come we never stay at your house?" I ask as my eyelids slide shut again.

"My house is . . . cold," he says.

"Like no heat?"

"Like no heart," he says, and my mind perks up.

Marlene told me he got the Pacific Heights mansion in his divorce. Marlene did most of Nicholas's creative work when he was a rising star at the agency, a newly married rising star.

"You make zillions of dollars. Why not remodel if it's got no heart?"

He clears his throat. "Not zillions. But I won't remodel."

"Why?"

Silence.

"Because that's where you lived with your ex-wife?" Only drunk would these words leave my mouth. When I'm sober, they simply lurk.

"Maybe."

"If the house has no heart, and you won't remodel it, why live there at all?"

Silence.

Then he says, "So she can't."

And there it is, a nugget of truth. Only with a dulled mind could I root it out. Only with a dulled mind would he let it slip.

I ask nothing more of him. His words expand in the room and settle. Like the fog, they find every corner.

So she can't.

His hand caresses my upper thigh. His mouth finds my neck at the base where it meets my shoulder, softly kissing at first, then trailing hungrily to my lips. Through my dullness, arousal blooms.

He strokes me between the legs, steady and slow, surely sensing my heat through my blue jeans. My body lights up. Tingles. My pulse jumps.

We slide to the carpet, mouths locked, with me underneath and Nicholas hovering above. He cups me again, massages me, draws the heat. I squirm. Warmth radiates out to my fingertips, my forehead, my toes. I run my hands up his arms and arch my back. Urgent. Ignited. My fingers find his neck and rake through his hair. He unsnaps my jeans and drags open the zipper.

"Let me," he whispers against my mouth.

I know what he wants to do. I have never let him.

"C'mon, baby, let me," he says, his tongue entwining with mine, but also pulling, dragging me forth. Still stroking me through my jeans, an inferno rages through my body. I ache for release.

He slides lower and kisses the rise of soft flesh on my exposed belly, then draws circles around my belly button with his tongue. Slipping lower, he nuzzles the triangular opening where my underwear peaks out from above the zipper. Lower. Lower. He kisses a trail, then rises over me, one hand curling over the top of my jeans and pausing, the other gliding in slow circles, lightly stroking my lower abdomen. It's as if he's drinking in the sight of me yet restraining himself, ready, eager for me to say the word so he can tug off my jeans and go down on me. Taste me. See me. Bring me to release.

I recoil.

And there it is, a nugget of my truth.

I spend no time exploring my reaction. I create a diversion by sitting up and kissing him deeply. I slide my hand over the bulge in his jeans and squeeze gently. He moans as I unbutton his shirt and roll it off his shoulders.

"No. Let me," I whisper against his mouth and he smiles and with the slightest pressure of my finger on his chest he falls onto the carpet, lifts his hips, tugs his jeans and underwear off and waits for the familiar touch of my mouth.

Even drunk, I know. Even drunk, I am aware of this walled off part of me. *Does Nicholas see it in himself?* I don't know.

Neither of us pushes the other. Neither questions. Ours is a pact about pretending not to notice.

I tell myself it's a relief to know, with certainty, that he won't stop and ask me why I won't let him go down on me. And listen well enough to hear what I'm actually saying no to, what I'm actually protecting. *From him? From myself?* I don't even know.

Too much thinking.

I lose myself in the buzz of pleasing him, of bringing him to climax, and then in minutes he is ready again, and he's inside me. Our bodies quickly find a rhythm, yearning, hungry, and we move in sync, joining, thrusting, fucking, and I tell myself it's all I really need. A moan escapes his lips and I know he's almost there and I open my eyes so I can watch his beautiful face relax into euphoria as he comes. He lowers himself, kisses me fervently, then rolls off me. We lay naked together on the rug in silence. While spooning, Nicholas falls asleep, his breath moving the hair at the nape of my neck.

Lobo sleeps just a few feet away, at eye level, with the upper half of his body off his bed, his belly exposed, and his favorite yellow lacrosse ball inches from his nose. He twitches, dreaming, rippling with electricity. He blinks. His paws flex. His hind legs kick out and puppy-like whines and yips burst from his slack jowls. He is far away, jubilant, maybe chasing a ball or a cat, running or hunting, with no part of himself locked out. No part of himself roped off.

His freedom and wholeness are unbearable to watch in this moment, so I leave Nicholas's warm flesh, and as I knew he would, Lobo awakens and lifts his head to watch me, ready for a command, ready for whatever comes next. I throw on shorts and a sweater, pull a cigarette from the pack I keep tucked away for emergencies, click Lobo's collar and leash on, and go outside.

Through the fog I can't see the park, but if the horse was still there, Lobo would tell me. The cold wakes me, cuts through my drunk, cuts through my sloppy mind. I drape the leash loosely over my thighs, light the cigarette, and tilt my face so the fog can mist my skin. Night in the city is never silent. In the distance, a siren blares, a dog barks, a motorcycle accelerates, and Taylor Swift's voice drifts from a passing car stereo.

I sink to the front step and Lobo quickly lowers beside me, sphinxlike, with his head high, his front paws extended, and his haunches curled under in case he needs to rise quickly and do something, be something . . . for me.

My free hand settles on his shoulder. Together we sit while I smoke and we search the dark, bracing ourselves for what might come, for what might appear. *Will we be ready?*

CHAPTER 27

I'm never drinking again.

"I'm never drinking again," I say.

"Hmm," Nicholas says.

"Ever."

"Hmm."

Cautiously, I explore the inside of my mouth with my tongue and find it thick and wooly from the wine, rough and bitter from the cigarette. Still wearing the sweater from last night and to my surprise, underwear, I stumble into the bathroom and brush my teeth. Twice. The second time is particularly frothy.

Nicholas lies on his side, facing the wall. Lobo races into the yard and pees while I prepare his food, but the moment he reappears, I set the bowl on the floor, crawl into bed, and close my eyes. I lie on my back and soon Nicholas does the same.

"What time is it?" he asks quietly.

"Seven-thirty." His fingers find mine under the sheet and we hold hands. Exhaustion hits me and I wonder where I got the strength to brush my teeth and tend to Lobo.

"I have a video call with Carlos in an hour," he says in a serious tone. My boyfriend retreats. My boss arrives.

"Hmm," I say.

"He wants to open a second office."

"Where?" My eyes are still closed. Listening and speaking are consuming all my strength.

"Las Vegas."

I attempt a complete sentence: "I thought you were going to say Los Angeles."

"No, that market's too tapped. He wants a location that's hungry."

"Vegas." I regress to one word where I belong.

"Vegas."

He squeezes my hand, then releases it. "I'm jumping in the shower."

"Hmm."

"Hi, Lobee dobee," he says. Lobo's collar jingles at Nicholas's touch, and his tail thwaps against the floor.

The running water lulls me to sleep and when I awake, Nicholas, naked, towels himself off at the foot of my bed.

"My brother's getting married," I say as he dries his chest.

"No kidding? Good for him," Nicholas says and starts on his legs.

"And he's having a baby."

He straightens. His wet hair stands on end. "Whoa. That's hard core."

"You don't want kids?"

"Sure. I'd have kids. A bunch of little me's running around. Handsome and witty," he says, drying his arms. I've never dated a man who is so naked.

"Inevitably, though, I'd screw them up. Then I'd have to pay for all that hypnotherapy. Aromatherapy. College. Their failed startups. Bail . . ." he says, with a far-off expression.

He flashes me a smile. "Just kidding. I love kids." He doesn't ask what I want. Instead, he pulls on his Calvin Klein boxer briefs.

"I need to take a few days off, Nicholas, so I can go home for Oliver's wedding." Saying it aloud springs my anxiety from its cage. It scurries around my fragile universe.

Vermont. Dad.

Tears quietly rise.

"Okay. How soon?" he asks, stepping into his jeans.

Mom's painting studio. Empty.

"In two weeks," I say.

He pauses with his fingers on his jeans zipper, as if calculating something in his head. "If you can get three boards done with slogans and art, Derek and I can present to PharmFresh without you."

Tell him the truth. Tell him you're a wreck about going home.

"I can do that," I say.

Fully dressed now, including shoes, he crawls onto the bed, lowers on top of me, and kisses me lustfully on the mouth. We kiss well. Our mouths fit.

A tear slips from my eye.

He wipes it away with his thumb. "Oh, baby, you'll see me again," he says, and I punch him lightly on the shoulder.

After the door clicks shut, I curl up on my side and watch The Tree outside my window. While its leaves quaver in the breeze, I let myself remember being a child and lying next to Mom in the tall grass beside her garden.

We had held hands and closed our eyes. "So we can hear the earth better," she'd said.

Silently, I had listened, straining to hear the earth's message for me, excited, thrilled, that something as big and important as the earth saw me, knew about me.

"I can't hear her," I whispered. Mom always referred to the earth in the feminine.

"Oh, she's there, honey. Listen again."

I had listened again. I even held my breath.

"All I hear are birds, wind in the trees, and crickets," I whispered.

"And how do you feel, hearing all of that?"

"Like they love me," I said. Mom had squeezed my hand, so I knew I got it right. She rolled over, kissed me on the head, and whispered, "Like I love you."

I am now a long way from there. *Would she recognize me?* A trail of half-burned candles slump like Greek ruins with gaping holes and sunken sides. Empty wine bottles shame me from the kitchen counter. In my mouth, tobacco wars with mint toothpaste, while my mind relives last night's sex—sex in which I was only partially present. Again.

I text Scottie.

Have to go east in 2 weeks. Can I leave Lobo with you?

What's east?

I'm from there.

Say whaaaaaat?

Vermont.

Ben & Jerry's.

Yes. Plus a few other things.

How long you gone?

5 days tops.

Bring me Ben & Jerry's T-shirt?

Of course.

Okay then.

CHAPTER 28

We have a good table. Nicholas plays golf with the restaurant owner's son, so with no reservation, we were whisked like VIPs to one of the prize four tops up on a riser. We're near enough to the glass façade for me to watch the passersby on Columbus Avenue, a major thoroughfare between North Beach and Chinatown, and central enough to afford Nicholas and Derek an unobstructed view of the patrons.

"How many of these diners do you know, Nicholas?" I ask.

"They're prospects, not diners," Nicholas says, and gives me a sultry wink. He might as well have leaned across the table and kissed me on the mouth. Derek's head snaps in my direction. I kick Nicholas under the table. *So much for our secret relationship.*

I attempt a countermeasure.

"So, this is new . . . going to dinner with you. Have you invited Derek and me out so we can talk about PharmFresh?" My voice sounds forced. And I strangle my napkin while I talk. I'm terrible at subterfuge.

Nicholas drops the orange peel garnish in his Negroni and swirls the low-ball glass. Not a drop of the Campari, gin, or sweet vermouth escape.

"Let's have some fun first," he says and brings the Negroni

to his lips.

"I'm all for fun," Derek says, and sucks the foamy head off his microbrew.

I take a sip of water. Some of it drips on my blouse.

"Ten o'clock. Bald. Fuchsia Ermenegildo Zegna suit. White shirt," Nicholas says.

"Is he Peet's Coffee?" says Derek.

Nicholas shakes his head.

"Uber?"

"One more strike and you're out."

"Odwalla."

"Odwalla's defunct, Derek. It died in Coca-Cola's arms," says Nicholas. "The guy in Zegna drinking Dom Perignon at the center table is the general manager of Harrah's in Vegas."

Derek nods. "Ben Santos said he heard a rumor that we're scoping out satellite offices in Vegas," he says.

Knowing the rumor is true and fearing it will be evident in my expression, I force my eyes away and feign interest in the twisted steel light array above our table.

"You think Ben Santos has a direct line to Carlos? Granted, Ben can bring a grown man to tears in a twenty-second Schwinn commercial, but nobody can anticipate our elusive owner's next move," Nicholas says. "Not even me," he adds and rejoins his Negroni.

"Then how do you know a GM in Vegas?"

I swallow. Derek is quick.

Nicholas's smile reaches his eyes. "I know everybody."

Derek shakes his head and takes a long drink of microbrew as our server, Elena, a stunning olive-skinned brunette, arrives. With cascading curls, a wide smile, and warm, almond-shaped eyes, Elena takes us through the posh restaurant's four-course prix-fixe menu with precision and charm, the latter amplified by her subtle Spanish accent. The moment her tantalizing spiel ends, Derek smiles up at her and addresses her in flawless Spanish. Elena beams, relaxes, and the two of them fall into a spirited exchange that culminates in laughter. Nicholas and I gawk. *Derek speaks Spanish?*

My mind flashes to the procession of pigeons outside the attic classroom in which I spent four years studying Latin at Westerly Prep. Eight semesters of Latin and the only phrase I can think of is, "*Puella est agricola.*"

Which translates to, "The girl is a farmer."

With a touch of envy, I watch Elena and Derek converse, newly bound by a language which appears to be representative of far more than simply nouns and verbs. Elena says something and touches Derek lightly on the shoulder. He replies. Their eyes lock. She blushes. He grins.

The girl is a farmer.

By the time we've reached the third course, a sumptuous honeynut squash terrine, the requisite PharmFresh discussion is long over, and Nicholas has grown uncharacteristically solemn. He knocks back his cabernet sauvignon and motions to a server for another bottle. While he waits he scowls at his empty glass.

I step in to fill the silence. "Where did you learn to speak Spanish?" I ask Derek, whom I'd previously and mistakenly pegged as a dumb all-American jock type.

"My mother is from Cozumel," he says.

"In the Yucatán Peninsula?"

"Yeah, just off the coast." He sips his microbrew.

Nicholas stares at something—or someone—over my right shoulder. A server refills Nicholas' glass, bows slightly, and leaves the bottle on the table.

"You grew up in Mexico?" I ask.

Nicholas's eyes follow someone walking behind me. It takes all my strength not to spin around.

Derek shakes his head. "No. I grew up here in San Francisco, but we spent our summers in Cozumel. We lived simply. Stucco bungalow. Bicycles. I've probably spent twenty percent of my life underwater."

I remember a summer in Vermont when I went nineteen consecutive days without putting on a pair of shoes. And forty-two days without brushing my hair.

A woman's voice breaks into my flashback. "Nicholas," she says. Her voice is throaty but feminine.

The light slips out of Nicholas's eyes. He lifts his chin in the barest of greetings.

I twist around as a tall blonde in a white cashmere pantsuit strides away from our table. Her slim figure and confident stride draw many eyes. Thankfully, it's Derek who asks the question.

"Nicholas . . . who was that?"

Nicholas drains his cabernet and meets my eyes.

"My ex-wife," he says.

CHAPTER 29

"She seems nice," Derek says with his eyes crossed.

Nicholas laughs and for a moment the clouds above him break. I can't study her and silently compare us; I'm stuck facing Nicholas and Derek and a colorful spectacle of nighttime city lights as I struggle to ascertain why I suddenly feel like a mistress.

Elena returns and describes our two dessert options: chocolate mousse with sea salt caramel or vanilla bean crème brulée. I force a smile. Nicholas drags a hand through his hair. Derek orders the chocolate mousse.

I find myself slowly rising and setting my napkin on my chair, excusing myself and weaving through the crowded tables toward the restroom. By force of will I walk instead of run, lock my eyes on the restroom sign, and breathe. No white cashmere pantsuit crops up in my line of sight, but my body braces for it anyway. I draw open the door, step into the cavernous, black-tiled bathroom, and stop beneath a beam of faint recessed light. The door clicks closed. Yo-Yo Ma wafts through invisible speakers and washes over me. Bach's Suite No. 1 in G Major, Prelude. I've listened to it a thousand times. I close my eyes. I lower my head. I unclench my hands.

A toilet flushes.

I'm washing my hands in the first of a trio of sinks when the white cashmere pantsuit penetrates my peripheral vision. My mind whirs and thumps like an overloaded washing machine. She strides to the wash basin farthest from me.

Don't look up at her. Don't—

I look up.

Our eyes meet in the mirror. I make a quick assessment: *Scandinavian supermodel.*

The corners of my mouth twitch but stop short of a smile. I drop my gaze and pump more frothy soap onto my clean hands. I'm scrubbing the nooks between each finger when she speaks.

"Are you prepping for surgery?" she asks.

My face reddens. Still, I meet her gaze in the mirror. Her light-blue eyes are nearly translucent. She raises an eyebrow as if I've already taken too long to answer her.

"Just a bit distracted," I say as I rinse my hands under a stream of lukewarm water.

She leans into her reflection and runs two fingertips across each cheekbone. Her complexion is flawless. She lifts her chin, then lowers it and turns her head side to side, examining her features with a satisfied expression. A shaft of silky blond hair falls forward. She tucks it behind her ear. It stays put.

"You work with him?" she asks, as she washes her hands.

"With whom?" I say, grateful that the position of the paper towel dispenser allows me to turn my back on her.

"Nicholas," she says with smooth familiarity—as if her lips and tongue have wrapped themselves around those consonants a million times.

"Yes. I'm on his creative team," I say as I dry my hands.

Suddenly she is beside me, extracting paper towels from the dispenser in two quick tugs. We are inches from one another. I resist the urge to move away, to concede my territory. I'm like a soldier defending her bunker even after the battle has been lost.

"You're with him?" she asks.

My heart thumps. *They're divorced. You have no reason to hide.*

Our eyes lock. She smiles, but it's joyless. Her Rose Prick Eau de Parfum encircles me. Sweet. Elegant. Thorny.

She tosses her crumpled paper towels at the hole in the countertop that conceals the garbage bin. The wad arcs over my shoulder, banks off the mirror, and disappears inside the hole. *Nothing but net.*

"Let me give you some advice," she says.

I beg my legs to walk away. I pray the door opens to a rush of chatty female diners who have to pee badly.

"He won't cheat on you," she says. "He won't forget your birthday. He won't leave the toilet seat up."

I don't want to hear what she has to say, yet I hang on her every word.

"But he won't ask you a question that he might not like the answer to. He would rather be with the version of 'you' that is perfect for him than know the 'you' that you truly are."

I think of our sex life and the wall I put up that he so willingly accepts.

"We have no secrets," I say.

She cocks her head, as if my lie has struck a dissonant chord.

I am a child in my mother's kitchen insisting that I didn't eat her baking chocolate even though it's all over my face.

Her eyes travel from my hasty ponytail to my slightly out-of-fashion strappy heels. Her demeanor softens.

"You seem like a nice girl," she says.

My body jolts awake. I'm walking away from her. I'm

reaching for the doorknob. Words are flowing from my mouth. "Have a good evening," I am saying over my shoulder.

The dining area absorbs me in a cacophony of clanking dishware, rumbles of conversation, and an occasional spike of laughter. I am not Carrie on prom night dressed in white standing up on stage drenched in pig's blood, but as I weave my way through the diners, I feel vulnerable and I fear that it shows.

Nicholas sits alone, sipping espresso from a doll-size china cup with his jumbo hands. It seems like hours since I last saw him. He motions for me to sit beside him in Derek's empty chair.

"Where's Derek?" I ask, as I drop next to him and push away the tall funnel-shaped dish that must have held Derek's chocolate mousse. I wish I had ordered one.

"At the bar chatting up Elena," he says.

Nicholas sets his espresso on the table and scoops up a bite of his own chocolate mousse, a firm, airy mound cut with swirls of whipped cream and curls of milk chocolate. I want to steal his spoon, eat the rest of his dessert, and then lick the dish. The bite disappears between his lips. He reaches for his espresso.

We have a clear view of his ex-wife as she slips into the chair beside the bald general manager of Harrah's at the center table. He squeezes her forearm. She lays her napkin across her lap. He says something to her, then scoots his chair closer. She smiles and reaches for her wine glass.

Nicholas's fingers intertwine with mine under the table. Surprised, I glance at our hands and up at him. His eyes are bloodshot and weary, but they hold mine with an intensity that nullifies all the activity around us. He leans over and kisses my cheek, then lifts my hand and kisses my wrist just below the palm. My body tingles. Warmth spreads through me. He gently tucks a loose curl of hair behind my ear. It stays put.

A server arrives to clear Derek's empty dish. Moments later he returns and sets a vanilla bean crème brulée in front of me.

I hate crème brulée.

"I ordered that for you, babe," Nicholas says.

I regard the repulsive custard with its lightly torched skin.

"Thank you," I say, and reach for the tiny spoon.

CHAPTER 30

My computer clock reads 4:00 p.m. I leave for Vermont tomorrow, but I still haven't bought a wedding present. Swiveling to face the window, I notice a party raging in the cube farm on the second floor of Wells & Menklin, the law firm across the street. The executive levels above are all unoccupied and unlit. I wonder if that's what's being celebrated. I rise and pull my mini-backpack onto my shoulders just as Nicholas, virile and deliciously handsome in a sherbet-colored dress shirt and faded jeans, pops his head into my office.

With every passing day it gets easier for me to justify not mentioning my conversation with his ex-wife in the restaurant bathroom. I tell myself I've almost forgotten what she looks like. *Scandinavian supermodel.* Okay, so I haven't forgotten.

"What time's your flight?" Nicholas asks for the third time.

"Six-thirty in the morning."

"Brutal. Want me to drive you?"

"Oh, that's sweet, but I'll take a cab," I answer, surprised he didn't lower his voice when he made the offer.

He steps into my office and closes the door behind him, his hand gripping the knob.

"You're staring," I say. "Do I have a latte mustache?" I swipe my upper lip with my index finger.

He shakes his head but continues to fixate on me.

"You know I'm going to be lost here without you," he says.

My stomach flutters in excitement, but I squash it by reminding myself that he could be talking about work.

"Marlene can pick up the slack. She'd do anything for you."

"That's not what I meant," he says, and I realize he meant he'll *personally* be lost without me. I blush and quietly curse myself for it.

"I think when you return from Vermont, I'm going to let the office know we're dating."

"You're no longer concerned that they're going to cry favoritism every time you assign me an account?"

"No. Your work speaks for itself."

Pride rushes through me. "Thank you, Nicholas."

"You're welcome, Beatrice," he says, in his formal voice.

I don't know what to do with my body. I really just want to jump over the desk and kiss him. Instead, I pick up a ballpoint pen and twirl it like a six-year-old.

"Besides, there may be more to announce," he says.

"When?" *What?*

"After."

I stop twirling.

"The PharmFresh account. They may have picked a slogan by then," he says.

"Right! PharmFresh. Of course." *Am I disappointed? Do I want him to propose?*

"I bought you something," he says, and grins. "A sort of going-away present. A going-away-temporarily present," he adds and darts out the door.

It's master-level ping pong. To and fro he bounces between boss and boyfriend. When he reappears, he holds a small spider plant. It's *very* small—a few fragile shoots—clearly the beginning of this plant's young life. He hands me the glazed turquoise pot, and I immediately touch the plant to be sure I'm seeing what I think I'm seeing.

"But it's real," I say, confused. He knows my dismal track record with plants—hence the plastic Ficus in my office.

"I think you're ready."

Still rattled by his surprises, I jokingly hold the plant away from me, in outstretched arms, as if it's an infant that might pee on me.

"Where's the nanny!" I cry comically. Nicholas's face falls. For the first time since we started dating, he appears hurt.

"You've got this," he says and takes a step backwards.

I give him a warm smile. "I guess we'll find out. Thank you for the plant, Nicholas." I say, hoping my lame joke has been forgotten. I lightly stroke the plant's delicate shoots between my thumb and forefinger. The growth feels sturdier than I'd guessed.

Nicholas runs a hand through his hair. We said goodbye this morning at my place, so I don't expect a drawn-out parting now.

"By the way, I saw the boards you left for PharmFresh. There was one clear winner."

"I thought so, too. Were the other two good enough to bring along as alternatives?"

"Definitely. Nice work," he says, and then smooths the front of his unwrinkled shirt. He stares at something on the carpet. He rolls onto his heels.

"One last thing," he says, fastening his eyes on mine.

"Yes?"

"I think I love you," he says. And leaves.

I stare at the backside of his curly head as he strides to his office. He doesn't even glance in my direction the entire way to his desk. I am rounding my desk to go to him when Derek appears at Nicholas's door, then shortly after, Emily, and then finally Marlene. The four of them launch into a discussion and my window of opportunity slams shut.

I think I love you.

I slowly organize my desk and gather my belongings. Two of my colleagues are in the elevator when I step in. We nod hello and it takes all my strength not to say, "He thinks he loves me."

At Neiman Marcus where I buy a silver wedding photo frame and a silver baby rattle, when the saleswoman asks me if I would like to apply for a Neiman Marcus credit card and save 15% on my purchase, all I want to say is, "He thinks he loves me."

And as I'm riding the steep "down" escalator in line with a string of women, women wearing sparkling wedding rings, women holding hands with their stylish young children, women with shopping bags from the men's department— clothes, I imagine, for their husbands—I sense I'm now part of something. A tradition. A lineage.

I remember the poster in the science lab at Westerly depicting the stages of man's evolution: small ape walking, medium ape walking, ape man walking, modern man walking. Only here at Neiman Marcus, it's women riding the escalator— a biological progression of the stages of evolution to proper womanhood: daughter, girlfriend, wife, mother.

The way it's supposed to be.

The way we're supposed to be.

"I think I love you" puts me in the lineage. It gets me on the poster. I'm not sure it's what I want, but maybe I don't have to know. Maybe I just let the poster show me, let it guide me.

Buoyed by the thought that my life might now be solved, I

allow one of the perfume-spraying ladies in cosmetics to spritz me with something spicy, and I smile at the scowling guard by the security sensors at the revolving doors. When I step outside, Union Square overflows with street vendors selling their art and homemade wares: jewelry, pottery, hand-printed notecards, paper mache, refrigerator magnets, and silkscreened T-shirts.

Despite the explosion of color, my eyes are drawn to a simple card table draped with a lacey white cloth. On it, the prism effect of the late afternoon sun animates a menagerie of glass figurines. A small, thin woman nods at me in greeting from behind the table. Her chestnut skin is deeply lined, suggestive of a long life hard-lived. Dressed in black, with a turquoise necklace, turquoise rings, and a silver bracelet, she appears to be about a hundred years old and extraordinarily fit.

I am unable to pass by without stopping. "Hello," I say.

"Hello." Her eyes are a stunning green with yellow flecks.

"Did you make these?" I ask.

She nods. "My mother taught me how to blow glass when I was a child." Her voice is strained and raspy. It's obvious her voice box has been damaged.

"Your mother?"

"Yes."

"She was untraditional," I say more as an observation than a question.

"Yes."

"An artist."

"Yes." She smiles as if she has been transported to a memory.

"May I pick one up?"

"Yes, please," she says, her curled fingers motioning to the entire collection. I wonder if she has arthritis or if her fingers prefer the position they take around the blowpipe.

Immediately, my hand gravitates to the horse. Mid-stride, it holds its head high, its mane flies, its tail trails in an animated swoosh.

"This is amazing," I say.

"Thank you."

"Your mother was a good teacher."

"She was good at many things," she says, glowing, as if the memory of her is itself a light source.

The words are out of my mouth before I even realize I'm thinking them. "My mother was an artist, too."

She nods and as our eyes meet; something passes between us. Understanding? Recognition? No. It's pride.

"I'll take this one," I say, horse in hand, and pull out my wallet.

CHAPTER 31

Unlike the airport in San Francisco, and in Chicago where I changed flights, the Burlington International Airport is the antithesis of international, with low-pile carpet, cozy wood-paneled nooks, and a plethora of live plants. Absent are the jarring loudspeaker announcements, the throngs of weary travelers, and the exhausting maze of wings and gates that seem to birth new extensions the moment you round a corner.

Even the national food chain vendors are absent. Here the eateries are local: Sweet Matilda's, August Farm, Blue Hill Coffee, and Cal's Burger House. I wonder if that's Cal himself over there behind the counter.

Oliver texted me as I was disembarking to say Dad would be picking me up. I make a beeline over to Sweet Matilda's, seeking baked comfort and courage.

From behind the counter, a woman my age with a Burton Snowboards cap and blunt blue hair acknowledges me with a quick nod. A black vine tattoo with red buds creeps around her forearm and trails up her bicep before disappearing under the sleeve of her T-shirt. Each of her fingers is adorned with a ring. Her belt buckle is a scorpion. She moves nimbly, pulling trays from the oven and cookies from the display case while the grumbling customer in front of me complains to her about airline delays. I expect the woman to lose patience, but as she passes the customer her box of freshly baked cookies, she smiles brightly and says, "I bet these will help with all of that."

The customer falls silent, almost trance-like, seemingly caught off-guard by the woman's kindness. She accepts the bag with two hands, as if it's precious cargo, and as she collects her rolling suitcase and spins away, she says "Thank you" with a dreamy expression that suggests the powerful cookies are already working their magic.

I scan the chalkboard menu and step to the counter. "Hi. One chocolate chip butterscotch. Two double chocolate chip. Oh hell, just give me half a dozen of each," I say, remembering how many people now live at the house.

"Sure thing," she says, and with a gloved hand, she selects cookies from the display. Perfectly shaped and bursting with chips, the cookies emit a smell so alluring it seems the entire airport has fallen in line behind me.

As we trade the box of cookies for my credit card, she squints and asks, "Do I know you?"

I was wondering the same thing.

"No, I'm from California," I answer, not yet ready to be here, not yet ready to claim it as home. I thank her and snake through the small airport, simultaneously drawn to and recoiling from the familiar surroundings.

I spot Dad and in the brief moment before he sees me, I pause and allow my shock at how much he has aged to register. Although still fit and alert, his buzz cut hair has gone salt-and-pepper gray, his frame is leaner, and I could swear he's shorter. The clothes and stance I recognize: a short-sleeved beige shirt, hands tucked into the pockets of long khaki shorts, athletic ankle socks, and double knotted sneakers.

His face softens when he sees me, and the push-pull in me

ratchets up.

"Hi there," he says, opening his arms wide for a hug. As if locked in an invisible tractor beam, I step in, but while he hugs me with two arms, I hug him with only one.

"How are you?" he asks into my hair.

"Good, good. I'm good." I babble and extract myself from his embrace. In my nervousness, I observe with horror, as one might a collision in slow motion, a stream of jabbering nonsense barreling toward my lips. "The flight was fine. No major delays. I had a window seat on both legs of the trip. Food was terrible, of course. I expected with it being Labor Day weekend that the flights would have been packed, but the one here from Chicago was pretty empty. Why don't we go stand in baggage claim?" *Breathe.*

Baggage claim occupies an area only forty feet away, so within moments we stand alone, together again, hands buried in our pockets. We assess the conveyer belt that isn't moving. We consider the cutout where suitcases will eventually burst through but where rubber fringe now dangles like doorway beads from the groovy '60s. We watch people and we silently read the walls: a welcome message from the governor, advertisements for Stowe resorts, and a humorous homage to cows, who reputedly outnumber humans in Vermont.

"From what I hear, you have a full house," I say, breaking the awkward silence. *Is it awkward for him, too?*

"Yes, Oliver and Rachel have been living with me for a few months now. I thought I'd see more of them than I have. With our conflicting schedules, we often only share a few meals together each week. Your brother keeps the refrigerator stocked with leftovers from the restaurant." He presses his palm against his flat abdomen and adds happily, "I eat like a king."

Oliver has been feeding our father and I haven't even acknowledged his birthday. I shove the comparison aside. "What about the university? Have classes started?" My eyes bore into the rubber fringed cutout in the wall, willing a suitcase to push through.

"The semester begins on Tuesday. I'm department chair now, which brings an extra layer of responsibility and complexity, but the position has its perks."

"Congratulations, Dad," I say, venturing to make eye contact. Beneath the baggage area's florescent lights, I see the crow's feet fanning out from the corners of his eyes, lines on his forehead and sagging skin on his neck—evidence of the passage of time, time and life in which I was not a part.

"Thank you." He bows his head slightly.

The conveyer belt sputters to life and as it rounds the bend in front of us, it squeals for grease. Bags begin appearing and as I pull mine off the belt, Dad says, "Here, let me," but I don't.

The silence bothers me less in the truck, especially as the city gives way to rolling farmland, views of Camel's Hump to the east and the blue peaks of New York State's Adirondack Mountains to the west. Dad's Ford F-150 smells new and I'm surprised to see he's splurged on leather seats.

"How long did your Toyota pickup truck last?" I ask.

"Oh, the transmission went about a week after you left for California. So that was what, five years ago?"

We fought, of course, as I was leaving for California. Well, I fought. Dad just stood there and when at last I paused, he walked away and spent the next several hours in his wood shop.

"I liked that truck. You taught me how to drive on it." I'm taken aback by my acknowledgment of happier times between us. *I'm slipping.* Must be the clean air.

I take note of his hands on the steering wheel, predictably

at the recommended 10 and 2, and I realize that I have his hands, not Mom's. Same long, slender fingers and rounded nail beds, a wide palm, and a splash of freckles across skin that tans quickly to golden brown. *In what other ways do I mirror him?* I squelch the thought.

"Are Grandma and Grandpa coming to the wedding?" I last saw them at graduation from Cornell. We all ate braised lamb at Moosewood Restaurant while Grandpa reminisced about his days at Yale. I had sent them one letter each semester apprising them of my studies. Grandma had responded with travel postcards from Sri Lanka, Scotland, and the Serengeti National Park. Neither of our notes contained more than a few sentences.

"No. They're in Osaka. Or Tokyo. Somewhere in Japan."

I haven't written them since moving to California. Grandma sent me a letter about the time I started dating Nicholas, but I've never read it. It felt like a piece of the past from which I was trying to escape.

We pull into our driveway, which has been paved since I was here last. The trees that were always unadorned now host a ring of bright red mulch around their bases. The lawn has been mowed to an inch instead of three, and the house, recently painted, is now gray rather than white. Two pots of pink begonias dangle from the eaves on the front porch. Along the foundation of the house, which had been overgrown since Mom died, the beds of hosta, iris, evening primrose, and black-eyed Susan grow neat and proud.

"Dad, what happened to this place?"

He chuckles. "Oli and Rachel's wedding happened. I painted the house two years ago and had the driveway paved last summer, but all the rest," he waves his hand, "is for the wedding."

"How many guests?"

"Thirty-five people last I heard. I've tried to stay out of it. Rachel's mother has been in charge."

I suspect my father is delighted to relinquish the lead wedding planner role.

Dad stops the pickup at the end of the driveway. He slides from behind the wheel while I spring out, leaving my belongings behind. Before I hug my brother or meet my future sister-in-law, there's somewhere I have to go.

CHAPTER 32

Despite the rain puddles, I kick off my shoes and sink my toes in the damp grass. From the outside, the art barn appears smaller than I remember and the stubborn, hanging door with which I used to have to wrestle has been replaced by a standard-sized door with a proper latch. I swallow against an upswell of irritation and start out across the glistening lawn. On a cement surface, my gait would be recognizable as stomping, but the spongy, rain-soaked ground beneath me is more forgiving. It masks the truth.

Yanking open one of the doors, I long for the graceful slope of the Mercedes' hood and headlights but am met instead by a concrete floor. Flipping on the light, it's obvious who occupies this space now. Waist-high, built-in wooden cabinets offer long, flat, work counters; while nails, screws, washers, and bolts, each in their own jar, line the shelves. I can still read the labels on some of the jars. Pickle relish. Peanut butter. Mayonnaise. My father: organized and unfailingly practical.

I make it as far as the base of the staircase leading up to Mom's painting studio before a voice intervenes.

"Beatrice," my brother calls from the doorway.

I whirl around. "Hi Oli." He's fit and strong beneath our hug. "You are still the best hugger I've ever known," I whisper.

He squeezes me tightly. "You're taller. When did you get taller?" I ask, assessing him from arm's length.

"I don't know. My life is a blur. Happened somewhere in there," he says, raking a hand through his midnight curls and leaving most of them standing on end.

A petite woman with shoulder-length auburn hair, pale skin, and disarming dimples appears with her hands pressed to the sides of her protruding belly, as if to steer it.

"This is Rachel," Oliver announces, stretching an arm around her shoulders and kissing her temple. "Rachel, Beatrice," he says, casting an open palm in my direction.

"Hi." I give a short wave, but Rachel breaks free from Oliver, walks over, and flings her arms around me. Her hair smells like lemons. Her embrace is firm and surprisingly comforting.

Rachel rejoins Oliver, then my father appears and the four of us congregate in this space which is now about something very different than it used to be, and everyone seems to be comfortable with the change except for me.

We talk about tomorrow's wedding—when the small tent will be erected, when the caterers will appear, when the guests will arrive—and I ask what I can do to help. I'm assigned last-minute house cleaning duties, assisting the florist, and greeting. Grateful for the tasks and the chance to get out of my head, I excuse myself with mutterings about needing to shower and wash off the airplane travel.

The house's interior startles me. The dull wood floors are now rejuvenated and polished. Doors that were once askew hang flush. Floorboards have lost their bounce and water stains have disappeared from ceilings. The vibe is welcoming but unrecognizably formal. Despite all that's changed, everywhere I look holds a memory.

I climb the stairs and stop, facing the long hallway. Transported in time, I am six years old again, sensitive and curious. Fearless. Free.

On my left is my parents' room where adult things happen: the murmur of conversation, giggles from my mother. To the right is the guest room, lifeless compared to the rest of the house, where folded laundry fresh from the dryer sits in piles for days. Then there's Oliver's room where everything is tiny. I'm afraid I will crush him with my bigness. At last there's my room, where I talk to my stuffed animals, draw horses the color of rainbows and know, with certainty, that I am loved.

The shrill ring of the landline phone in the kitchen jolts me into the present. My bedroom door creaks as I open it. The room hasn't changed. Sumptuous yellow walls that are soothing and soft and a stark contrast to the darkly stained hand-me-down bedroom set that once belonged to my grandparents. The bookshelf overflows with my Westerly textbooks and a sheepskin still pads the swivel chair in which I used to do my homework. The mobile of nuts, bolts, and screws that Dad made when I was a child hangs motionless, waiting for an audience.

The suitcase I had left in the truck now sits by the bureau. *Dad.*

The door to the bathroom between my room and Oliver's is slightly ajar, so I close it before falling onto my narrow bed.

Memories rise. I can almost smell my sweaty soccer uniform in a heap on the floor after a game hard won. Feeling empowered, proudly checking my body for bruises—spoils of war—I'd slip into a hot shower and watch mud circle the drain. I remember staring at this very ceiling when I was home from Cornell during holidays, vividly aware I was barreling toward a point in my life where I could be whoever I wanted, live wherever I chose. I recall the camping trip and Oli's horseback riding accident, Cowboy and Winter, and turning around in Arizona instead of continuing to California and Ginny. *Ginny. Whatever happened to Ginny?*

Like an unstoppable wave, the months immediately following Mom's death rush over me. I remember Dad always knocking on my door to tell me dinner was ready or to ask me a simple question. He'd never enter my room uninvited. Oliver's nighttime sobs, the sting of the frigid bathroom floor tile, the comforting nook between the shower and the toilet.

Sorrow settles on me like a blanket. I bolt upright and dig around in my backpack for my phone. I text Nicholas.

`Home.`

Within seconds he responds.

`Home sweet home.`
`Sweet - ISH.`

Seconds pass. Then a full minute. My fingers hover over the keys. I type then erase. Type, then erase. Finally, I type:

`You love me?`

I feel small and needy the moment I hit send.

`I do.`

Say it, just say it. It will make everything better and for all you know it's true.

`I love you too, Nicholas.`
`Talk soon. Don't go all flannel on me.`

I don't feel better. I text Scottie.

`How's Lobo?`
`Sleeping on Javier's leather Eames lounge chair.`
`Bad dog?`
`Good dog bad Javier.`
`What'd Javier do?`

Nothing. Me cranky.

Me too.

Go be with your family. There's no place like home.

Trying, Dorothy.

CHAPTER 33

There are no bugs, rain clouds, or drunken uncles. Forty guests sit in folding chairs beneath a brilliant September sun, while a cooling northerly wind fans their skin. Tasteful contemporary dresses rustle. Romantic updos and braided ponytails flitter. Suit jackets swing from seat backs.

I stand alone about ten feet behind the last row, taking it all in. The yard has been transformed. White lattice partitions and standing vases of calla lilies create a charming perimeter for the ceremonial space. Tea lights twinkle from tree branches. Chiffon streamers tumble from tiki lamps. But in the distance, the same northerly breeze rattles through the old stable and corral and bends the overgrown wildflowers in the long meadow. Out there—land forgotten. In here—space renewed.

Past and present. The moment asks me to acknowledge their contiguity not as a tragedy but as a natural progression, the cycle of life. Endings. Beginnings. A perspective I've resisted gathers inside me and tries to coalesce into a thought. I wrench my mind away, smothering it before it can take shape.

Rachel's mother, whom I met at sunrise this morning, wears cobalt blue and floats along the end rows clasping hands, whispering in ears, and against the occasional burst of wind, stabilizing her elegant wide-brim derby hat with a French-manicured hand. She is both event architect and onsite facilitator, and I've yet to see her sweat or hear a hint of frustration in her voice. The florist, caterers, and the wedding cake have arrived on time. The wedding officiant has arrived early. The bartenders have arrived sober. And the plumbing in our house has held up.

Despite the camaraderie and excitement surrounding me, I grip my cell phone, hoping that it will give me the signal and beam me up. The wedding is not unpleasant. It's . . . gentle. Years of city life have left me suspect of anything less than frantic. I scan the revelers in search of trouble, a protester, or a burgeoning argument, something to help me regain my bearings. Instead, I see a group of young women in the third row collapse into giggles, and several rows behind them I watch a man wrap his arm around his partner's shoulder.

I lift a flute of champagne from a passing server's tray. In the front row, my father rests his hand on the empty seat beside him. I don't know whether he's consciously saving it for me or unconsciously saving it for my mother.

I empty the flute in one long swallow. My cell phone vibrates. *Scottie.*

> Beam me up Scottie.
> Would if I could. Lobo question for you.
> Uh oh. What did he eat?
> Loaf of kalamata olive bread.
> Sorry.
> Cork from Javier's Chardonnay.
> Whoops.
> Dryer lint.
> That's a first.
> Thought I'd give him coconut oil. Help move things along.
> Let me know how it ends up.

Lol. What r you doing?

Waiting for my brother to walk down the aisle.

You have a brother?

Yes.

Older younger?

Younger.

Gay straight?

Straight.

He's getting married?

Imminently.

Why isn't Nicholas there with you?

I type, *Because Vermont is,* then erase it. I type, *Because the men in my family are,* then erase it. I type, *I didn't think he'd,* then erase it.

Work.

If I was your man, you wouldn't be at that wedding alone.

I wish I wasn't at this wedding alone.

Ceremony is starting.

Catch the bouquet?

Not sure.

Let a girl who wants it catch it.

Thank you.

For what?

I don't know. For being kind.

For taking care of Lobo.

Pachelbel's Canon in D Major filters through the cacophony of chatter and laughter. A petite cellist in Birkenstocks and a lanky keyboard player in a bowler hat handily quiet the crowd with their skilled rendition. I set my empty glass at the end of the bar and make a beeline for the vacant seat in the last row, but my body doesn't stop there. A tickling feeling along my neck propels me forward until I find myself plunking down beside my father at the very front.

My heart thumps. This is not what I'd intended. *How did I end up here?*

Oliver saunters past in a slim cut burgundy suit and takes his place by the gray-haired officiant wearing a silver dress and hoop earrings. I am suddenly nervous for him, as if he's onstage in a vast, packed auditorium readying to sing a cappella or recite original poetry. I grip my seat to stop myself from launching up and . . . what? Tackling him? Dragging him away? Standing with him?

Standing with him.

My breath catches in my throat.

The music transitions to the "Wedding March" and Oliver, who has yet to glance my way, fixes his gaze on the spot behind us where his fiancée is supposed to appear. The shuffling behind me confirms that many in the crowd have likewise spun around to witness her arrival, but my eyes remain locked on my little brother.

Wind lifts his tie and pushes a flop of curls off his forehead and, as a collective *ahh* slips from the guests' mouths and a pregnant Rachel processes up the aisle, past and present fuse before my eyes. Oliver the boy. Oliver the man. Oliver the son. Oliver the father.

His hand reaches out. Rachel takes it.

CHAPTER 34

Three mushroom caps, a salmon kabob, and two glasses of champagne later, I sneak away from the festivities, ditch my wedge heels, and head to the abandoned stable and corral.

Careful not to snag my chiffon dress, I duck through the fence. My feet leave the firm lawn for deep, shifting sand. I pause to admire the scene. *Nothing has changed.*

The first of the stable's two stalls overflows with musty hay bales, milk crates, a watering trough, and a pail. The second offers a home for a tractor attachment that resembles a freakishly oversized spider. On the walls, cobwebs creep from every angle in a mass descent. In the rear corner, an overturned sawhorse lies among straps, crates, and remnants of a wagon. I find what I'm searching for on the ledge below the sole window—a Chock full o' Nuts coffee tin. Beneath its warped and faded plastic lid are the box of matches and hard pack of Marlboros I'd hidden the day before I moved to California.

I draw the stale tobacco into my lungs and welcome the surge of chemicals and an immediate but tenuous sense of equilibrium. After a day celebrating love, union, and community, I am compelled to feed the part of me that feels lacking in it. I flip over a milk crate and sit, the corral and the efflorescent meadow stretched out before me.

"You are the prettiest fire hazard I've ever seen," says a voice from the fencepost. With his suit jacket, tie, and dress shoes discarded, Oliver seems more himself. He untucks his white button-up shirt, lets the wrinkled fabric drape over his trousers, and ducks through the same spot in the fence as I had.

"Busted," I say, lifting the cigarette as evidence.

"If smoking didn't make me puke, I'd join you."

"Needing to puke is just something you have to push past."

"I never had your stamina."

"You never had my desperation."

"I never had your courage."

"You never needed it, Oli. You weren't running from anything."

A comfortable silence settles in. Oliver leans against the doorframe and contemplates the view. I make smoke rings and track them as they shape-shift in the breeze and then dissipate.

"Why are you so mad at Dad?" he asks, without a detectable shred of condemnation.

My mind flashes to our fight in the kitchen after Mom's memorial service. Like a gunslinger, I had stood in the doorway hungry for a fight.

"All that time Mom was taking sleeping pills. Where the hell was he? How did he not notice? How did he let it go on?" I take a puff and exhale toward the corral. My heart gallops. "Maybe he knew she had let herself get pregnant on purpose. Maybe it had festered in him all those years and when she finally started to suffer the consequences of her deception, some part of him felt she deserved it."

"I suppose it's possible," Oliver says and crosses his arms.

"Mom had gotten messy. Emotionally untidy. And Dad refuses to acknowledge disorder. He pretends it doesn't count for anything. That it isn't a legitimate form of communication.

Mom was obviously crying out for help, and he refused it. To me that's—" I drag on the cigarette and blast the smoke skyward. "Unforgivable."

Oliver lugs the sawhorse from the corner of the barn, sets it beside me, and sits.

"The last straw was when he announced he was cleaning out Mom's painting studio. That was it for me." Adrenalin floods my senses. I feel light-headed. I lean forward and rest my elbows on my knees. The pool of deep sand in the corral glitters pink in the evening sun. It holds my gaze. Steadies me.

Oliver leans forward and mirrors my pose, his elbows on his knees. My voice softens. "He seemed so unaffected by Mom's absence," I say. "He soldiered on, stoically on, but her death rocked my world. Shattered me. We couldn't be more different."

I consider what little remains of my cigarette—a pathetic stump—and wonder how I could have smoked it so quickly. With one final pull, the ember ignites the edges of the filter.

Oliver leaves my side and reappears with an empty can from somewhere in the recesses of the stable. He carefully extracts the smoldering cigarette butt from my fingers, drops it in the can, and sets it on the dirt floor. We both watch as the cigarette releases last-gasp tendrils of smoke before puttering out.

"Have you ever talked to anyone about how you feel?" He says while rubbing the space between my shoulder blades in slow, hypnotic circles.

My gaze finds the pink corral again. "I don't really let people know me."

Oliver gets a faraway look. "You're tolerable," he says. "And you make decent coffee. And you dress okay."

His loving humor dislodges a block somewhere inside me.

"Oliver, I don't even think I know me."

"You're beautiful and sensitive and strong. You're kind. Independent. Full of heart. And you see things most people don't notice."

Tears rise in my throat on a wave that feels too big and too unpredictable for me to permit its passage. I exhale through my mouth. Swallow. Tamp down the flood.

"Talk to Dad," he says. "Before you leave for California, try and talk to Dad."

I close my eyes and nod, then rest my head against his shoulder. Oliver strokes my hair as if he's petting a cat. I purr.

"Good kitty," he soothes. "That's a good kitty."

He wraps his arm around me.

"I'm sorry I haven't been in your life," I say. "I guess I shut you out, too."

"I've missed you," he says.

Fingers of pink light in the distant meadow bloom reddish gold as the sun sinks on the horizon. A legion of crickets chirp and cavort.

"How come you're okay, Oli? You're a husband, for god's sake. In ten seconds, you're going to be a father."

"Doesn't mean I know what I'm doing," he says. "Doesn't mean I've got it all together. Hell, I miss Mom. I miss her every day. Am I rushing my own family hoping I'll miss her less? Possibly." He brushes dust off his thigh then goes still. "It's difficult with you being three thousand miles away. And when you're away, you're *gone*."

"I'm sorry."

I lace my fingers through his. We sit linked and watch the first of the evening's shadows creep into the corral. "I thought when I came home this time, she'd be here," I say. "I thought if I felt her presence, I could reclaim a part of me. But I haven't.

She seems more dead than ever."

Our eyes lock and we are children again, raw and floundering. But instead of amplifying my sense of loss, seeing it reflected in his eyes makes me feel less alone. We fall into a fierce hug.

Voices on the other side of the wall drag Oliver to his feet. He kisses me on the forehead and then ducks through the fence in the same spot through which he had entered.

"Bob, Fran. Are you having a good time?" Oliver asks. "Have you seen the view from the hill yet? There's a bench up there my dad built from a maple tree that lightning had struck." Their voices retreat as he guides them away from me. Away *for* me.

I peer at my hands resting on the rich, luxurious fabric of my dress, then past my knees to my bare feet where dust now clings to the skin between my toes. I'm not repelled by the grime; it's strangely comforting. I dig my feet deeper into the dirt and grit, fire up another cigarette, and watch the light give way to darkness out in the meadow.

CHAPTER 35

Sunday morning, I wake to chickadees, goldfinches, and cardinals serenading me from the oak outside my window. I listen with my eyes closed as remnants of the dream I was having fade—a dream in which the birdsong had woven itself. When at last I open my eyes, morning sun drenches every surface. Warm and soothing, it amplifies the richness of my bedroom walls. It's as if I'm waking up in melted butter. Butter. PharmFresh. B'udder. Big on taste, not on your butt-er.

Am I her?

I roll onto my stomach and toss my pillow to the floor. My toes curl around the bottom of the mattress and my arms flop off the sides. I am a huge walrus sprawled on a wee rock. My cheek sinks into the freshly laundered sheet. The faint smell of lavender fills my nose. *Rachel.* Dad would only ever buy unscented.

The house creaks. I listen for footfall, but the squeaking has no rhythm. I snuggle deeper. The wedding ceremony replays in my mind. Oliver and Rachel waited until all the guests had left before they themselves slipped away for two nights at a spa in Stowe—a wedding present from Rachel's mother. Oliver left me the keys to his pickup truck and while hugging me, whispered in my ear, "Talk to Dad."

Rachel embraced me again. We've hugged more than we've spoken to each other; but I know I like her.

I throw on shorts, a light blouse, and my flip-flops. On the staircase, I make a point of stepping on the creaky spots. The pot of what smells like fresh coffee in the kitchen lures me.

Wandering around the first floor with my steaming mug, I'm happy to discover Oliver's guitar on a stand in the sunroom. I was afraid he had stopped playing. Beyond the living room windows, my father, in his uniform of khaki shorts and a T-shirt, digs on his hands and knees around the base of one of the willows in the yard.

"What are you doing?" I ask when I reach him.

He wipes his forehead with a soil-covered glove and leaves a trace behind on his skin. "Rachel's mother had a landscaper drop about a yard of dyed mulch to help spiff up the property," he says. I count six more trees bearing identical cherry-red rings. He shakes his head. "It's deep and it's everywhere." He hinges forward and continues clawing the mulch toward him, away from the trunk. After several passes, roots peek through, and he dusts them off with the care of an archeologist on a fossil dig. The backside of his shirt clings to his sweat-soaked skin.

"Can I help?"

"You could get me the wheelbarrow."

I swallow the last of my coffee, set the mug on the front porch, and fetch the wheelbarrow that's perched outside the art barn.

"Why not use a shovel?" I ask when I return.

"I don't want to damage the roots."

"But it's a sixty-foot tree."

"It doesn't matter how big the tree is, you can kill it if you compromise its roots," he says while he works. "The bulk of the nutrients come up from the ground through the root system, so when the root flare is covered with a foot of mulch like this, oxygen flow is compromised, and the tree can eventually suffocate. It's a slow process. A slow death."

I am aware that this is the most I've heard him say since I've been home.

"If mulch can kill the tree, why does everyone use it?"

"Because it's pretty." He throws handfuls of mulch into the wheelbarrow. "Your mother was much better at all this than I am," he says offhandedly.

With his rare mention of Mom, I forget that we're talking about trees. My mouth gets dry.

"Your mother could walk out front or in the garden and be still for a minute or two, and the plants would seem to tell her what they needed. 'Trim me. Fertilize me. I need more sunlight.' At the time I didn't give her enough credit. Now I think she was on to something."

He keeps working while I, transfixed and mute, wait for words to come forth. They take an agonizingly long time.

"Why didn't you help her?" I blurt.

"With the gardening?"

"No, the sleeping pills." He tosses more mulch into the wheelbarrow. I continue to talk to his back. "You must have known she was taking them. Even I knew—at least since the camping trip. I heard the four of you in Grandma and Grandpa's living room."

"I knew, Beatrice. I even spoke with her physician. He felt they were an appropriate part of her recovery."

"From?"

"He suspected it was postpartum depression."

"He suspected?"

"Yes."

"And the sleeping pills were still an appropriate part of her recovery *ten years* after Oliver was born?"

With that he stops. When he faces me, his mouth has tightened into the line of controlled anger that I rarely glimpse but immediately recognize. "There was more to it than that."

"Dad.

"There was more to it." He peels off his gloves. "Your mother was . . . larger than life. I spent a lot of time in her shadow." He wipes his forehead with the heel of his hand. "But she refused to sever ties with her father even though he was a . . . "

"A tyrant," I say, finishing his sentence and unwittingly establishing solidarity between us. I quickly smash it. "You should have done more."

"I did more than you could understand."

"Tell me. Tell me what you did."

"It's between your mother and me. It's private, Beatrice."

"How convenient."

He shakes his head, clenches his jaw. His lips press so firmly together, they almost disappear. He's still on his knees. Beads of sweat gather at his temple.

He meets my glare. "I tolerated years of dismissive, condescending behavior from your grandfather. Those Mercedes he sent? Every time they arrived, every time your mother drove them, it was a reminder of my inadequacy."

A light breeze blows my hair away from my face. "But she loved you."

"Did she? Deliberately going off birth control so she could get pregnant? That's not a loving act." His gaze sweeps the property. "I wonder if she thought all this would distract her from her yearning to create art. A Vermont farmhouse. A woodworking husband. Chickens roaming in the yard." His eyes meet mine. "She started to retreat from our relationship the moment you were born. She loved you. She loved your brother. But I think she wanted to be a mother more than she wanted to be a wife."

"So you let her self-destruct. You were angry."

"She died in a car accident, Beatrice. She didn't self-destruct."

"She'd been gone for years."

"I did what I could. I did my best."

"Silence was your best?"

"You've been silent."

I step backward. He's right. *Why do I choose silence?* Protection. *From what?*

"She made choices, Beatrice. I couldn't choose for her. Just like I can't choose for your brother . . ."

A ladybug lands on my forearm.

". . . or for you," he finishes.

I know even before I say the words that they aren't true. "Sounds like maybe it's just easier for you . . . letting Mom go, letting me go." He flinches as if I've struck him and sinks onto his heels.

I leave him that way, gather my backpack from the house, climb into Oliver's pickup truck and drive off. As I turn onto Steeple Road and head west toward Lake Champlain, it's unclear to me whether by leaving I am protecting myself or protecting him.

My fingers grip the steering wheel. A flash of movement draws my attention. I drop the gearshift into fourth and realize the ladybug is still on my arm.

CHAPTER 36

I am encapsulated in blue, from the cloudless sky to the turbulent lake to the reflection of Vermont's mountain skyline in my rearview mirror. The ferry rises and falls while its engine drones steadily on. The temperate wind rushing through the pickup's open windows reminds me of summer more than fall. Seagulls perch on the bow, proud and alert, their feathers fluttering.

I don't remember consciously choosing to cross the lake, but when I found myself among a line of vehicles at the Kingston ferry buying a one-way ticket to Wildham, NY, it felt right. Although my insides churned as I maneuvered onto the sturdy ferryboat, I have since been lulled into submission. Cocooned in the rocking, steel cradle, weariness has set in.

Up ahead, a small coastline community rises up around the tiny Port of Wildham. A smattering of restaurants and tourist shops lines the water, while across Route 42, stone homes, centuries old, loom like centaurs from a forgotten age. While commerce and residences intermingle in the foreground, a forest rises, unfettered, behind them. The ferry bounces between the gargantuan pylons before settling into position at the dock and I type into my phone what I can remember of the property's address. The WiFi is spotty and I have only one bar of charge, but a map eventually loads. I slide the gearshift into first and leave the comfort of the steel craft.

The pickup engine transitions smoothly. I've forgotten how much I love driving a stick shift, but soon Route 42, winding, banked, and unpredictable, demands my focus. I downshift around a bend, then accelerate and upshift. Oliver's truck, my copilot, offers no resistance. It simply wants to *go.*

As the road steepens northwest from the lake, a bank of frothy, gray clouds builds on the horizon. Around me, undeveloped forest gives way to empty pastures and abandoned dairy barns. Mounds of bald tires and rusty farm equipment dot the landscape, while plastic, instead of glass, covers farmhouse windows. Lawns have turned to dirt beneath American-made pickup trucks and cars.

I'm surprised on the rare occasions when the landscape offers a small, pristine farm with livestock-filled pastures and matching barns. Hoop houses afford them year-round growing. Solar panels power their farmhouses. Foreign-made hybrid vehicles fill their driveways. These must be the newcomers, the first-generation farmers with graduate degrees and investors, selling CSAs, organic, grass-fed beef, and homemade kimchi.

As I pass through this community with feet in two worlds, I wonder if there are any bridges between them. I wonder what each has to teach the other.

Not until Ethel's Dew Drop Inn appears do I realize that I am traveling the stretch of road where my mother died. I wait for tears, for tumult in my system. My heart rate picks up, but there's no emotional descent.

Drive.

It's the loudest word in my head.

With no vehicles on my tail, I decelerate as I near the street sign. *Is this the road?* I take it and immediately feel I've entered an enchanted forest. To my right, I catch glimpses of the glimmering lake beyond the trees, and to my left a deer bounds deeper into the forest, penetrating the thicket with agility and ease. I brace myself once again for a spike of emotion, but there is none. It's as if I am answering a call.

Cabins whose docks I vaguely remember having been visible from the lake, appear periodically, with luxury SUVs angled out front. I count five mailboxes before arriving at the main entrance, a dirt lot with an L-shaped garage where the property maintenance equipment used to be stored. I downshift and slow to minimize the kick of dirt from my tires. The lot is empty as I cross and eventually pick up the access road that I believe meanders over to the lake and then up to the cabins on the eastern shore. Despite the plethora of bright orange "No Trespassing" signs nailed to posts, fences, and occasionally a tree, I cruise on.

Several people are gathered at the small beach from which Michael John's brothers launched their sailboat to "attack" and capsize us. When their unfamiliar faces dart my way, I raise my hand in a casual wave. They stare but wave—concerned, but ever polite.

Just passing through. Nothing to see here, I say to them in my mind.

A proper sign marks the road up to Dunder Ridge, but there are no tire tracks, no evidence the access road has recently been used. I continue past, up a small rise, and then relax as nature takes over. A rabbit races across the road and zigzags off into the brush. A statue-like falcon perched on a high branch launches into flight. My head finds the headrest. I revel in the smell of pine trees, and after a long exhale, I allow the edges of my memories here to resurface.

The turn off to Michael John's cabin appears sooner than I

remember, perhaps because we only ever walked this road. I slow and crane my neck to get a glimpse of his cabin, but his driveway is too steep and the forest is too thick.

A short distance later, the road curves sharply right, banked by a lush, untrodden meadow on the left. I round the bend and imagine a parallel arc in the lake somewhere below. The road descends gradually and somewhere along the way it morphs into Ginny's driveway. I inch along and wonder, for the first time, what I will do if cars are parked out front. This is Labor Day weekend, the unofficial end of summer. *Surely there will be people here.*

There are none. It's as if the cabin has been expecting me.

I slip from Oliver's truck but only make it a few steps before the grandeur of the cabin stops me. With picture windows and skylights, a continuous wraparound deck, Swedish Cope logs and a sleek, symmetrical design, the cabin is even more beautiful than I remember. I walk unhurriedly around to the rear deck, which has felt like my destination since the ferry docked in Wildham, but all that awaits me are four empty Adirondack chairs, tight and flush, neatly stacked side tables, and a covered grill. Wind chimes stir from the eaves, bringing life to the otherwise deserted scene.

What did I expect to find? Who did I expect to find?

I cup my hands and peer through the glazed windows. Gone are the overstuffed couches, the brass floor lamps, the glossy pine coffee table, and the plush, colorful rugs offered up like lily pads across the wide plank hardwood floors. Now, chrome and white leather curved sofas dominate the space, accented by frosted glass side tables and black leather footstools. The only color springs from the trophy suspended from overhead beams: a fifteen-foot sailfish with a majestic dorsal fin—eternally diving but never able to land home.

"What am I doing here?" I say aloud to my reflection in the glass.

"What *are* you doing here?" asks a voice behind me.

CHAPTER 37

I spin around. The man takes a few steps toward me. He's my age and a bit taller than I am. His thick, straight hair falls into coffee-colored eyes, so dark it's hard to tell where the irises end and the pupils begin. Wearing Ferragamo slides, Patagonia trail shorts and shirt, and a few days of stubble, he emanates both affluence and approachability.

"I'm trespassing," I say.

"That you are," he says in an unmistakable New York City accent.

"Michael John?"

Recognition brightens his face. "Beatrice."

"Hi."

"You staying here again?" he asks.

"No, I live in California. I'm just here, I mean, here in Vermont, for my brother's wedding. I came to the cabin," I say, gesturing at the window through which I'd been peeking. "Well, I don't know. I guess I came to see if this place was real or a figment of my imagination."

"Ouch. You know how to hurt a guy." He puts a hand over his heart.

Our eyes lock. We both smile. The tug is there. The tie. It feels good—familiar—even after a decade.

My eyes drop away first.

"My brother got married yesterday. Sort of a shotgun thing." As soon as the words leave my mouth, they sour. I find his eyes again. "I don't mean that. It was a heartwarming ceremony, and they are very much in love. And very pregnant."

Michael John shows no outward reaction to my words, but his eyes remain trained on me. I wait for him to offer superficial pleasantries about marriage and babies, but instead he slides his hands into his pockets and cocks his head. *He's appraising me.* I run a hand through my hair and wait for my self-judgment to kick in. *What should I be wearing? Am I thin enough?*

I flash him a smile. "I can't believe you're standing there," I say, derailing my own critique.

"I can't believe you're trespassing again," he says, shaking his head. His stance is relaxed, but his gaze is penetrating. I squirm.

"New owner?" I ask, signaling to the cabin.

"Yes. From Washington, D.C. He's not here that often. I think he's a lobbyist. Oil and gas."

I nod as if that explains the stark furniture and the dead fish. "You come here often?"

He chuckles, and I squeeze my eyes shut, aware too late that it's a classic pickup line. He graciously lets me off the hook.

"Whenever I can. You get to Vermont often?"

I glance up at the darkening sky. "Not so much. But with the new baby . . . Maybe. I don't know. Do you have kids?"

"No, but I'm an uncle several times over."

I could ask his nieces' and nephews' names. I could ask what he does for a living, but in my head the questions sound like they're for strangers. And we are not.

"You curious about the lake?" he says.

"Oh no, is there a Starbucks on it now?"

"You think I'd let that happen?" he says, opening his arms in mock injury.

"Not if you could help it," I say. Then I pause. "Is it up to you?"

He raises an eyebrow and glances sideways. The effect is youthful and mischievous.

"You're in charge?" I ask.

He shrugs.

"Of the whole thing?"

He beams.

"Michael John . . . you're king of the lake?"

He rolls onto his heels. "Yep. I'm Aquaman." Then he touches his head. "But without the Fabio hair."

I laugh. "So what do you do?"

"I protect underwater civilizations from tyranny and exploitation," he says, deadpan.

"Seriously," I say, although I'm still smiling. "What are you in charge of?"

"I'm the volunteer president for the association of families who together own the property, which includes the lake."

"Oh. I think I prefer Aquaman."

"Me too, but somebody has to run the meetings."

"Do you still sail?"

"Not as often as I'd like. Do you have a few minutes, or are you on a tight trespassing schedule?"

I chuckle. "I have time."

He motions toward the lake. "Let's walk and talk."

I nod. He politely steps aside for me to go first.

"Oh thanks, but you go," I say, enjoying the sight of him.

He leads the way along the path. A pair of red squirrels dart for cover.

"The woods are as dense as they were ten years ago," I say.

"I'm surprised the fossil fuel lobbyist hasn't carved them up so he can get a better view of the lake."

Michael John shakes his head. "He can't," he says over his shoulder. "It was one of the first rules that passed under my watch. I want to make sure the cabins remain invisible from the lake so when you're on the water—or in the water —" he motions toward me in acknowledgement of where I was when we first met, "—all you see is forest."

"With only docks to indicate where the cabins are."

"Exactly."

We round a bend. Soon I hear the water striking the shore, rhythmic and sure like a distant drum. With each step, the sound amplifies until a dark blue—almost black—expanse materializes behind the trees. The wind skims my ears. My pulse races. A sense of urgency rises in me that I cannot explain.

I stop at the dock while Michael John continues to the end. He spins around, shirts and shorts flapping, and opens his palms to the sky.

"This wind would test our sailing skills!" he shouts. Then he glances skyward at the steely clouds and out at the roiling lake. He slides his hands into his pockets and resumes the relaxed stance he had on the deck moments earlier.

Snippets of my time here a decade ago fight for my awareness. Watching him disappear into the woods with his fishing pole. Hanging side by side on the hull of our turtled sailboat. Racing behind him along the water's edge toward the siren's scream. I toss my head.

Enough. Enough with the remembering.

I kick off my flip-flops, lean into the wind, and set off across the dock to join him. The spectacle is breathtaking.

"It's the most beautiful lake I've ever seen," I say, marveling at how unchanged it appears. Steady. Ancient.

He stands motionless. I steal a glance at his profile. He appears transfixed. My nerves urge me to keep talking, but as the wind sweeps over my face and lifts the hair off my neck, I settle.

Movement on the shoreline draws my attention. I watch as the air current stirs the trees, synchronizing and enlivening them. It gently thwarts a hawk's flight above me, and it churns the water into frothy ridges before me. It fills the silence. It touches everything.

The temperature drops.

CHAPTER 38

His voice startles me. "Storm's coming," he says over the howling wind.

How long have we been standing together?

I fill my lungs and slowly exhale. I can't leave here without saying the words. I choose a focal point on the horizon and muster some courage. "I never thanked you," I say, elevating my voice so he can hear me.

"For what?" he says, stepping closer.

"For taking me in that summer, showing me around, for sailing, horseback riding, cliff jumping." I remember the kiss and feel my skin flush. I lower my gaze to the undulating water. "I had so much fun with you those two weeks and then—with my mom—you were so . . ." My words dry up. Fail me.

"I never forgot," he says, turning toward me.

I fasten my eyes on his face.

"I don't know," he says, "maybe because we were young. It was easy with you. Familiar." His expression grows solemn. He glances over my shoulder as if the words he seeks are there. Then he meets my eyes. His cheeks redden. "Your mother. Being there with *my* mother when the state trooper told you what happened. The way you and your brother collapsed. I didn't know how to handle it."

"You handled it fine," I say over the blasting wind.

"I should have gotten your phone number or your email or something. It all happened so fast. I didn't know what to do. I didn't know if you would want to hear from me."

Say yes. Tell him yes.

I swallow.

Our eyes meet but neither of us moves. A zigzag of lightning slices through the shadowy clouds. The connection between us crackles. A single raindrop pings my nose.

"Storm's here," he says. "We should go."

I don't want to go. "Okay," I say.

He follows me through the rustling forest and up the stairs to the deck. My senses are alive, bristling with awareness that I am retracing the steps I took the evening I learned of Mom's death. *These were my last steps as a girl with a mother. And the same person accompanies me now.* I listen for his footfall. The creaking floorboards beneath his feet reply.

Aside from family, Michael John is the only person in my world who knew me when I was someone who looked forward to what life might offer, instead of fearing what it might take away. She's gone. *And I have guarded myself against loss ever since.*

Stop.

Thinking.

I pause by the living room window through which I glimpsed my fate all those years ago. The wind slips across my skin. Michael John's reflection appears in the glass. I walk on. In moments we arrive at Oliver's truck. The cabin and forest buffet us from the wind.

I open the driver's door and recall the soothing pressure of his mother's hand between my shoulder blades, bracing me while the trooper changed my life with a few words.

"How's your mother?" I ask.

He shakes his head. "Still taking care of everyone. Nine grandchildren are keeping her busy."

"She's amazing, she—"

"She liked you," he says. "From the moment she saw you in my T-shirt looking roughed up." He bends over and picks up a stone. "I suppose it's the ER nurse in her. She knew you were tough." He tosses the stone, and we both watch it disappear in the brush.

"Please tell her I said hello." My voice cracks.

"I will."

Raindrops pepper us. I pick at a seam in the upholstery on the front seat instead of climbing in. "What made you come over here to the cabin?" I ask.

He shrugs. "I don't know. Just a feeling." He steps past me, peeks into the pickup's empty bed, and leans against the truck. I want to go to his side. I want to touch him. My body won't move.

His eyes cut to mine. "I'm sorry about your mother," he says. Rain dots his face and shirt, but he doesn't even flinch.

"Thank you," I say. Something expands in my chest. Presses against my lungs. A helium balloon readying to burst. I can't let it. I won't let it.

I hop up into the truck. The seat is cold.

"Can I give you a lift?" I say.

"No thanks. I think I'll take the trail."

Raindrops strike my left thigh and forearm, impelling me to move. I slide off the seat. My feet hit the dirt, and I face him. He hasn't budged. He's still relaxed against the bed of the truck, his hands disappearing into his pockets. Only now his wet head tilts slightly in amusement. I take two quick steps closer and kiss him on the cheek. He gathers me in his arms. The bubble inside me strains. My throat closes.

"Let me know if you move to the East Coast," he whispers into my hair.

I nod against his neck. I'm afraid to speak. Afraid of what will flood out. I leave his embrace and jump into the pickup, shut the door, and roll down the window. The engine fires, and I click on the wipers. I move quickly, not because I want to leave him, but because I'm afraid of how intensely I want to stay.

"Beatrice," he says. He's inches away, standing at my open window.

I meet his gaze. A seriousness has befallen him.

"I'll see you again," he says.

My voice sounds thick. "See you again," I say.

But I don't know if the statement is true.

CHAPTER 39

I drive too fast. The pickup bucks and bounces along the winding dirt road. Protesting. Reproving. I grip the wheel more tightly, but I don't let up off the gas. Rain blows in through the open driver's side window. My front left tire splashes through a mudhole and spatters me. I glance in the rearview mirror. My face is speckled. My wet hair plasters to my cheek. I press on.

Soon the turnoff to Dunder Ridge appears on my right. The beach area, which was populated on my way in, should be up ahead on my left. I slow and downshift. I drag my fingers through my hair . . . *as if that will make me look less like a serial killer.*

By the beach, a petite woman in white capris and a lime-colored polo shirt tugs on a little boy's hand seemingly to get them out of the rain and into the Audi SUV parked nearby. The woman shields her hair with a magazine while she says something to the child, who promptly pulls away from her, tilts his head, and snaps open his mouth to catch the raindrops. At the sound of my engine, they turn in unison. As I pass, the woman stares but the boy gives me a wave fit for a hometown hero in a parade. I honk in response—two quick blasts—and in my side mirror a man steps into view, collects the boy, and makes for the Audi in long, impatient strides.

I round the bend and spot the paved road that leads to the exit. Instead of feeling relieved—I couldn't have pushed the truck harder to get here—the balloon reconstitutes itself inside me. I downshift to second gear and fight the urge to turn around. Within seconds the final few hundred feet of dirt road are behind me.

The truck sounds eerily silent on the pavement. Every quarter of a mile or so, the rain seems to escalate, as does the pressure in my chest. I close my window and flip on the windshield defroster. At the stop sign that marks the end of the private property, I sit and idle. In my rearview mirror a heavy mist rises off the pavement—obscuring passage—as if the gateway to an enchanted world is slowly closing.

Resignedly, I slide into first gear and pull out onto Route 42. Within moments the storm grows to a gale. A torrent of water cascades over every window. A headwind slams into the front windshield and grille. I lean forward, driving nearly blind with the defroster whirring and the wipers tacking. I flip on the hazard lights.

Descending the mountain in a crawl, I reassure myself that the storm's going to pass, she's going to move on. Then a gust of wind strikes with such force that the pickup fishtails violently. I pull my foot off the brake and steer into the spin— muscle memory from years of icy winter driving. I face a wall of rain. There appears no safe way forward until a neon orange mailbox appears—like a flair—on my right. I swerve in.

Muddy and marred by deep ruts—now pools—the driveway offers passage only if I traverse it in first gear. In the microsecond of visibility between wiper blade strokes, I see branches and slam on the brake. A tree has fallen, thoroughly blocking the roadway.

I kill the engine, root around in my backpack, and pull out

my phone. Dead. The truck may as well be dead, too. I can't see out the windows and if someone pulls in quickly, will they see Oliver's truck in time to stop before they hit it?

I pound the dashboard. Rain pounds the roof. My hand throbs.

I am a sitting duck. My instinct says *go*. If there's a mailbox, there must be a house.

I reach around behind the bench seat hoping, praying, Oliver has an umbrella or a jacket tucked there. Sure enough, my fingers connect with slick fabric, and I draw out a windbreaker with the logo of his alma mater, Culinary Institute of America, on the breast. I pull it on, take a deep breath, and step into the deluge.

Within seconds my flip-flops are swampy and useless, so I leave them and tiptoe through the branches of the fallen tree. Once beyond it, I jog. My feet sink into warm muck, even along the side of the driveway where instead of lawn, I find tall grass, wildflowers, and a tattered fence.

A pasture.

The windbreaker offers little rain protection, so now it and my blouse fuse to my skin, while my shorts drag on me like a weight belt. Mud splatters on my shins, knees, and thighs. *This is absurd.* I keep fighting, keep jogging, even as the barrage of rain on my face forces me to squint. I push a patch of wet hair off my nose and mouth.

Up ahead on the right, a white farmhouse materializes. I race to it. There's no porch, no overhang, nothing to hide under, just bare steps up to a door. Rain sheets off the gutterless roof and hammers the ground by the cement foundation. Light glows in an upstairs window, so I bang on the door. Nothing. I rap again. Nothing. A battered Chevy with a bed full of trash bags sits beneath a tree around the far side of the house.

"Helloooo!" I call out. No response. I bang again. Nothing.

I spin around and rest against the door and there, directly across from me, is another road. *It could lead nowhere.* I shake my head, determined to find safe shelter. Through the torrential rain, I can't see Oliver's truck, but I glance in its direction anyway. I know what returning to the truck has to offer. I give up on jogging and walk down the newfound road. With each step warm mud sucks at my feet. Water shoots from my dangling fingertips and drips from my brows, and soon I find myself at the rear of a faded, lopsided barn.

I spot a crooked gate to the left and slog over. With my fingers around the latch, I scan the area. Missing from the high grass are feeding troughs and water stations, which tells me a herd isn't living in there. The grass is barely trodden except for a single path leading to the front of the barn. The air smells mild, with no trace of cow manure or the pungent food scraps pigs would be eating. If a bull resides in there, I'm in trouble. Big trouble.

I breathe deeply and exhale. I'm tired of being wet. I'm tired of pushing. Tired of trying. Tired of fighting.

The gate moves silently. I slip through and close it behind me but leave it unlatched in case I have to exit quickly. I follow along the side of the barn where the roof overhang offers a narrow swath of respite from the downpour. When I peek around the corner, I brace myself for the worst: a massive head rising from a muscular form, horns, a ring in a nose, and rapid snorts of warning.

Nothing's there but pasture and that single path snaking away.

I round the corner with my shoulder flush against the barn and I slink toward the door, which is cracked open a few feet. I hold my breath and listen for animal sounds from inside the barn, but all I hear is the rain hammering the tin roof. I rest my head against the outer door frame. A shiver travels up my spine. My muscles stiffen. I'm drenched. There isn't a single dry spot on me.

The opening is inches from my face. I lean over and peer in.

Nothing but darkness.

I step inside.

CHAPTER 40

My eyes adjust slowly as the punishing rain swallows up any ambient sounds. The space is rectangular, open where I stand, but at the opposite end it's too dark for me to discern what's there. Beside me, seemingly random items hang from nails: a New York State license plate, a plaid shirt with the sleeves torn off, and an oil-stained John Deere cap. A narrow ledge runs along the wall, home to a tin of chewing tobacco, a mug with a broken handle, and a frayed welding glove.

Above the drum of rain, an animal exhales through its nose, triggering a surge of adrenalin through my body. On the balls of my feet, I whip around, poised to bolt. I can make out only an outline: a head high, ears perked straight up, the rise of withers, the graceful curve of a long back, the bump of hindquarters.

I step toward the noise, and my forehead meets a dangling string. I tug and a single overhead bulb in the center of the barn struggles to life. It's a draft horse. A Belgian Draft. I recognize the breed from one of the posters in my childhood bedroom. But the thick, full mane on this Belgian, although straight at first, bunches into a twist of matted twigs and thistles. The mane's color is exquisite: blond—Southern California beach-blond—not brassy, bottle-blond. The Belgian's coat, encrusted in dirt and mud, is golden.

The horse considers me but makes no move to leave its stall, the partitions of which are the height of my shoulders. Its body rises well above them. This horse is huge, and there's no gate on the stall—nothing to keep it from leaving.

"Hello, horse," I say, and its ears twitch. I step closer, grateful for the dry surface beneath my bare feet and the reprieve from the storm, which is rapidly fading from my awareness despite the continuing barrage on the roof and the cascade by the door.

It doesn't occur to me to maintain a safe distance, watch the horse while it ponders me, and wait for the rain to let up so I can get out of here. Instead, I gradually close the gap between us. The horse remains still, but its eyes, weary and curious, follow me. Watch me.

Stopping at the Belgian's side, I realize with its head up, I couldn't touch its ears if I tried. The animal is formidable, with the physique of a retired working horse: broad chest, big, square hindquarters, wide neck, and sturdy legs. But there's more. A trail of gunk leaks from the corners of its chestnut eyes. Its belly is caked with mud and an old scar, raised and hairless, with a jagged Frankenstein stitch, snakes over protruding ribs. Its tail, coated with feces, hangs only a few inches, then wads up in a clotted ball.

I glance beneath its haunches. Female. A mare.

"Hello, mare," I say and stretch my hand out, palm up. She lowers her head and sniffs my skin. Her whiskers tickle my palm. I slowly touch her jaw and run my hand up the side of her face and as my hand slides higher, her head drops. I rub her forehead and underneath her bangs, I discover a crescent moon-shaped mark, delicate and symmetrical, as if drawn by a steady hand with a fine brush.

Hammered onto an interior post of her stall is a square piece of tin. I have to get up close in order to read what's etched on it. K A T E is scrawled in child-like handwriting.

"Hello, Kate," I whisper and slide both hands along her neck, rubbing in circles, knocking off the dirt as best I can while I go. Her head continues to hang low, so I rub high along her crest beneath her mane, my fingers and thumbs kneading into the tightness, massaging, stroking, inching slowly across her withers and over to her shoulder.

She sniffs my knees, my thigh, and Oliver's windbreaker, then suddenly her nose is pressing at my ear through my damp hair, sniffing, inhaling. I am breathless, paralyzed.

"I don't know what I'm doing," I whisper, and as she lowers her head and I gently extract three burrs from her mane, I realize I'm not talking about horses.

She plants her right leg forward and sweeps her muzzle over her knee—left side, right side—purportedly to relieve an itch. I spot a curry comb hanging from a nail. The puck-like oval with flexible rubber spikes fits perfectly in my palm. My fingers curl comfortably around its knobby rim. I move in, rest my left hand against Kate's chest, and with my right hand rub the curry comb across her neck as if I'm waxing a car in looping, interlocking circles. Small ones, big ones. I slowly work my way to her shoulder, then up to her withers. I make circles along her leg and across her wounded belly. Over her flank and down her legs. With each stroke, I leave a trail of raised hair that shows me exactly where I've been and where I still need to go.

She releases a long breath and flicks her matted tail.

"My god, you're beautiful," I say and set the comb aside. I lean into her neck, lightly touching my nose to her coat so I can breathe her in. Heat—life force—radiates from her body, and beneath the surface, beneath the muck and the gunk, beneath her solitude and her scars, I sense her pride. Her vitality. Her unbreakable spirit.

The balloon in my chest strains against my lungs. I close my eyes against it. Then a memory consumes me.

I am eleven years old, standing in the shade of the lean-to, stiff and parched, while Mom rocks Oliver against her chest with tears trailing over her raw cheeks. Her eyes fix with horror on the horizon as if she's watching a replay of Oliver's accident—one that doesn't end with him alive in her arms. I know I am invisible to her in that moment, and Oliver is everything. I turn away and watch as Cowboy dips a blocky sponge into water and gently wipes Winter down. Despite the heat and the scorching sun, despite her tremendous size, the mare trembles. *She'd been running for her life, yet she'd taken care not to kick my brother.* Powerful and brave yet full of fear, Cowboy says about the horses. See the cracks and flaws, but instead of walking away, love them more.

Instead of walking away, love them more.

I return to the present. *Instead of walking away, love them more.* The thundering in my chest sweeps up my throat and explodes inside my head as a single word.

Forgiveness.

It washes over and through me, from my crown to my heart to the soles of my feet. Opening. Allowing.

Then I see my mother in my mind's eye the summer she died—only about a decade older than I am now. Searching. Regretful. Imperfect. *We are not so different.*

I run my palm lightly over Kate's scar.

Forgive your mother.

I bury my head in my hands.

Forgive your father.

I let the balloon of air I'd been holding in my chest release at last.

Forgive yourself.

I lift my blurry gaze. My skin prickles with heat just as tears rush forward, but I make no move to wipe them. Then a wave of love engulfs me. Love for the grand creature in front of me, for Oliver, for Nicholas, for Michael John, for my dog, for the rainstorm, for my wet clothes, for the strangers at the wedding, for the baby who's on the way . . . and then I feel her.

She fills the barn and encircles me like a blanket.

I am tucked into her, coddled, held.

She is everywhere, and in my head I hear her say, *I am with you.*

All my resistance falls away. I rest my body against Kate's, bury my fingers in her golden coat, and surrender while my mother holds me.

CHAPTER 41

The doors to Dad's workshop, formerly the Mercedes' berth, are propped open when I pull into the driveway. My shorts chafe. I'm waterlogged, starving, and strangely euphoric, but I can't let another minute go by without talking to him.

"Dad," I say from the doorway.

Startled, he springs up from the vice over which he was bent. His hands rest on a tubular shaft of wood. "You're home," he says.

"I am. I went over to Ginny's cabin, got trapped in the storm, stuck in a farmer's driveway, and then met a Belgian Draft horse."

"Impressive. All I've done is carve a few legs for a crib."

I nod and survey the rear of the garage while mustering up the courage to speak. A tidy assortment of rakes, shovels, and brooms hang parallel from wooden hooks. Clippers of every imaginable size and purpose—sorted small to large—dangle from wall pegs. Velcro straps hold tightly coiled hoses and cords.

"I owe you an apology. What I said was untrue and unkind. I'm still sorting out—Mom—how I feel about her—about losing her—and in the meantime I think I've needed to blame someone. I think I needed someone to be at fault."

Neither his expression nor his stance changes. In no way does my father divulge what's going on inside him.

"I guess I chose you," I add.

He wipes his hands on a rag, walks over, and leans against the opposite doorframe. "I would have asked your mother to marry me even if she hadn't been pregnant. She was the most exciting woman I had ever known . . . and the most complex."

A rabbit nestles by the garden where Mom and I used to lie together in the grass.

"So, the pregnancy didn't force the marriage?"

"It forced the timing, not the marriage itself."

An old knot loosens within me. Relief seeps in.

"You lost your mother when you were around my age," I say, trying to recall the story. "To cancer?"

Dad nods. "I was fifteen. She'd been ill for years before she died. Bedridden. Frail. My father and I figured out how to cook and run the house and my uncles helped us keep the dairy farm afloat. Dad died of a heart attack two years later. I sold the farm and the cattle, paid off all the debts and used what little was left to buy a truck that would get me to Cornell."

"They gave you a full scholarship?"

"All four years."

My gaze rests on our farmhouse, resplendent with fresh paint and new windows. But the blinds in my parents' bedroom are drawn—as they've always been.

"Was it hard seeing Mom retreat to her bed like your mother had?"

Dad runs his thumb over the callouses on his left palm. His brow furrows in contemplation. "It was familiar. In retrospect, I wish I had been more alarmed by her withdrawal." His attention shifts to the farmhouse. "I suppose your mother and I rebuilt our childhood experiences."

"In what way did Mom recreate hers?"

"She felt isolated as a child despite the abundance of resources at her disposal. I think her secret about her pregnancy and later, her depression, left her feeling similarly cut off."

What parts of my past am I recreating? Where are my blind spots?

"May I show you something?" Dad asks.

I follow him up the rear staircase to the loft where Mom's painting studio used to be. Paint bespatters the floor. The mobile of swans waits expectantly for a breeze. A countertop overflows with mason jars crammed with hardened brushes, mangled tubes of acrylic paint, and triangular mini sponges. A crusty washcloth drapes over a water jug. Palettes, dotted with dried colors, pile up below the windowsill. Mom's easel sits across from a child-sized chair, and atop her stool her smock drapes, its ties nearly touching the floor. This is the painting studio of my childhood; this is Mom's world. This mess . . . it's a shrine.

"You didn't clear it out. You left it as she had it."

"I did."

Then it hits me. Abstract portraits in fiery reds, oranges, and purples claim nearly every inch of wall space. The brush strokes are fat and bold, but somehow the subjects' intricate features and delicate emotions flow through. A joyful elderly man. A skeptical, bespectacled woman. An earnest child with Downs Syndrome. Like glinting jewels, each work reflects a precious fragment of my mother and together, they complete the picture of who she was. I recall the sensation I had had as a child that she was keeping parts of herself hidden. I see them now. Confidence. Bravery. Power.

"Dad . . ."

"Beatrice."

"You mounted and hung her paintings from college."

"They remind me of her essence—of who she was beneath her self-doubt."

"I remember Ginny visiting and the three of you talking about the critic who gave Mom a negative review. Was he really the reason she decided she would never make it as an artist?"

"His criticism was a blow, for certain. She'd heard only rave reviews up until then. But I think she could have gotten past it if she had believed in herself. And if she'd been willing to let go of all hope of pleasing her parents."

My mind scrambles to try and integrate all the new information. "This is her show. Her permanent show."

He nods. "I feel as if she's close by now."

"Is that why you moved your shop downstairs where the Mercedes used to live?"

"Yes."

I was wrong. I had a whole story in my mind, and it was all made up. He wasn't erasing her; he was joining her, as best he knew how.

"There's one painting in particular I think you should see." He pulls a furled canvas from a low shelf and unravels it. "I wanted you to be able to decide how you'd like it mounted."

It's the portrait of me that Mom started when she was pregnant with Oliver. Colorful and vibrant, it suggests a return to her former artistic self. Her true self. But only half of my face appears.

"Too bad she never finished it," I say.

"She told me it was done."

"The left side is, but the right side is just an outline. A suggestion."

"She said you were growing up so fast and changing so

much that she wanted to leave it blank."

"I thought she lost interest in it."

"No. She lost interest in trying to capture you, to capture someone who was still . . . becoming, was I believe the word she used."

Mom. "I wish I'd known her better those last few years. I was so mad at her."

"She disappointed you."

"At Ginny's cabin, the summer she died, she tried to bridge the gap with me, but I wouldn't let her. Oliver did, but I wouldn't even let her *begin.*"

"You thought there'd be time. We all did." He walks to the disheveled counter.

"How do I make this right in my life, Dad? I'm tired of battling this sense of . . . incompletion."

"There will be a way. You'll see," he says. His fingers move swiftly to transform a pile of tubes into one uniform row, side by side. I walk over and lay my hand over his to stop him from cleaning up the mess. Understanding slowly registers across his face, and he gives my fingers an appreciative squeeze.

"Leave it alone?" he asks, eyeing the disarray.

"Yes."

"I don't do well with disorder."

"I know, Dad."

He lowers his gaze to rest on our hands. My eyes follow his.

"I lose my bearings," he says softly.

"I know."

He flips his hand over to hold mine. Clasped, they settle on the countertop, intertwined and motionless, beside a mound of colorful paints—like two orbiting planets temporarily at rest by their sun.

We tighten our grip.

CHAPTER 42

Headlights sweep across my bedroom as I towel dry my hair after a gorgeous, scalding shower. I wonder what Michael John is doing. Is Kate grazing in the pasture now that the storm has passed?

Downstairs, the kitchen door squeals open and snaps shut. Even through the floorboards, the surprise and delight in my father's voice is evident.

"Well, hello," he says.

"Hi," Oliver and Rachel say in unison. "We're home," Oliver adds.

"I see," Dad says.

"We were booked for a second night, but—"

"I couldn't sleep—" says Rachel.

"Rachel couldn't sleep," Oliver says. "So we thought we'd come home early."

Silence.

I picture my father nodding with his hands thrust in his pockets, unaware of what Oliver is subtly asking.

"I hope that's okay," Oliver says.

"Of course," my father says, coming to life. "I'm glad you're home. Here, let me help with the bags."

"I thought I'd make us all dinner," Oliver says. "Dad, you

hungry?"

I draw my attention away from their conversation and pull on a pair of shorts from my suitcase. Instead of choosing one of the blouses I'd packed, I rummage through the top drawer of my old dresser, which is stuffed with T-shirts, none of which are folded. I smile. Folding didn't occur to me until I watched my college roommate put her clothes away. Ironing didn't land on my radar until Nicholas asked to borrow my iron one morning before work. I told him it was broken, then bought one the next weekend. It was my first.

A periwinkle-blue wad catches my eye. I hold it up. Soft cotton fabric. Frayed hems. Riddled with creases. The shirt was one of my favorites. I slip it on.

In the hallway, I nearly bump into Rachel, who's walking with her fingertips skimming the wall.

"You okay?" I say.

She draws a hand to her belly. "Yeah, I just need to lie down," she says. I open their bedroom door for her.

"Did you get a chance to use the hotel spa?"

She disappears into the dark room and flicks on the bedside light as she gingerly lowers herself onto the mattress. In the amber glow with her hair falling forward, she resembles a shy teenager. Innocent. Vulnerable.

"I had a foot massage," she says, lifting her feet so she can see them over her enormous belly. "I wasn't up for the other stuff."

I drop my shoulder against the door frame and cross my arms. "Oliver did the deluxe spa package, didn't he?" I say.

She meets my eyes and smiles. "Plus water shiatsu."

"He was probably the only guy in the pool, surrounded by a bevy of ladies."

She nods. "And he wore the swim trunks with the dancing

dinosaurs."

Pride washes over me.

She fixates on the far window. "I love my husband," she says, as if the feeling is so vast, it can't be contained within her body.

Goosebumps flush my skin. "And he loves you," I say. Our words hover and dance in the dim light. "Have a good rest," I say, and make my way down the hall.

In the kitchen, my father sits at the table peeling carrots into a compost pail and Oliver stirs a saucepan on the stove. Most of the cabinets are open, their contents already strewn across the countertops. A cutting board is piled with fresh herbs. Pots teeter in the sink. There's flour on the floor.

"Hey," Oliver says, as I fill the sink with soapy water. "I hear you had an adventure."

I share the high points while I wash the pots, but I leave out Mom's appearance in the barn. He balances his attention effortlessly between his caramelized onions and me.

"Dad, could you cut those carrots into half-inch sections?" he says over his shoulder after my story has finished.

"Sure. Diagonally?" Dad says.

"Please."

I clear space on the counter, lay out a dishcloth, and arrange the pots to drip-dry. Behind me, Dad begins chopping. *Thwack.* He pauses between each strike to allow the measuring stick in his mind to calculate a perfect half-inch. *Thwack.* I glance over at him, huddled over the cutting board, his glasses poised at the tip of his nose.

Oliver cracks open the oven door and releases a plume of aromatic steam that races toward the ceiling. I smell chicken and garlic and something sweet—a familiar scent that I can't quite place.

"What's on the chicken?"

"Maple syrup, soy sauce, and garlic," he says, reaching into the oven with a meat thermometer.

"You've come a long way, Oliver. Remember the kielbasa and macaroni?" I say, moving on to wash measuring cups, rubber spatulas, and what appears to be every spoon in the house.

"What's wrong with kielbasa and macaroni?" he says, spreading his arms dramatically.

"Two times a week?"

"Yeah, but I switched up the macaroni—elbows on Tuesdays and shells on Thursdays."

He sets the sizzling roasted chicken on an oven mitt beside the stovetop.

"I think we ate pasta twenty days out of every month."

"I liked your kielbasa, Oliver," Dad says. "It had a good char on it."

"It was burned," Oliver and I say in unison and laugh.

"That chore chart," I say, as I rinse handfuls of spoons. "I remember vacuuming but never dusting," I say.

"Bringing in firewood," Oliver says.

"Cleaning the chicken coop," I add.

"And we each did our own laundry," Oliver says.

"You know I still wash my whites and colors together in the same load?"

"How are your clothes not pink?" he says.

"I wash in cold water," I say, and flash him a toothy smile.

He covers his eyes as if he can't stand the sight of me. I smile wider.

"I don't remember putting our communal stuff in the washing machine . . . like these dish towels," I say, tugging at the one slung over my shoulder.

"Or bath towels," Oliver says.

"I don't think we ever mopped."

"Or cleaned the fridge."

"And that porch light was out for what . . ."

"Six months."

"It was an easy fix. Just a lightbulb."

"Yeah, but it was high up," Oliver says.

"It required a stool," I say.

" . . . and a lightbulb."

"Where did you get the idea for a chore chart, Dad?" I ask.

"From your grandmother." Dad ambles over with the carrots. "She even made suggestions about what to put on the chart."

"Well of course she did. She would know. She has maids," I say.

Dad shakes his head, sets the cutting board beside my drying dishes, and pulls a can of Rolling Rock beer from the refrigerator. "No, you don't understand. By suggesting what I put on the chart, she was giving me permission to ignore everything else." He pops the tab and takes a long sip. "And that meant a great deal, coming from her. She was letting me know that nothing mattered but the basics." Oliver and I go stock-still. All humor evaporates. "Your grandmother knew that getting you kids involved was important. Even with simple things like vacuuming. It wasn't about what you did, it was that we did it together. We each had a role. We each did our part. She believed it would help us heal," he says, "as a family."

Oliver and I fasten our glassy eyes on one another.

"Grandma," Oliver whispers, shaking his head in wonder.

"She wrote me about a year ago," I say.

"What?"

"I haven't read the letter. I couldn't imagine that it would make me feel good."

"She might surprise you, Beatrice," my father says.

I'm still processing his statement when Oliver says, "Whatever happened to Ginny?"

Ginny.

"She fell in love with an older man and moved to London. He's a duke."

"Of course he is," my brother says.

Dad returns to the table. His expression goes grim. "Speaking of your grandparents . . . they haven't seen us together since Beatrice's graduation."

"That's right. Beatrice missed mine," Oliver says and thwacks me with a dishrag.

I cover my eyes.

"I think we should all go visit them next time Beatrice comes home. They can meet their first great-grandchild," Dad says. "Your mother would like that."

CHAPTER 43

From the waiting area by the gate, I soak up my last view of the Green Mountains, a triple chocolate chip cookie in hand. A young mother holds an infant in the seat across from me, a far-off expression adding age to her face. *How will Oliver and Rachel fare as young parents*? They weren't as rested and rejuvenated as I thought they would be when they arrived home from the resort last night. The baby is due any day now. Their lives are about to change dramatically. It would stress me out too.

My mind relives last night's dinner.

During the meal, Oliver put on a vintage James Taylor CD and sang along, but he replaced some of the lyrics with baby-related commentary. "Something in the Way It Spits Up." "How Sweet It Is When There's Only Pee in the Diaper." Rachel came downstairs from her nap, and we crowded around the kitchen table and feasted. It was nearly midnight by the time we finished eating and washing up, and we were acutely aware the next time we were together, there would be one more at the table.

I sleep on the plane to Philadelphia and then again on the flight to San Francisco. Nicholas meets me outside the security check point.

"Welcome home," he says into my hair as we hug.

Is this home? Where is home?

"Thanks," I answer.

Over the loudspeaker, nonstop recorded greetings and safety instructions are interrupted by crackling announcements in twice the volume. We are alerted to gate changes, lost items ready to be collected in baggage claim, and lost people hoping to "meet their party" by the ticket counter.

"Has the airport always been this noisy?"

Nicholas shrugs and squints at me with concern. I dodge bodies left and right. I seem to be on the wrong side of every encounter while Nicholas flows gracefully through the crowd, for him a parting sea. I slow his pace so dramatically that he eventually drags me over and puts his arm around my shoulder to hustle me along.

At baggage claim, nearly everyone talks, either to the person beside them, to the child running away from them, or to their cell phones. I search the crowd, hoping to recognize someone who was on the flight from Vermont. At the other end of the carousel, I recognize a teenager in a dark green UVM T-shirt whom I remember waiting in line in front of me to buy cookies. He, too, chatters on his phone, animated in conversation, gesturing, laughing . . . acclimating.

"Babe. Where are you?" Nicholas breaks my trance.

"I was just seeing if there was anyone here from the Vermont flight."

"Easy. Find the flannel," he says sarcastically. I don't respond.

Strapped into his BMW, we stop and start amidst throngs of traffic all the way to my apartment. We wait to get around construction and fender benders. We wait to change lanes. We wait for green lights. Whenever I can grab a glimpse, I lock my eyes on the water in the San Francisco Bay, a reprieve from the concrete and steel and a reminder of what makes this city so magical.

Nicholas pulls into my building's driveway and I'm speechless. The Tree in front of my bedroom window is now a stump. He carries my suitcase upstairs and while he's in the bathroom, I text Scottie.

I'm home. What happened to The Tree?
Cable repair truck.
Huh?
Bad brakes.
That was our only tree!
BOOM bye bye.
Can I come get Lobo?
Do you have the Ben & Jerry's T-shirt?
Yes.
Then yes.
Okay, be right up.
Lobo isn't here. Javier walking him at the Marina.

Ugh. My heart aches for my dog, but I catch myself before complaining.

Thx for taking such good care of him.

We ♡ your Zen dog. Come up in an hour.

I hang up and toss my phone onto the bed. With The Tree gone, I have an unobstructed view of Lafayette Park's occupants: Tai Chi practitioners, dog walkers, and mommies with blankets and babies. In the few minutes since Nicholas and I arrived, the fog has rolled in, diffusing the bright notes of the sun and thickening the air with dampness. The women gather up their little ones, the dog walkers pull up their hoods, and the Tai Chi practitioners carry on as if nothing has changed.

Behind me, the bathroom sink water runs and stops, the

door opens, and then silence. I feel the tug of Nicholas's gaze, willing me to spin around and acknowledge him, but the park holds my attention. Through the dense gray, now nearly a wall of fog, I watch the shadows shape-shift and imagine that one of the dark silhouettes is a flicker of ears, a flutter of mane, and a swoosh of tail.

"Beatrice," Nicholas says.

Please don't be naked. I spin around.

Fully clothed, he stands beside my bed, his brows knotted with concern.

"I have to run to Sausalito to meet with Randy Brothers about their social content."

"Okay."

"And tomorrow I'll be in Santa Clara consulting on a brand storytelling campaign for an apparel startup."

"Okay."

"So I won't see you until tomorrow night."

I lock my jaw to stop myself from saying "okay" a third time.

He extracts his watchband from beneath his shirtsleeve cuff and glances at the dial. "Let's go out to dinner when I return from Santa Clara tomorrow. Maybe drive to Half Moon Bay."

My mind fumbles past "okay" and hunts for actual words. "I'd like that."

"I'll have news from PharmFresh by then. We'll know if they selected one of your slogans."

I fall silent and remain still.

He squints at me. "You okay?"

"Yup."

"You sure?"

Don't say yup. "Yes."

"So how come I'm over here and you're all the way over

there?"

I have no answer. A hint of color warms my cheeks and I drop my gaze, but I don't move. He rounds the end of the bed and draws me into a hug. I am fully present as he holds me, fully engaged as he kisses my neck, my ear, and my mouth, but by the time my front door clicks closed behind him, I am back at the window searching for horses in the shadows.

CHAPTER 44

The office is a ghost town. I drop my bag on my chair and survey my desk: Post-its, fine-tipped Pilot pens, extra-large monitor, ergonomic keyboard, and a mouse pad emblazoned with a steaming mug of coffee. The photo has the intended effect; I contemplate the bustling coffee shop nestled beside the Wells & Menklin law firm, which, at present, is uncharacteristically ablaze on every floor. The partners must be on the premises.

I'm scrounging for my credit card when Derek strolls in.

"Nicholas says we'll hear from PharmFresh today," he says as he tosses a small chocolate orb high into the air and catches it in his mouth.

"So I'm told," I say, and he eyes me quizzically. *I've been away on vacation. How would I know that?*

He offers me a chocolate. I scrunch my eyes. "Espresso beans," he says, correctly interpreting my question. I shake my head. "I'm hoping after their line of spray foods, we get a shot at their Cheeze-All products."

Rapid fire, he pops two chocolate-covered espresso beans into his mouth.

"Those don't give you the jitters?" I ask, pointing to the beans in his palm.

He grins. "I don't get the jitters," he says, and holds out a hand—rock steady—to prove it. Another bean disappears between his lips.

"What's Cheeze-All?" I ask.

"Powdered cheese that's guaranteed not to clump," he says.

"How can they promise that?"

"Cellulose powder."

I make a sour face.

"It's not that bad. Just an anti-caking agent. They chemically treat raw cellulose and refine it to a microcrystalline powder and add it to the cheese."

I lean over and write on my Post-it pad, "Don't forget to throw out your powdered cheese." He reads it, smiles, and sets a lone chocolate-covered expresso bean on my desk before turning away.

The sky is clear and the sun blazes as I leave the lobby and step out onto the sidewalk. A lull in traffic tempts the jaywalker in me, but my boots have a treacherously high heel, so I walk to the corner and stand with the rule-abiding pedestrians at the crosswalk.

On the opposite side of the street, a handsome man in his forties leaves Wells & Menklin and travels the short distance to the coffee shop without lifting his gaze from his cell phone. His suit shimmers. The fabric is blue, but in the sunlight, it twinkles with silver and lavender undertones.

It's mermaid yet manly. I can't drag my eyes away.

He must sense me staring because as I reach the coffee shop, he acknowledges me with a nod and holds the door open for me. His eyes are brown with gold accents. His tie and dress shirt are identical shades of cornflower blue. His watch is platinum.

"Thank you," I say, then smile and glance down. Twenty-four hours ago, I was sitting in the airport in flip-flops, eating a chocolate chip cookie for breakfast, and watching the sun rise behind the Green Mountains. I feel ill-equipped to engage with a hotshot lawyer wearing a magical mermaid suit. Still, as I slip past him and step through a luxurious brume of spicy cologne-scented air, I allow myself to imagine riding in his Gulf Stream, shopping with his Amex Black Card, and touring his vineyard in Tuscany. Then I all but knock over the two men waiting at the end of the ordering line.

"Sorry," I say to them.

"No worries," says the guy on the left.

The lawyer materializes beside me. "You work nearby?" he asks in a rich, rumbly voice.

My eyes meet his. "I work at the ad agency across the street. You?"

"Wells & Menklin," he says.

I don't share my theory about hierarchies and his firm's office lights. I'm not sure I'll be able to form a complete sentence under his penetrating watch—a look he's probably cultivated through treacherous cross-examinations and riveting closing arguments.

I quickly scan his face for an imperfection: a sag of skin, rogue stubble, a pimple. He's clean-shaven, exfoliated, and serum drenched. My mind flashes to my father in a sweat-soaked T-shirt dragging mulch from the willows' root collar with a dirt smudge across his cheek and Oliver sipping coffee with pillow head and a guitar in his lap.

"Litigation," the lawyer says. He must have thought I'd been pondering his legal expertise.

"You enjoy it?" I ask.

"Wouldn't want to do anything else," he says.

The line inches forward.

"Where are you from?" he asks.

I think of our sagging Vermont farmhouse and the night a storm blew the kitchen door open, and we awoke to find fifteen chickens camped out in the living room.

"Martha's Vineyard," I say, searching my memory for the name of the road where my grandparents live. *Please don't ask me.*

"I have a summer home there," he says.

"It's beautiful," I say.

"Too many tourists, but they're avoidable," he says.

We shuffle forward.

"These days I prefer Paris," he says.

I nod. I've never been to Europe.

"Or Norway," he adds.

I've never even been to Florida.

"Or the Balkans," he says.

I try to spell "Balkans" in my head. *Is it 'aul'?*

"But when I can't leave the country, I just get out the convertible and drive the Pacific Coast Highway."

His mermaid shimmer begins to fade.

I glance up at the chalk board menu on the wall behind the baristas, even though I know it by heart. The lawyer pulls his phone out and punches out a text with manicured thumbs. While he's silent, I eavesdrop on the conversation between the two young men in front of us. The one on the left has untidy wet hair and a twist in his tie beneath his collar. The one on the right wears a bike helmet and a messenger bag.

"I was out before sunrise this morning," the guy with wet hair says to the messenger. "I hoofed it from my apartment with my board under my arm. Scared a few racoons."

The messenger chuckles.

"'Course I was thinking about work the whole way over, but

the second that cold water hit my wetsuit, I forgot about it."

The messenger nods.

The line moves forward.

"The tide was strong, but once I paddled out past the pull, it was just me, the seagulls, and the ocean swells. A few good waves came straight away, but I let them pass. I just sat and bobbed on my board, watching the stars fade. Then a band of pink light crept onto the horizon—pale at first, but soon it got so dark it was practically red."

I lean in so I can hear him over the rising din of the café.

"Even though I knew it was coming, nothing could have prepared me for the moment the sun broke the horizon." He shakes his head. He seems to be searching for words.

My eyes rest on the cascade of blonde-tipped ringlets hanging past his collar.

"The waves got righteous after sunrise. I rode on pure adrenalin. My heart was thumping. Forgot the city was even there."

"Awesome," the messenger says.

"I had a few gnarly wipeouts, but then I caught this mega wave, and it was like the ocean took hold of me, you know? Like it was talking to me and showing me how to be with it. How to ride it. I don't know. I can't explain."

"It winked at you," the messenger says.

"Yeah. But it was more than a wink," the surfer says. "I rode that wave almost to the shore. I always wipe out before then. I've never ridden to the shore. The ocean . . . I swear it was communicating with me." He clears his throat. "Or something."

A voice cuts through. It's the lawyer, still by my side. I don't know how long he's been speaking.

"Pardon me?" I say to him.

His face tightens in irritation. *He's accustomed to having women's undivided attention.* He moves a half step forward in front of me. *I'm being dismissed.* One of the café's recessed ceiling lights now shines like a spotlight on his head and shoulders. And suddenly I see . . . gray roots. A thinning spot. And his suit . . . is simply blue. The silver and lavender undertones, all the shimmer and magic—the mermaid—was the sunlight.

I slip away, step outside, and lift my face up to it.

CHAPTER 45

Restless. Distracted. Time creeps by. Around noon, Nicholas texts and tells me to leave work early and he'll pick me up at my apartment at 3:00 p.m. I hop on a Muni bus and slump in the rear seat like a teenager, free at last.

Lobo bounds off the foot of my bed and greets me by dragging his body across my legs, back and forth, as a moose in the wild might use a tree to relieve an itch. I throw on jeans and sneakers and Lobo and I walk up Clay Street to Alta Plaza Park, climb the broad, tiered staircase, and stand so we face the breeze and the stunning southern view. A man strolls by with his cat on a leash and nods at me in solidarity, as if the walking of an animal is what binds us, not the species of animal being walked. I smile at him and a few moments later, marvel at his dignified composure when his Maine Coon cat suddenly flops on her side and starts to groom her groin.

Soon after, I'm applying mascara with a churning stomach in front of my bathroom mirror. The rumbles aren't the whine of hunger but a growl of warning, so every action of preparedness for dinner with my boyfriend happens in a sort of painful slow motion. As if I am meant to take special notice. As if, somehow, it's the last time.

The Pacific Ocean crashes against the coastline along

Highway 101 all the way to Half Moon Bay, a small town about thirty miles south of San Francisco. I take Nicholas's hand for the early part of the drive, but soon the winding 101 demands both of his hands on the wheel.

I'm relieved that Nicholas talks about work throughout our dinner of enchiladas, tamales, and chile relleno at Alejandro's, one of my favorite restaurants in the Bay Area. Started by their grandparents who emigrated from Belize, three sisters now run Alejandro's but serve the same traditional menu the restaurant was founded on.

I'm scooping up the last bit of grilled pepper with my soft corn tortilla when Nicholas shares the news. PharmFresh chose one of my slogans for their national campaign. "B'udder: the lighter side of delicious" won. Nicholas orders a bottle of champagne while I secretly search for excitement to start on slogans for their next two products: "Eggz on the Run," a liquid egg substitute, and "Mighty Moo," a whole milk replacement beverage. I wonder how long before "Cheeze-All" lands in my lap.

Nicholas smiles broadly and seems genuinely proud of me. In spite of my growing concerns about my compatibility with the work I'm doing, I smile and let myself receive his appreciation. Let myself be celebrated.

Then my phone dings.

Hello. We are at UVM Medical Center. Rachel is in labor.

It's my father. I didn't think he even knew how to text.

Everyone okay?

Yes. Same OBGYN who delivered you.

Our journeys will begin in the same hands. Interesting . . .

Wish I was there.

I will keep you posted. Labor is expected to take a while.

My fingers hover over the keys.

"What's going on? Who is it?" Nicholas asks.

My head remains lowered while I stare at the alphabet on my phone.

"Babe?"

My fingers fly over the keys, and I quickly hit send.

I love you, Dad.

His answer appears immediately.

Love you too.

I beam at Nicholas. "My sister-in-law is in labor."

We order flan "to go" and between it and a surprise order of paella for Scottie, Nicholas's car smells almost as good as the restaurant. Instead of heading home by way of the slower, winding, Pacific Coast Highway, Nicholas takes Route 88, the East-West connector between the coast and the interstate. I want to return to Lobo. I want to be home when Dad's texts arrive with news about the baby.

Route 88 climbs, winds, and threads through a massive grove of eucalyptus trees, grand and stoic, with shedding trunks and dense, waxy, blue leaves. On either side of us, the road drops off dramatically to a forest floor from which one hundred-foot trees rise majestically. We seem to be driving in the treetops, nearly touching the cosmos. At this time of day, drenched in early evening sun, with winds rolling off the ocean, light penetrates the leaves and cuts between branches, sending angular shafts that swing and pulse. *It's light that plays tricks.*

I notice the car before Nicholas. It's on our side of the road but faces toward us at an odd angle. Only three of the car's wheels touch the pavement; the front grille twists off the road and disappears into the grayish trunk of a towering eucalyptus.

"Do you see the car?" I ask, lightly touching his thigh.

"I see it," he says, and his BMW responds instantly, quietly decelerating.

The scene appears lifeless; no one moves outside the vehicle and no passersby have stopped. As we get closer, steam snakes from the grille. The car has lost its battle with rust while its mismatching yellow hood and green body give it a cartoon quality.

Something totters across the rear seat.

"I think we should stop," I urge.

"No. I'm sure they have cell phones."

The BMW moves swiftly. I have precious little time to peer in as we pass. The windows are open but with the car facing the opposite direction, the driver is nothing but a slumped form. All I can grab is a glimpse of who's in the rear seat.

It's a toddler, two or three years old, wearing nothing but a diaper. It stands with its arms straight out on either side. Eyes wide. Mouth open.

Screaming.

CHAPTER 46

Stop! The word builds in my chest before erupting from my mouth. "Stop!" I yell.

"What the hell?" Nicholas says and pulls over. I unbuckle my seat belt and leave it loose in my lap as he slows the BMW. I am already running to the other car when I hear him shout my name, but the only call I am answering is the one from the child.

The window on the passenger side is open and the seat is littered with McDonald's wrappers, a pack of Camel cigarettes, and cans of Pepsi. On the floor lies a new diaper and a half-empty baby bottle.

"Please, take my boy," a young voice pleads. She couldn't be more than sixteen. Her long coal black hair, damp with sweat, sticks to pale skin inflamed by tears. The heavy mascara that once accentuated stunning light blue eyes, now stains her cheeks and darkens the waterway of tears over her cheeks and throat. A cropped black tank top narrowly covers her bra-less chest. Her cutoff shorts ride high. A large bruise brands her thigh. Her feet are bare.

The steering wheel protrudes from the dashboard at a downward angle, pinning her hip, twisting her upper torso and locking her in place. She braces her upper body with her right forearm, her elbow jammed into the console between the front seats. She can't reshuffle. She can't sit up. She can't reach her child.

From the rear of the car, the same light blue eyes stare at me from beneath a crop of raven black hair, but on the boy, the effect is otherworldly. With one hand braced on the car seat beside him, he stands, bow-legged and trembling, while his other hand supports his sagging, gaping disposable diaper. His body is stocky, his belly beautifully rounded, his arms and legs sturdy and full, but his skin, from head to toe, is filthy.

At the sight of me he stifles his cries and immediately starts hiccupping. With each powerful jolt, his little body lurches. A teardrop flings wide, clears his belly and lands on top of his foot. I smell baby shit, cigarettes, and fear.

"Call 9-1-1!" I yell to Nicholas, who stands by the trunk of his car with his arms folded across his chest. He pulls his phone from his pocket.

"Please, lady, take my boy!" the mother begs, her lower lip swelling. At the sound of her panicked voice, the boy's sobs recommence.

"Will he let me? He doesn't know me!" I say over his cries. A vehicle whizzes past, the displaced air forcing me flat against the car.

I hear Nicholas's voice. "They're on their way!"

"Just take him, lady, please take him!" the mother pleads. I lean in, unlock the front seat, and flip it forward out of the way. I reach out to the boy, but he recoils against his car seat—one he must have let himself out of after the crash.

"It's okay," I say soothingly. His mouth pinches into a frown. His eyes widen, shiny with tears, and dart between his mother's lowered head and me.

"Go with the lady," the mother urges, her voice thin with

desperation.

He eyes me warily.

"Go with the lady . . ." she whispers.

I grab the unused diaper from the floor by the front passenger seat and set it on the roof. Then I draw in a long, deep breath and lean into the car. I don't reach out to him this time. Instead, I study him and imagine him building sandcastles on the beach in Half Moon Bay, splashing in the shallow water, and burying his feet in the sand. I picture those luminescent eyes wide with delight and his little body rippling with excitement. The back of my neck tingles. My chest opens. I smile at him.

"It's okay," I promise, and he seems to hear me this time because he lets go of the car seat and lifts his arms. I slide my hands beneath his armpits and pull him slowly, carefully out the passenger window and draw him to my chest. He clings to me, buries his face against my neck, and wraps his legs around my ribcage. I hold him tightly, take the diaper off the roof and walk around behind the trunk of the car, as far off the road as I can get.

Another car zings by.

The boy is a fireball in my arms, radiating heat and sweat, vibrating with adrenalin. I slip off his soiled diaper and let it plunk to the ground, then as best as I can, I pull the clean one on and fasten the tabs.

I'm suddenly aware of the wind whirring through the trees and the play of light that before was a trick and but now seems more like company. I lift my face toward the sky, drink in the steadiness of nature around me, and lightly scratch the space between the boy's shoulder blades.

In my arms, the child's breathing steadies. In the BMW, Nicholas leans against the driver's headrest. In the crashed

Ford Escort, the crown of the young mother's head slowly lowers.

We have all surrendered.

The boy doesn't lift his head when two rescue vehicles arrive, their lights flashing. One squad member sets up flares, another jogs to the Escort, another walks to the BMW, and the fourth one strides to me.

"Is this your son, miss?" the squad member asks, her voice clear, her enunciation crisp. She's a few inches shorter than me, sinewy and fit, with velvety ebony skin. I can't read the emblem on the breast of her T-shirt, but above it is embroidered the name "Castro" in capital letters.

"No, he belongs to the woman in the Escort," I say, suddenly aware that I'm swaying side to side, rocking the child. I don't remember when I started doing that.

"You're with the BMW?" she asks.

"With Nicholas, yes."

She doesn't ask who Nicholas is. She seems to know exactly where our conversation needs to go.

"Was there an accident?"

"No, we were passing and I saw the boy and he was screaming, but I couldn't see the mother and it was just bad," I ramble.

"Are you injured?"

"No."

"Was the child in a car seat?"

I recount the details as best as I can, but my mind isn't processing information logically and methodically. Her questions are short and specific, while my answers stumble and wander. She asks to examine the boy but instead of taking him from me, she guides us to her rig, opens the doors, and steers me by my elbow so that I sit on the end, my legs dangling.

The boy moans when I try to pull away from him. She squeezes my forearm and shakes her head and mouths, "Don't move him." I hold still as she explores the boy's head, neck and shoulders, then slides her hands along his arms and out each individual finger. She palpates his spine and hips, each leg, and each foot. Finally, she slips her hands around to examine the boy's chest and belly and in doing so, grazes my breasts. I don't flinch; her touch is remote, clinical. There is no misinterpreting her intention.

A fire engine and a county sheriff's car arrive, and I watch as they work on extracting the young mother from the Escort.

"The child appears uninjured," she reports, "but he'll need a thorough examination at the hospital."

"Okay," I mumble and she nods and rejoins her colleagues as they carry the young woman, now fitted with a neck brace and strapped to a stretcher, to the ambulance.

Every inch of skin or fabric where the boy and I connect fuses with sweat. He slumps in my lap, snoring lightly. I have to hold his torso and brace his neck to keep him from lolling backward. His hands have slipped off my lap and curl open, palms up, in total release.

The rescue woman reappears. "Miss," she says. "Please bring the child to the ambulance so he can ride with his mother."

"Is the mother going to be alright?"

"The full extent of her injuries is unclear."

"So I should just walk over there?"

"Yes," she says.

"Thank you."

She smiles, but it doesn't quite reach her eyes. I wonder how she manages, witnessing so much trauma and death.

I can't see the mother's face. When I arrive at the

ambulance, her feet are nearest to me and her head and torso disappear beneath wraps and straps. When one of the rescue squad members opens his arms for me to hand him her son, I am certain the boy will awaken and howl, but he remains lost in sleep—puffy, limp, and oblivious to our separation.

Nicholas cracks a window the moment I slide into the car and pull the BMW's heavy door shut. In a vehicle that smells like a delicious meal from a gorgeous seaside restaurant, I smell more like what gets discarded in the dumpster around back.

We drive in silence. I am acutely aware Nicholas and I have just landed on different sides of something significant. I can't unravel it or name it, so I stare at the warm lights of the city as they rise and cool darkness falls. Then I lean my head against the window, close my eyes, and think of Oliver, Rachel, my father, and the new baby—who might already be on the planet, might already be safe in their arms.

CHAPTER 47

On my kitchen floor, Lobo gnaws on a raw beef bone. He steadies the bone between his front paws, which have grown slick with saliva and flecked with gobs of marrow. His eyes are wide and wild.

Nicholas sits hunched at the kitchen island with his head in his hands. Feeling only slightly soothed by my shower, I pad barefoot over to the sink wearing a T-shirt and leggings, my hair damp and unruly. I pour myself a glass of water, but instead of taking a seat beside Nicholas, I sit on the floor near Lobo.

"This day has been all wrong," Nicholas says.

My phone dings.

Rachel still in labor. Under close watch. Text you when I know more.

Ok!

I set the phone beside me and sip my water. "It's been a crazy day," I say, "a crazy, unpredictable day." I scratch Lobo's hind leg and he shifts away from me in fear I might snatch away his prize. The moment I pull my hand away and tuck it under my thigh, he resumes his gnawing.

"What you did," Nicholas lowers his hands so I can see his blazing eyes, "was irresponsible."

"Irresponsible? That child was upright, conscious, terrified, and basically standing in his own shit."

"She could sue you."

"I had to take that chance."

"That's naive."

"It's humane."

"She had a cell phone."

"She was pinned under her steering wheel."

"That could have gone a million different ways wrong."

"And you considered all of them. The absolute worst possible outcomes are what you based your choices on."

"For good reason."

"I can't live that way. I won't live that way."

"What way?"

"Fearing strangers."

He shakes his head. He seems as uncomfortable arguing as I am. The grind of Lobo's teeth tearing at raw bone amplifies the tension.

"I bought this for you while you were away. Actually, I bought it just before you went away." He pulls a light blue Tiffany's box from the pocket of his jacket and sets it on the counter. "I was going to propose at dinner, but you were so distracted. And then the accident . . . that child . . . and now I'm sitting here wondering who you are."

Adoration and rejection wash over me in one tangled swoop. Nicholas's ex-wife's image drops into my head. Her Scandinavian beauty. The way she cornered me by the towel dispenser in the restaurant bathroom. Her words of warning.

"I think you should open the box," he says.

I rise and stand across from him at the island counter. He slides the box halfway between us and leaves it. I slide it the rest of the way toward me and open it. I know little about diamonds and their cuts, but I do know when I see something beautiful. And this ring is stunning: a large diamond flanked by two sapphires on a mirrorlike setting that I believe might be platinum.

I want to lift the ring out of its box, slip it on my finger, and live a fairytale. I want the ring to put to rest all my questions and uncertainty about who I am. I want it to fill in all my holes and show me the right way forward. I remember my father's words. *There will be a way. You'll see.*

"It's beautiful, Nicholas," I say, mesmerized, but I don't touch it.

The gemstones sparkle and wink. *We can save you. We can make it all better.* I want the ring to decide for me. California is where I belong right now. I'm doing work that suits me. Nicholas is the right partner for me.

"Try it on," he says, but my hands don't move. Nor do his.

We stare at the ring.

Lobo tears cords of fat from the beef bone.

Silence can't protect you, Beatrice.

I clear my throat. My heart thunders in my chest. "You just said you are wondering who I am. Do we know each other well enough to get married?" I ask.

Startled, his eyes cut to me. "What kind of question is that?"

The words fly out of my mouth. "I met your ex-wife."

"What? When?"

"The night you, Derek, and I went out to dinner. I ran into her in the restroom."

"How did you know she was my ex-wife?"

"She stopped by our table, remember? White cashmere pantsuit?"

"I couldn't care less what she was wearing."

"Well, she was in the bathroom when I went in. And she spoke to me."

His mouth slips open, then snaps shut. "I don't like this," he says and rockets off the stool. His eyes travel around the kitchen as if he's searching for a trap door into a parallel reality where this conversation isn't happening.

"I didn't like it, either." The exquisite ring spellbinds me. Light jumps off the diamond, cool and sharp, while the sapphires glimmer, warm and oceanic. I curl my fingers possessively around the box.

"What did she say to you?"

I meet his gaze.

"She asked if I was with you."

"And you said . . ."

"I didn't say anything . . . which she correctly interpreted as 'yes.'"

"Well, that's great," he says.

"You were going to tell the staff anyway. Why does it matter if your ex-wife knows?"

"Because it's none of her business. Because I should be able to decide what she does and doesn't know about me."

"You can't control what she knows, Nicholas."

He stretches his neck and rolls his shoulders, but his body appears just as rigid afterward.

"What else did she say?"

I expect a lie to roll from my lips. A lie to quiet the storm. *Nothing. She said nothing.* "She said you'd prefer to know the me that is right for you than know the me that I truly am."

"That's idiotic," he says and drags a hand through his hair. "What if those are the same people? What if you, truly you, are right for me?"

Heat rushes to my face. Thoughts collide in my mind. He

plants his hands on his hips. His chest heaves. Then his eyes fall on me. Penetrating. Unwavering.

"I do," he says.

"'You do' what?"

"You asked me if I thought we knew each other well enough to get married, and my answer is I do."

The collision in my head clears. Two words remain.

I don't.

My mind pounces and circles them like prey. *How can I kill this thought? How can I kill this truth that, if allowed to survive, will force change in my life?*

"Beatrice?" he asks.

CHAPTER 48

I survey the apartment. All that remains is what I'm taking with
me: jeans, long-sleeve shirts, sweaters, my laptop, and an ice-
packed cooler of raw chicken necks. My furniture, high heels,
and miniskirts are tucked safely in storage, just south of San
Francisco. It took Scottie and me four trips on Sunday in my
rented SUV to get everything moved. Tucked in the glove
compartment, we found a CD someone had left—Joni Mitchell's
Ladies of the Canyon. Turns out it was Scottie's mother's
favorite album, too. He set his feet up on the dashboard and we
sang "Big Yellow Taxi" aloud with all the windows open.

From my bedroom, I watch traffic stream steadily up Gough
Street, a couple stroll hand in hand along Sacramento, and in
Lafayette Park about a dozen Tai Chi practitioners flow in
graceful unison. It strikes me as unfair that life should appear
to roll along as usual out there when for me it's rife with unrest.

Lobo circles me. He's underfoot every time I move, his gaze
trained on me like an expectant child.

"We'll go for a walk later," I assure him.

On my way to the bathroom with Lobo on my heels, my
phone dings. *Scottie.*

When r you leaving?
Three hours.

What's Lobo doing?
Herding me like a cattle dog.
He's afraid you're leaving without him.
I pause while his words sink in.
How did I not know that? I glance at the electric toothbrush on my sink as if it, too, is a foreign object.
Put him in the car while you pack it.
Really?
He'll probably want to sit in the driver's seat.

I lower to the edge of the bathtub. Lobo lies on the bathmat, facing me. My eyes travel over his graceful silver form, from his long rudder of a tail to his majestic square head. On his forehead, a single gray hair protrudes. *When did that appear?* My fingers loosen around my phone. Scottie texts again.
You still there?
I'm here.
Now you'll have time to get to know Lobo.
Yes.
He's an amazing dog.
Yes.
And you're an animal whisperer. You just don't know it.
Seriously?
Yep. Btw Javier has rented your apartment.
Already?

I wait for his usual rapid-fire response. Thirty seconds later—an eternity for Scottie—my phone dings.
But there's no replacing you.

My chest swells with emotion. My fingers hover over the alphabet. *Don't be clever. Tell the truth. Like he did.*
Scottie. You've been my closest friend.
Love you, girl.
Love you too.

I'll swing by later. I have something for Lobo.

Kalamata olive bread?

Dryer lint.

I laugh aloud and snap on Lobo's collar and leash. Out front, he pees on the stump where The Tree once stood, then sails into the rear seat of the SUV. Moments later, when I return with a suitcase and a tote full of toiletries, he watches from the driver's seat, his eyes tracking me over the rim of the steering wheel.

My muscles and limbs protest with every loaded trip between the apartment and the car. Still, my senses are on full "Nicholas alert." I've barely seen or heard from him in the two weeks since the roadside car wreck. And the proposal. I slump in the passenger seat while my mind retraces last Friday, my final day at the agency.

Nicholas had missed the morning gathering held in my honor—an alleged hot sauce emergency with the Randy Brothers.

I finished up all my work around 2:00 p.m. but still, no Nicholas. Eager to be around in case he returned, I filled my time by sifting through file drawers that I knew held nothing meaningful, stringing together loose paper clips to form a chain-link necklace, and seeing how many consecutive rotations I could elicit from my swivel chair.

At 3:00 p.m., I ducked over to the café across the street and like a stalker, sat by the window with my eyes fixed on our building's entrance. A soy latte and two biscotti later, I started to accept that the roiling in my gut was not over-caffeination but fear I'd never see him again.

At 4:00 p.m., as I was leaving the café, I nearly collided with the Wells & Menklin attorney in the blue suit. He showed no signs of recognizing me, but graciously stepped aside to let me pass.

At 4:30 p.m., Derek kissed my cheek and slipped me a bag of chocolate-covered espresso beans. Although my other colleagues were friendly, I couldn't shake the sensation as I turned off the lights and closed the door to my office, that several sets of eyes were already redecorating it.

Lobo's joyful whine jerks me into the present moment, and I find myself still in the passenger seat with a pile of disks in my lap.

"You're really leaving," Nicholas says.

I pop up out of the car and release a waterfall of CDs onto the floor mat. Nicholas' face appears drawn, his bearing beleaguered. A shadow of stubble darkens his jawline. His lavender dress shirt falls crinkled and untucked over faded blue jeans. A few wisps of hair peak out from the "V" of his open collar, and I fight an impulse to walk over and gently press my lips there. I'm struck by the sorrow in Nicholas' face and pained by the knowledge that I am the cause of it. He solemnly pets Lobo's head and is rewarded by a jubilant thwap of tail against the console.

"I didn't think I'd see you again," I say, pushing the hair out of my face and wishing I was wearing something more attractive than a 49ers T-shirt and shorts.

"I needed time," he says, glancing at Lafayette Park, then fastening his eyes on me. Wind ruffles his hair. "You didn't say, 'yes.'"

I come around the hood to his side of the car but pause by the wheel well. "I didn't say 'no'" I say, holding his eyes.

"What does that even mean? You're going to Vermont. I'm in California. How can we figure out if we're right when we're apart?"

My mind scrounges around for the perfect response, but quickly accepts defeat. "I don't have a clear answer. All I can say is this move doesn't feel permanent. I just know that I can't start a new life until I've made peace with the old one." I cross my arms, hoping to mask the nervous quiver in my hands.

His eyes sweep over the park again. "Is this about my ex-wife?" he asks.

"The Scandinavian supermodel? No."

He gives in to the tiniest of smiles.

A thread forms between us. A link. My solar plexus stirs.

"I don't like that she spoke to you," he says.

I nod.

"She does whatever she wants. She doesn't waste energy considering the ramifications of her behavior on other people."

I nod.

"Once she got what she wanted from me, she left."

The stirring in my abdomen builds to a dull throb. "Are you sure you're over her?" I ask.

He gazes past my shoulder up Sacramento Street, then scratches Lobo's ears and chest. "I'm still angry," he says.

My gaze drifts down the sidewalk and Nicholas studies the roof of my rental car while we acclimate to honesty. A knot gathers in my throat.

"I lost my mother when I was a teenager. She died in a car accident."

I swallow. It's as if the truth has robbed my throat of moisture.

I sense his eyes on me. With the toe of my sneaker, I trace a crack in the cement. "Instead of facing her death, I cut off parts of myself. I fell in line. Joined the pack. I bought into the game of busyness and striving and powering through . . . and now I'm tired. And I want to feel better. I want to feel whole."

An elderly woman crosses Gough Street with four golden Pomeranians, each one under ten pounds. They don't dart and yip; there's no tangling of leashes. The animals march side by side, heads high, tongues out, tails curled over their hind ends, as if their only wish is to help give their fragile owner ballast in an unpredictable world.

Nicholas comes to me, pushes my hair aside, and kisses my temple. His warm hand slides across my back and rests at the base of my spine. "I'm sorry about your mother," he whispers against my skin.

I slip my arm around his waist and tuck my head against his neck. My lips are inches from the "V" I had wanted to kiss. I do it now.

"I'm sorry about your wife."

He nods and tucks a stray hair behind my ear and when our eyes meet again, he doesn't try to hide the sadness that has lingered beneath the surface since we first met. I see it now for what it is, and I realize that we have both been grieving.

Wordlessly, we fold into one another, chest to chest, bodies pressed. He smells of Bleu de Chanel. Cedar and sandalwood. I close my eyes and will my senses to imprint every detail of the moment into memory. After some time, he speaks against my ear. "The spider plant I gave you. You're bringing it with you."

He must have spotted it in the rear seat with the blown glass horse I'd bought from the artist in Union Square. I nod, unable to find my voice amidst rising tears.

"It's still alive," he says incredulously.

I beam with pride.

"This isn't goodbye," he says.

I feverishly wipe at my deluge of tears. He covers my hands with his and gently draws them downward. Our eyes lock. Tears leak and rush over my cheeks. Droplets pepper my chest. His mouth finds mine, his lips hungry and familiar. We intertwine again, meld again, and then part.

CHAPTER 49

In the gray. It's where I spend most of my time these days, between the black and white of blind faith and certainty. Between how life is and how I think it's supposed to be.

The crisp October air raises chill bumps from my skin. I button Oliver's flannel shirt and grab Dad's rake while Lobo sniffs intently along the perimeter of the corral, unlocking its archives and reading its backstory.

As I drag the last of the old hay into a pile in front of the barn, I am reminded how much friendlier my thoughts are when I'm exercising. Dad helped me get the spider-shaped farm equipment out of the stall last weekend and found a farmer through Front Porch Forum who not only wanted it but was willing to let us borrow his trailer in exchange. We propped the sawhorse, pails, rope, and remaining odds and ends at the edge of the driveway with a "Free to a Good Home" sign, and they disappeared before the sun did. All that's left for me to contend with are the cobwebs, the straw, and this molded hay.

By the time I've finished, I've stripped off Oli's flannel shirt, my skin shines with sweat, and the nippy air is a welcome relief. I stand and let the mosaic of orange, red, and yellow fall leaves remind me of the inevitability of change. Last time I was here, those trees were green. I'm living squarely in the change now. It's far easier than anticipating it.

I peel a cobweb from my neck and consider my appearance: filthy hands, dusty jeans, a baseball cap I've worn for five consecutive days, and not a stroke of mascara. *What would Nicholas say?*

Nicholas.

I set the rake against the wall and kneel on the dirt floor. Lobo notices my new position and races over, as if it's the invitation he's been waiting for. Like a grounding cord, his silky coat, velvety, floppy ears, and radiant joy steady me instantaneously.

Make the phone call. The thought has been cycling through my mind for days. Instead of rejecting it again, I allow it to rest and take root, and as Lobo and I set off on our walk, my thoughts wander into what I might say.

We pass by the sugar maple beneath which my mother and I used to lie, our bodies snug, our fingers laced. I recall the cool earth, the tickling grass, and the pools of warmth where our skin touched. Amidst the crickets, the cauliflower clouds, and the hypnotic in-out of our breath, we sometimes fell asleep. She told me once that she used to lie in that exact spot when she was pregnant with me. I remember my young mind having to stretch into the idea of my having been anything other than the six-year-old I was in that moment. The news that I had been tiny enough to fit in her belly was both shocking and exciting. But having no memory of living insider her—*How did I eat? Was it dark?*—a burst of vulnerability and fear had swept over me. I remember tightening my fingers in hers. *When I get older, will I forget this moment, too?*

Lobo instinctively picks up the lightly worn footpath that hugs the perimeter of the field, and he bolts ahead. He's out of sight for most of the walk except every ten minutes or so I catch a glimpse of him standing perfectly still in the wildflowers and the tall grass, his tail up, his head craned around, and his eyes searching for me, waiting for me. Once I am in full view, he darts off.

An hour later, Oliver greets us through the screen door. "You miss me?"

Lobo bounds to him and although it's unclear to which of us Oliver was talking, I smile and let the scene flood my senses. My childhood home. My brother in the doorway wearing oven mitts. His sleeping infant upstairs. My dog at his feet. The whir of my father's table saw humming from the art barn. The overlay of past and present which was so unsettling just weeks ago at the wedding, now feels precious.

"I smell eggs," I say as I close the kitchen door behind us.

I wonder how long it will take for eggs and toast to stop triggering thoughts of B'udder, PharmFresh and sprayable dairy replacement products. On my last day in the office, Marlene had told me Emily, the youngest creative on our team, had been assigned "Eggz on the Run" and "Mighty Moo," but my name was still recorded as lead creative for the account. Maybe for client optics.

Or maybe because Nicholas believes I'll soon return.

Will I return?

"I'm whipping up a little frittata," Oliver says as he peeks in the oven. "Spinach, feta, scallions and dill." He tosses the oven mitts on the counter and adds, "I thought I'd liquify a piece in the blender and feed it to Isabelle."

My face twists in horror.

"It's never too soon to plant the seed for a career in the culinary arts."

"You scare me."

"Rachel wants her to be a concert pianist. Or a marine

biologist."

"Maybe for now we just focus on hoping her poop gets solid."

Oliver clasps his hands in prayer.

"So where is my little niece?"

"Upstairs napping. She should start stirring any minute."

"I've got to make a phone call," I say, grabbing my cell from the kitchen table. "I'll do it upstairs and bring Izzy down when she wakes up."

"Good plan," he says. "That will give me time to find the blender."

Sitting in my childhood bedroom at the end of my twin mattress with my cell phone in hand, I realize that I have arrived at yet another line in the sand. I can stay on this side and discredit the nudge that's been prodding for days or I can accept the risks that crossing the line demands of me. My heart flutters with nerves. The phone turns to lead in my palm. I punch in the ten digits. My call is answered on the third ring.

"Hi, it's Beatrice," I say.

"Hello."

"I'm in Vermont."

"I know."

I clear my throat and search for the words that were flowing so easily out in the field. They elude me like a mischievous toddler.

Just be real. Show yourself.

"I've been thinking about forgiveness," I say. "It's been on my mind a lot."

Izzy coos from her room.

"My mother asked for my forgiveness, but I withheld it and for years my refusal festered like a wound that wouldn't heal." I peel a fragile strand of cobweb off my jeans. "You and I don't know each other very well . . . maybe we were both hoping the other would be something different."

I rise, cross the bedroom, and confront my reflection in the mirror. "But this is me," I say to my vibrant eyes, wild hair, and dusty cap, "and I'd like for you to know me. I'd like to know you."

My grandmother clears her throat. A rush of embarrassment and regret courses through me.

"Death changes us," she says. "And nothing can prepare you for outliving your child." She pauses. My embarrassment recedes. "I think often, 'What would Lily do? What would Lily say?' She was the soft one in the family. Her father and I were always trying to toughen her up, but now that she's gone, I realize that we had it backwards. Lily wasn't supposed to harden. Her father and I were supposed to adopt more of her gentle nature. She was the bloom on our thorny stem."

I envision my grandmother sitting in her pristine living room staring out at the sea and my mother standing behind her with hands resting on her shoulders.

"I don't intend to make the same mistake twice," my grandmother says.

Isabelle's low whine draws me to her doorway. I release a deep breath. Courage blooms inside me.

"I received your letter, Grandma, but I didn't read it until recently. I guess I wasn't ready." Isabelle flails her arms. "You had offered to share photos of Mom when she was a child and letters she had written to you when she was falling in love with my Dad. Does your offer still stand?"

"I'll bring them to you," Grandma says. "That way we won't be interrupted."

I smile at her phrasing. She knows her husband.

Izzy's eyelids fly open. A howl is sure to follow.

"Isabelle is waking up. I have to go to her," I say.

"Tell my great-granddaughter that I can't wait to meet her," she says.

"I will, Grandma."

The moment I enter the kitchen, Oliver opens his arms to take his daughter from me. As I pass Izzy over, she punches her tiny fists in the air like a rock musician winding up the crowd.

"So, Bea, what are you going to do?" Oliver asks.

I flash him my most mischievous grin.

CHAPTER 50

The pasture covers more acreage than I realized, but its condition is as rough and raw as I remember. The land resembles a graveyard, with fallen tree limbs rising like crooked fingers from the earth and an abandoned tractor, all but overtaken by wild shrubs, collapsing into itself, surrendering to fate.

I know to proceed slowly after the orange mailbox, that the drive will be marred by ruts, potholes, and no shoulder. Thankfully, someone has taken a chain saw to the downed tree and has pushed the logs and the branches to the side. Oliver's truck and the trailer squeeze through, but barely.

A white-haired man, bent from age, steps from the house and stands in the middle of the driveway, the smoke from his cigarette accompanying him like a ghost. I wave, but he ignores me, spins on his heels, and heads toward the barn. Despite his uneven gait and the noticeable hitch in his step, he moves quickly, as if his body is trained to push through pain.

I wait while he opens the flimsy gate. His long-sleeve red flannel shirt, bulky on his stringy frame, is tucked neatly into baggy jeans, which appear to be held in place by a leather belt, rather than his hips. The narrow strip is cinched so tightly that the excess leather circles halfway around again. I wonder how many years it's been since he weighed enough to fill out those clothes. He moves methodically, pushing one bony arm through the webbing of the metal gate, lifting it at the crook of his elbow, and walking it out to its full extension.

I open my window and pull up.

"Can ya' back it?" the man says, instead of, "Hello."

His cigarette bobs between tight lips. His eyes are bloodshot, his skin is wrinkled and sallow, and there's a resignation in his expression that reminds me of the sinking tractor out in his pasture.

"I can't. How about I do a U-turn out there in your field?" I ask, smiling wishfully.

The corners of his mouth upturn slightly, but he doesn't give in to it. Instead, he drags on his cigarette. "Ahh, hell, go ahead," he grumbles and swats the air, as if my trailer-backing ignorance and I are a winged nuisance.

While bouncing and clattering across the untrodden pasture, I silently pray nothing punctures my tires. I know enough to make a wide turn in order to avoid jackknifing, but I don't dare glance over at the old man, fearing I'll lose my confidence. He was probably hauling trailers in middle school.

At last, the truck's grille faces the open gate, and the trailer extends straight out behind me. The man stays put, smoking, assessing.

I grab the halter and the lead rope I bought at an equine supply store, stuff two carrots in my pocket, and slide out of the pickup. The man makes no move to join me or to interact in any way, so I just give him a small wave and duck around the rear to prop open the trailer doors with bungee cords.

"You know what you're doin'?" he asks, as I hurry to the barn.

No.

"Yup!" I answer.

He shakes his head. "You can't do nuthin' with her, ya know," he says, but I am already at her stall.

"Hi, Kate," I say, snapping the carrot and laying both halves on my open palm. She snatches them up, then sniffs my hand and my hair, searching for more. I feed her the other carrot and stroke her neck while she chews.

To slip the halter over her ears, I have to rise up on tippy toes. She doesn't flinch or retreat; she seems unphased by the activity, intent only on the food. I buckle the halter, hold the lead rope in one hand, and massage her shoulder with the other, circling, soothing, and lightly running my fingers over the snaking scar on her belly. Still chewing, she explores my forearm. I reach up to extract a knotted ball of thistle from her mane, one of many that together give her the appearance of a 1950s housewife with a head of curlers.

"You ain't got her haltered yet?" the old man hollers.

"All set," I yell. "Just leaving something here for you." I tuck a $100 bill behind the "Kate" nameplate on her stall. Since my first phone call to ask if I could adopt her, he has never mentioned money. Paying him feels right, but handing it to him does not.

I step away from the stall, then freeze. My brain thunders with uncertainty.

What am I doing? I don't know how to do this.

"This" . . . care for a horse.

"This" . . . change my life.

"This" . . . trust.

Kate watches me from her stall, completely still except for her jaws, which grind and pulverize the remains of the carrot. I turn to leave, forgetting all about the slack lead rope in my hand. She lumbers free from the stall and falls in at my side, or maybe it's me who falls in at hers. As we emerge from the barn, she quickens her pace, exhales sharply, then tosses her head— mane flying, as if in triumph. Healed. Sovereign. As if she has already let go of the trauma in her past.

"She's all broke down," the farmer says, unwilling to see anything else. With curled fingers he pulls the cigarette from his lips and reminds me, "You can't ride her. Bad joints."

He's right. Her body clicks and pops with every stride.

"I'm not going to ride her."

My toe hits a rock and I nearly stumble. The huge horse doesn't even twitch.

"She ain't loaded in a trailer since god was a boy," the farmer says. I glance over as he pulls a fresh cigarette from the breast pocket of his flannel shirt and lights it from the glowing remains of his last one. "I hope you ain't in no hurry," he adds, then he repositions himself, gate in hand, relaxed and settled, just in time for the show. It's not malice I sense from him; it's amusement.

Shoulder to shoulder, Kate and I stand at the trailer's entrance. The man at the equine supply store suggested I tie a satchel filled with alfalfa inside to help encourage her to load. The satchel appears tired and underwhelming. *Will it be enough to entice her?*

A breeze pushes the hair off my face. Kate snaps her tail. I fill my lungs and look upward to the cloudless sky, clear and vast, then at the empty trailer, a harsh steel box with cutout windows.

"Help me out here, Mom," I say.

I can feel the old man's eyes on us.

"Come home with me," I whisper to Kate.

And without pause, she does.

Acknowledgments

My heartfelt thanks to:

Book coach Michele Orwin for riding shotgun since the novel's first comma-ridden draft.

Rachel Cadwallader-Staub for her beta reading and animal whispering.

Lorraine Fico-White for rousing me out of a passive voice.

My Atmosphere Press team for their professionalism and guidance.

Fran Allen and the Donovan family for lending me a bunk on their ranch and igniting my journey with horses.

About Atmosphere Press

Atmosphere Press is an independent, full-service publisher for excellent books in all genres and for all audiences. Learn more about what we do at atmospherepress.com.

We encourage you to check out some of Atmosphere's latest releases, which are available at Amazon.com and via order from your local bookstore:

Icarus Never Flew 'Round Here, by Matt Edwards

COMFREY, WYOMING: Maiden Voyage, by Daphne Birkmeyer

The Chimera Wolf, by P.A. Power

Umbilical, by Jane Kay

The Two-Blood Lion, by Nick Westfield

Shogun of the Heavens: The Fall of Immortals, by I.D.G. Curry

Hot Air Rising, by Matthew Taylor

30 Summers, by A.S. Randall

Delilah Recovered, by Amelia Estelle Dellos

A Prophecy in Ash, by Julie Zantopoulos

The Killer Half, by JB Blake

Ocean Lessons, by Karen Lethlean

Unrealized Fantasies, by Marilyn Whitehorse

The Mayari Chronicles: Initium, by Karen McClain

Squeeze Plays, by Jeffrey Marshall

JADA: Just Another Dead Animal, by James Morris

Hart Street and Main: Metamorphosis, by Tabitha Sprunger

Karma One, by Colleen Hollis

Ndalla's World, by Beth Franz

Adonai, by Arman Isayan

The Journey, by Khozem Poonawala

Stolen Lives, by Dee Arianne Rockwood

About the Author

Photo: Andy Duback

At various times, Annie has lived in a train car, studied at an Ivy League university, dumpster dived, traveled with governors' spouses, hand-milked goats, lost hope, kept secrets, and seen ghosts. She lives in Vermont.

Connect with Annie at **annieseyler.com**

CPSIA information can be obtained
at www.ICGtesting.com
Printed in the USA
BVHW042217041222
653455BV00001B/9